Praise for RITA® Award-winning author
IRENE HANNON

Rainbow's End
Irene Hannon

Steeple
Hill®

Published by Steeple Hill Books™

STEEPLE HILL BOOKS

Steeple
Hill®

Copyright © 2007 by Harlequin Books S.A.

ISBN-13: 978-0-373-15075-5
ISBN-10:   0-373-15075-X

The contents of this book may have been edited from its original format. The publisher acknowledges the copyright holders of the individual works as follows:

RAINBOW'S END
Copyright © 2007 by Irene Hannon

Excerpt from A COWBOY'S HONOR
Copyright © 2008 by Lois Richer

www.SteepleHill.com

Printed in U.S.A.

And God will wipe away every tear from their eyes.
And death shall be no more; neither shall there
be mourning, nor crying, nor pain anymore,
for the former things have passed away.
—*Revelation* 21:4

Chapter One

The little boy was watching her.

Startled, Jill Whelan froze. She had no idea how long her young visitor had been crouched in the shadows of the large boulders that separated her sunny meadow from the dark woods beyond, but she sensed that he'd been there quite a while. If he hadn't shifted position to keep her in sight as she moved across the field, she doubted whether his presence would ever have registered in her peripheral vision. Now that it had, however, the tense lines of his body warned her that he was poised to run at the slightest hint of detection.

Instead of making eye contact she resumed gathering wildflowers, salvaging as many of the profuse July blooms as her large basket would hold before the angry clouds sweeping across the sea battered the island with a flattening torrent of rain and wind. So far, she'd gone about her task with the same singular focus and intensity she brought to her painting, which also helped explain why the solemn-eyed, brown-haired little boy hadn't caught her attention before. Now, she was acutely conscious of his scrutiny.

As she bent, reached and clipped, savoring the vivid colors of the perfect blossoms, he continued to stare. That didn't surprise her. She was used to people gawking. She was also used to people keeping their distance. Her appearance made adults uncomfortable and, on a couple of occasions, had even frightened small children.

This little boy, however, seemed more cautious than scared. As if he wanted to communicate with her. Yet something was holding him back. And for once she didn't think it was the disfiguring scars that covered most of the right side of her face.

But then, what did she know? After two years of self-imposed isolation on this outcrop of rock in the San Juan Islands off the coast of Washington State, her once-keen people skills were rusty, at best. Still, she knew all about loneliness. And she could feel it emanating from the little boy in an almost tangible way that tugged at her heart.

With slow, deliberate steps, she eased closer to him. Out of the corner of her eye, she noted the grimy, oversize T-shirt that hung on his thin frame. His unkempt hair didn't look as if it had seen a comb in weeks. And a large smudge of dirt on his face obscured the sprinkling of freckles that spilled across the bridge of his nose and onto his cheeks. He was about six, maybe seven, she estimated.

Odd that she'd never seen him before. The adjacent property, which abutted Moran State Park on the less-populated eastern wing of butterfly-shaped Orcas Island, had never shown any sign of habitation. Unless, of course, you counted the occasional black-tailed deer that wandered onto her property to see if she'd replaced any of her deer-resistant plants with something more suited to their tastes, or the raccoons that came to forage in her trash bin. But Mary Lynn, at the tiny grocery store a few miles down the road, had mentioned once that an old hermit lived there. If so, he'd earned that label, because Jill had never seen any evidence of his existence. So who was the little boy? Could he be lost? Hungry? Injured? Did he need help?

Her nurturing instincts kicked in, and she set the basket on the ground, then slid her clippers into the back pocket of her jeans. After dropping to one knee, she adjusted the brim of her hat to better shade her face, then turned toward the boy.

His eyes, blue as the summer sky, widened in alarm when they met hers. For a second he froze, much like the deer she often startled on her twilight walks to the shore, a quarter of a mile away. Then he half rose from his crouched stance, prepared to run. When Jill remained motionless, however, he held his position and stared back at her.

"Hello there. My name is Jill. What's yours?"

Sometimes the husky quality of her once-soprano voice still surprised her—especially after she hadn't used it for a few days. It occurred to her as she spoke that she hadn't had any contact with another human being since her once-a-month shopping trip into Eastsound to stock up on essentials, and that had been…how long ago now? Five days, maybe?

Instead of responding, the boy stood and, with one more fearful glance in her direction, took off at a run into the deep woods behind him, where the shadows of the firs and cedars quickly swallowed him up.

Sighing, Jill reached for her basket and rose. It seemed the skittish little boy didn't need her, after all. Perhaps he'd just been shocked—and curious—about her appearance. It wouldn't be the first time she'd drawn that kind of unwelcome attention.

Nor, unfortunately, would it be the last.

* * *

The lashing rain slammed against the windshield of Keith Michaels's older-model compact car with enough force to render the wipers almost useless despite their valiant effort to keep up. And the waves pounding the jagged shore just a few feet below the narrow, dark road did nothing to ease the tension in his shoulders. With each mile that passed, he was sorrier that he hadn't thought ahead and realized how difficult it would be to find a place to stay over the Fourth of July weekend. Except the imminent holiday hadn't even registered in his consciousness. For the past year, the days and weeks had blended together in one long, gray blur. Weary now after months on the road, he'd hoped the San Juan Islands would offer him a quiet, out-of-the-way spot in which to figure out what he was going to do with the rest of his life.

Well, Orcas Island might be about as far away from Ohio as he could get in the contiguous—more or less—forty-eight states, but this remote speck of land was way more populous than he'd expected. When he'd seen the congestion in tiny Orcas Village as he'd driven off the ferry, he'd been tempted to turn around and get back on. Except his had been the last boat of the day. Meaning he was stuck here overnight.

And now he was driving the back roads on what could very well turn out to be a wild-goose chase. Still, it was his best hope of finding a place to sleep tonight. He wasn't about to try and set up his tent in this torrential downpour. And every single inn and bed-and-breakfast he'd passed had displayed No Vacancy signs. Considering the pricey tabs and the sad state of his finances, he supposed that was a blessing in disguise.

In any case, a garrulous checker at the grocery store in Eastsound, where he'd stopped to buy a deli sandwich, had picked up on his plight in no time. She'd suggested that a "widow lady" she knew of might be willing to give him the use of a small cottage on her property for one night.

"I live down her way, and I try to chat with her a bit when she comes in here every few weeks," the woman explained. "She doesn't rent the cottage out as a rule, and mostly keeps to herself. But I expect she might give you shelter from this storm that's brewing. She's always taking in stray critters." The woman had laughed and planted her hands on her ample hips. "She's got an account here, so we have her number. Shall I give her a call?"

A widow lady who took in strays. She was probably one of those eccentric old women who had forty cats on the property and kept newspapers from ten years ago piled up in a spare room, Keith mused. But what choice did he have? "Sure. Why not?" he'd responded.

"Hey, Beth, cover for me a minute, will you? I need to call out to the Whelan place."

A perky young woman with long blond hair, wearing a cropped shirt that skimmed the waistband of her low-cut jeans, came up behind the woman. "Sure thing." She gave Keith a smile that could be just friendly…or inviting. He didn't trust himself to make that judgment anymore. But he figured it must be the former. After all, he hadn't shaved in several days, his own jeans were threadbare and faded, and his black leather jacket was scuffed and worn. He didn't see how any woman could find him attractive. Then again, considering the current Hollywood heartthrobs, maybe the dangerous, bad-boy image was a turn-on.

Best not to take chances. He stepped back and turned away to stare out of the store's plate glass window. Large drops of rain were already darkening the pavement, and lightning slashed across the sky, branding an angry streak onto the inky blackness and outlining the looming profile of a nearby mountain. The mood could only be described as ominous—and depressing. Which somehow seemed fitting for this last stop on his year-long journey. A journey he'd hoped would lead him to answers, to healing, to resolution—even back to God.

Instead, he felt just as lost, just as empty, just as broken as he had twelve months before when he'd set out on his quest. All he had to show for his travels was a bunch of photographs stuffed in a box in the back of his car. At first, he'd snapped dozens of images a week. But as the months had worn on, he'd taken fewer and fewer pictures. He'd stopped developing even those three months ago. The film from his recent efforts was still wound in tight coils, hidden inside a handful of dark spools he'd tossed into an empty fast-food bag.

Where did he go from here? he wondered. The answer was elusive, and despair swamped him, much as the sudden torrent of rain was flooding the streets. He'd reached the end of the line. Literally. There was nowhere else to run.

"Looks like the phone's out over at the Whelan place." The older woman's voice intruded on his thoughts and he turned, grateful for the interruption that gave him an excuse to delay the tough questions for another day. "But you could ride on out there. She'll be home."

"How far is it?"

"Twelve, fourteen miles."

His spirits took another dive. The last thing he wanted to do was drive more than a dozen miles in this storm. "You're sure there's nothing closer?"

"Sorry. Every place is full. A lot of mainlanders come for the Fourth. Make their reservations months ahead. There's not a camping site or room to be had anywhere this weekend on the San Juan Islands. You can trust me on that."

He didn't need to trust her. He'd seen the No Vacancy signs himself. He supposed he should be grateful the woman had come up with the "widow lady's" cottage. Except gratitude wasn't something that came easily to him anymore. Or at all.

"Okay. Thanks." He dredged up the words from somewhere. "Can you tell me how to get there?"

A few minutes later, his sandwich in one hand and scribbled directions in the other, he'd stepped into the rain and dashed for his car. Now, after thirty minutes of snail-paced, white-knuckle driving, he figured he must be getting close. Although his stomach was rumbling, his sandwich lay uneaten on the seat beside him. Navigating the pitch-dark road required his full attention. More so as he approached his destination, when the pavement narrowed and the center line disappeared.

The woman at the store had said to watch for a blue mailbox with a sign underneath that said Rainbow's End. Up to this point, he'd seen very few mailboxes—and none that matched the woman's description. Of course, he might have missed it. His headlights could barely illuminate the deserted road, let alone pick out the occasional side road that branched off. And he wasn't about to retrace his steps. Worst case, he'd ease onto the shoulder—if he could find one—recline his seat, and catch what sleep he could right there. In some ways, that might be preferable to staying in some hermit's cottage, anyway. In fact, the more he thought about it, the more appealing…

All at once, a small deer darted in front of the car, no more than a flash across his headlights. Shocked, Keith slammed on the brakes and yanked the wheel to the left, skidding to a stop at the edge of the pavement, mere inches above the flooded ravine that ran alongside the road. As he stared at the turbulent, dark water, waiting for the pounding of his heart to subside, he drew a shaky breath. Talk about close calls. He might not be all that excited about life anymore, but he sure didn't want his to end in a drainage ditch.

When at last his pulse slowed and he raised his head, his eyes widened in surprise. A few feet in front of him was a washed-out blue mailbox and a chipped, peeling sign. Though the letters were faded, the words were discernable: Rainbow's End. If his headlights hadn't been angled in this exact direction, he'd have missed it.

Once upon a time, Keith would have attributed such a coincidence to Providence. Now, he just considered it good luck. Or perhaps bad, depending on what he found at the end of the rutted gravel lane beside the mailbox, he amended. But he was bone-weary. And at least the steep, tiny byway that wound up into the woods held out the hope of shelter from the storm. At this point, he didn't even care about eccentric widows, stray cats or old newspapers. All he cared about was a protected place to wait out the storm.

He just hoped it was dry.

At first, Jill didn't notice the thumping sound that blended in with the unremitting rumble of the thunder. But when thumping turned to pounding, she realized that there was a person on the other side of her front door. An impatient person, if the increasingly aggressive banging was any indication.

Considering her scarcity of visitors, Jill could only stare at the door, dumbfounded. Madeleine from the art gallery had stopped by two weeks before, but no one had set foot on her property since. Unless you counted the little boy earlier today. But he hardly qualified as a visitor, considering he'd stayed on the perimeter of her land and avoided contact. Unlike the person on the other side of her door, who was making it clear that contact was his or her precise intent.

Another crash of thunder boomed through the dark house, and Jill jerked, sending a beam from the flashlight in her hand bouncing off the opposite wall. Without electricity, the warm, comforting home she'd created was dim and shadowy. She'd put a battery-operated torch on the kitchen table, and another on the table at the base of the stairs. But they didn't provide enough light to dispel the gloom, or make her feel very secure.

This sense of edginess, of unease, was new. Despite her isolated location, she'd never worried about her safety. Not once in her two years on the island. Then again, she'd never had a visitor at night in the middle of a raging storm. But her caller *was* knocking, she reminded herself. People who were up to no good wouldn't announce their presence.

Her concern abating, Jill walked to the door, pausing to peer through the sheer curtains that hung at the window beside it. The visitor standing on the porch was hidden from her view, but she could see the blurred outlines of a car pulled up beside the steps. As she reached for the lock, she tried to think of some reason why anyone in their right mind would drive all the way out to her place in this kind of weather. When she couldn't come up with even one, her hand faltered.

All at once the pounding started again. "Hey, if you can hear me in there, please answer the door!"

A man's voice. An irritated man's voice. Jill's hand fell to her side and she took a quick step back. Perhaps she should just ignore him. If she didn't respond, he'd assume no one was home and go away, wouldn't he? Then she'd be safe. Holding her breath, she leaned closer, listening for evidence of retreat.

Instead, as the silence lengthened, she heard a heavy sigh of frustration—audible even over the sounds of the storm.

"Look, a woman at the grocery store in Eastsound said you might have a cabin I could rent for the night," the man called out. "She tried to phone, but your line is out. I really need a place to stay."

This time, Jill heard the weariness in his voice. The I've-had-about-all-I-can-take-before-I-fold tone. Only someone who'd been there would discern it beneath the thick coating of frustration.

Closing her eyes, she sent a plea heavenward. *Lord, my heart tells me to help this man. He sounds like he's in need of kindness. Please keep me safe as I follow the example of the Good Samaritan.*

With sudden resolve, Jill tucked the flashlight under her arm and flipped back the dead bolt. But she kept the chain in place, cracking the door no more than the sturdy links would allow. Since the man on the other side was in shadows, she aimed the flashlight at his face.

Muttering something she couldn't make out, he threw up his hands to deflect the intense beam of light. "Could you lower that a little? Try aiming at my chest." His tone was gruff, but he sounded more relieved than angry.

A flush rose on Jill's cheeks as she complied with the stranger's request. "Sorry."

A couple of beats ticked by before he moved his hands aside, as if he was afraid she might pin him with the light again. Then he stared back at her with wary, watchful, cobalt-blue eyes that seemed as uncertain about her as she was about him.

And that was plenty uncertain. Because once Jill got past his eyes, the rest of him scared her to death. Even in daylight, the man on the other side of the door would have made her nervous. His shaggy dark hair was damp and disheveled, and the stubble on his jaw was so thick she wondered if he was just unkempt—or trying to grow a beard. A leather jacket that had logged more than its share of miles sat on his broad, powerful shoulders, gapping open to reveal a chest-hugging T-shirt.

An alarm went off in her mind, and she reduced the crack in the door by the barest margin. But the man noticed. His eyes narrowed, and for a moment Jill was afraid he might try to force his way inside. Her grip tightened on the handle as she prepared to slam the door if he made one wrong move.

The tension emanating from the woman in the house was palpable, and Keith knew he had but a few heartbeats to put her at ease before she shut the door—and left him to face the raging storm with nothing but his car for shelter. Not an appealing prospect. Not when he was this close to a real roof and a dry bed. Yet he couldn't fault her caution—or her alarm. Considering her remote location, she was wise to be careful with strangers. And he didn't exactly look like the boy next door.

As for what *she* looked like—he had no idea. Although his eyes were starting to return to normal after being seared by that blinding light, all he could see through the thin crack in the door was a shadowy form. Not that her appearance mattered. The important thing was that she was his ticket to shelter…*if* he played his cards right. Hoping that she wasn't too spooked by his appearance to listen to his story, he stuck his hands in his pockets and took a step back, keeping his posture as nonthreatening as possible.

"Like I said, the woman in Eastsound told me there was a cabin on the property that might be available for the night." He did his best to sound conversational rather than desperate. "Everything else on the island is booked because of the holiday. She tried to call, but your phone seems to be out. I could sure use a place to stay. The storm's bad."

As if to reinforce his comment, a jagged flash of lightning strobed the sky, followed by a boom of thunder that rattled the window beside Jill. In the wake of that aerial display, the rain intensified. The wind was sweeping sheets of it over the porch railing. Beads of water glistened on the man's leather jacket, and he took his hands out of his pockets to turn up the collar. Yet he didn't step closer, even though such a move would have offered him more protection from the rain.

The notion of having this strange man on her property was disconcerting, but Jill saw no recourse. She couldn't send him back into the storm. That would go against every principle of her faith. And the cabin was on the other side of the meadow, after all. It wasn't as if she was opening her door and bringing a stranger under her own roof. Still, she hesitated.

When the woman didn't react to his first entreaty, Keith tried again. "I know you don't usually rent the cabin, but could you make an exception for one night? I'm willing to pay whatever you think is fair."

Taking a deep breath, and praying that she was making the right decision, Jill spoke at last. "No...I mean, yes, you can stay there. But there's no charge. You're welcome to use it for the night. I'll get the key."

Before he could respond, the door shut and Keith heard the lock click back into place. Surprised by her sudden acquiescence, he stared at the closed door, letting his good luck sink in. He had a place to stay. A haven from the storm. The tense muscles in his shoulders began to ease, and he let out the breath he hadn't realized he was holding. The woman who lived in this house might be eccentric, but she had compassion. *Bless her for her kindness, Lord.*

Twin furrows appeared on Keith's brow. Now where had that come from? Although such blessings had once been routine for him, he hadn't offered one for two long years. Yet the request had slipped out. Force of habit, no doubt. A result of weariness and relief rather than a firm belief that the Lord might listen—let alone answer.

The lock rattled again, and once more the door opened no farther than the chain would allow. A hand slipped through, holding a key, and Keith reached for it.

"The cabin's about a hundred yards east of the house at the far side of the meadow. It's rustic, but it does have running water. There's a narrow, overgrown graveled track that leads to it across the edge of the field, off the driveway. If you need…" As their fingers brushed, Jill's words trailed off. The man's hands were like ice! One thing she'd discovered since coming to the island—even nice summer evenings could be cool, and stormy nights were apt to be downright chilly. This man hadn't learned that yet. She cleared her throat and retracted her hand. "There's a portable propane heater in the closet if you get cold."

"Thanks. Are there candles out there?"

"I don't keep candles on the property." She turned away briefly, then her hand reappeared through the crack, clutching a large flashlight. "This should get you through the night. I expect the power will be back on by morning."

The husky quality of the woman's voice intrigued him. She didn't sound old. But it wasn't a young voice, either. Curiosity about his temporary landlady warred with the need for shelter. Shelter won. Besides, it was obvious that he wasn't going to get more than a shadowy glimpse of her tonight.

"Thanks. I'll be fine."

As he took the flashlight and turned away, directing the beam on the path in front of him, he sensed that she was watching him. Making sure, perhaps, that he followed her instructions and went on his way. And that was fine by him. He'd much rather have a woman intent on getting rid of him than one who...

Unbidden, an image of Susan Reynolds flashed across his mind. Blond, vivacious, attractive—and lethal as a viper. Keith's mouth settled into a thin, grim line as he slid behind the wheel. He'd never known hate until she'd swept through his life like a hurricane, leaving death and destruction in her wake. Never known the kind of all-consuming rage that could rip a man's heart to shreds and leave him helpless and bereft and destroyed, railing against the God who had once been the center of his world. Crying "Why?" into the black void that had become his life, with only the hollow echo of his question coming back in response.

A crash of thunder boomed across the meadow as his headlights tried with limited success to pierce the gloom. The rain beat against the roof of his car in an incessant, pounding, staccato beat. Gusts of wind buffeted the vehicle as he struggled to stay on the obscured, overgrown track, and find his way in the darkness when all the forces of nature seemed to be conspiring against him.

But Keith knew he was close to his destination. That if he persevered, in a couple more minutes he'd find physical refuge from the storm around him.

He just wished a reprieve from the storm within was as close at hand.

Chapter Two

It wasn't noise that roused Keith from a deep slumber the next morning. In fact, the stillness was absolute. Instead, the culprit was a cheery beam of sunlight that danced across his face and tickled his eyes until he finally gave in and opened them.

For a few seconds, he lay motionless, taking stock of his surroundings—his usual orientation ritual after a year of waking up in a new environment on a sometimes-daily basis. What wasn't usual, however, was the odd sense of…*peace,* was the word that came to mind…that enveloped him, like the cozy, soothing warmth of a downy comforter on a cold winter night. Calm had replaced the restlessness that had been his constant companion for more months than he cared to remember. The question was, why?

His mind went into rewind. He was on Orcas Island, in the widow woman's cottage where he'd taken refuge from last night's raging storm. A storm which had now blown out to sea, if the rays of sunlight slanting through the grimy windows of the tiny cottage were any indication. His location didn't seem to offer the answer he sought, however. But whatever the cause, this sense of serenity was a balm to his soul. Instead of trying to analyze it, he'd just enjoy it while it lasted.

Throwing back the patchwork quilt on the double bed that was crammed into the miniscule, spartan bedroom, Keith rose and stretched muscles stiff from too many hours behind the wheel. His wet jeans and shirt lay on the floor where he'd dropped them the night before, when he'd been too weary to do more than kick them into a soggy heap. Stepping over the limp pile, he padded into the only other room in the structure—a combination living-eating area that was furnished with an eclectic mix of odds and ends. A tiny galley kitchen was tucked into a corner alcove, the door to a bare-bones bathroom beside it. Not quite the Ritz—but at least it was dry.

Cleanliness was another story. When he bent to pick up his bag from the floor, then dropped it onto a dated plaid couch, a puff of dust rose, generating two monumental sneezes. His landlady might be charitable, but her housekeeping skills seemed rusty, at best.

Fifteen minutes later, however, fortified by a hot shower and clean clothes, Keith took a better look at his temporary home and revised his assessment. This didn't seem to be the sort of place that required housekeeping. Although the cottage was furnished, suggesting that someone had lived here at one time, it now seemed to be used more as a storage shed. Several wicker baskets were piled on the kitchen counter beside the crumpled paper from the sandwich he'd wolfed down last night. A stack of boxes labeled Miscellaneous Kitchen Items stood beside the couch. And artist supplies were piled in one corner. An easel, blank canvases, brushes of different sizes, a bag of rags, some well-used palettes. Had the previous tenant been a painter, he wondered?

A sudden, loud rumble from his stomach distracted Keith,

reminding him that his eating habits of late had been dicey, at best. His appetite had vanished along with the life he'd once known, and these days he only thought about food when meals were long overdue and his body began to protest. Considering that his diet yesterday had consisted of a doughnut and a deli sandwich, the hollow feeling in the pit of his stomach wasn't surprising.

A quick inspection of the cabinets in the tiny kitchen and the refrigerator yielded nothing edible, as he expected. Why should an unused cottage be stocked with food? He'd been lucky to find a dry—albeit dusty—place to lay his head.

Shoving his palms into the back pockets of his jeans, he wandered over to the window and looked across the field toward the widow's house. The compact two-story structure looked far more trim and tidy than his humble abode, and a lush, well-tended garden edged the foundation. Except for a missing piece of light gray siding on the second level—storm damage, he speculated—it seemed to be in pristine condition.

As if to confirm his theory, a figure in a bulky jacket and wide-brimmed hat, wielding a large ladder, appeared around the corner of the house. From his distant vantage point, it was hard to determine the age, weight or even gender of the person, though he or she was struggling a bit with the awkward piece of equipment. Was it the widow? he wondered. But when the ladder was turned, lifted and propped against the house with minimal effort, he dismissed that notion. Most older women wouldn't have that kind of strength. Still, he'd gotten the impression that the widow lived here alone. And there was a certain grace of movement, an inherent lithe fluidity in the person's posture, that suggested femininity. Perhaps the figure in the distance was, indeed, his landlady. If so, she seemed quite capable in the handyman role.

Another rumble from his stomach reminded him that he needed to scrounge up some food. But his conscience nagged at him. The woman had, after all, given him shelter from the storm—at no charge. The least he could do was repay her kindness by taking care of the siding problem. His father had instilled good carpentry skills in him, and he could bang out that job in ten minutes. Maybe that wasn't the way he'd planned to start his day, but it was the right way.

Trying to ignore his protesting stomach, he slid his arms into his jacket and stepped out into the cool, clear morning air. As he set off down the gravel path—*road* was way too generous a term for the narrow, overgrown lane he'd negotiated across the field last night—the world seemed somehow fresh and renewed. The still-damp leaves of the trees glistened in the morning sun, and the song of the birds was the only sound echoing across the quiet air.

At least it was until the woman began to hammer. As the discordant pounding reverberated across the tranquil stillness, shattering the contemplative mood, Keith increased his pace. The sooner he offered his services, the sooner he could restore the peace that had soothed his soul.

So intent was Jill on her task that she was oblivious to her guest's approach until he called out to her from the foot of the ladder.

"I'd be happy to lend a hand with that."

Startled, she lost her grip on the hammer, then watched in horror as it plummeted toward the ground, heading straight for her visitor's head. If he'd been less alert, the results could have been nasty. As it was, he jumped back and it landed with a dull, innocuous thud on the wet ground.

A warm flush crept up Jill's neck as she tucked her head

into the collar of her jacket and stared down at the man. In the light of day, his presence was even more disconcerting—and unsettling—than it had been last night. With the golden morning glow illuminating his upturned face, there was no question that underneath the stubble and shaggy hair, he was a good-looking man. Close to forty, she estimated, though she couldn't tell if the lines on his face were the result of age or weariness. As he raked his fingers through his hair, she realized that it was much lighter now that it was dry. A medium, sun-streaked brown. His striking, cobalt-blue eyes were vivid in the daylight, though there was a dullness in their depths that spoke of defeat and disillusionment. Right now, however, they were regarding her with a wariness that suggested he wasn't sure whether or not she'd dropped the hammer on purpose.

"Sorry. You startled me." She set the record straight.

The tension in his features eased. "Then I'm the one who should apologize. Why don't you let me take care of that for you?"

"Thanks, but I can handle it."

"I owe you for last night. Besides, I'm a carpenter, so a job like that is a piece of cake for me."

The man didn't seem in the least inclined to budge. But Jill was used to handling maintenance on her own. She didn't need his help. Yet despite the extensive rehabbing she'd done on her house, she wasn't all that fond of ladders. Or heights. Sensing her indecision, the man grasped the ladder to steady it.

"I'm sure you have better things to do than deal with storm damage. Come on down and let me take care of it."

Capitulating seemed the quickest way to end the conversation, and once on the ground she could make a fast break for the house, Jill reasoned. With sudden decision, she climbed down in silence.

Back on solid earth, she stuck her hands in her pockets and buried her chin deep into the collar of her coat, keeping her face averted. At five foot six, Jill wasn't short. But the man beside her was a good five or six inches taller. "Thanks. I do have some things to attend to in the house," she murmured.

As she turned to go, a capricious gust of wind snatched her weathered, wide-brimmed hat, tossing it into the sky. With a gasp of surprise, Jill lifted her head and attempted to grab it, but it was already beyond her reach. As she watched, the man's hand shot out and his sun-browned fingers closed over the brim, retrieving it from the wind's grasp. Then he turned to her.

"Looks like the wind…" The words faded from Keith's lips as he stared at his landlady, stunned. Up to this point, she'd given him no more than a shadowed glimpse of her countenance. Now, though her face remained in profile, he realized that the old, wizened widow he'd expected couldn't be more than thirty-five. Fiery highlights in her wavy, light brown hair sparked in the morning sun, calling attention to the long, lustrous tresses that had tumbled from beneath her hat. Wispy bangs brushed her forehead above wide, hazel eyes flecked with gold, and below a straight nose her lips were full and slightly parted. If the voice didn't match the woman from last night, Keith would never have believed that this was the eccentric widow the storekeeper in Eastsound had described.

Yet there *was* a different quality about her. She hadn't yet established eye contact with him. In fact, she was doing her best to keep her face averted. Why?

Curious, he held the hat out to her, letting it slip from his fingers as she reached for it—forcing her to angle his direction as she bent down to grab for it. That move bought him only a quick glimpse of her face. But he saw enough to get his answer. One that shocked him to the very core of his being.

The woman's flawless beauty, which he'd admired in profile, was marred almost beyond recognition on the right side of her face by a large, angry scar that started at her temple, nipped close to her eye, then followed the line of her cheekbone south, catching the very corner of her mouth as it trailed down to her chin.

Before he could mask his shock, the woman straightened. Jamming the hat back on her head, she stared at him for several long beats of silence. Then her expression shifted in some subtle, but disturbing way. It was as if something had shattered inside her. Not in a dramatic way, like a crystal vase smashing into pieces on the floor. It was more like the network of fine cracks that spread across the surface of a piece of pottery when the protective glaze becomes crazed.

Whatever it was, Keith didn't have a chance to analyze it because she turned with an abrupt move and almost ran toward the back of the house. As she disappeared around the corner, her hurried footsteps sounded across a wooden surface before a door was opened—and closed.

At one time in his life, Keith had been good at dealing with distraught people. They'd sought him out for his compassion, his understanding, his sensitivity. Well, those skills had deserted him today. He'd gawked at the woman, stared at her as if she was some freak in a circus sideshow. He'd been rude, tactless, inconsiderate, thoughtless…in other words, a jerk. Of all people, he should know better. He had plenty of scars of his own. They just weren't visible. But if they were, they'd be as disfiguring as his landlady's. Maybe more so. And how would he like it if they drew the kind of look he'd given her?

The short answer was, he wouldn't.

The bigger question was, how did he make amends?

It had been a long while since Keith had interacted enough with another human being to risk hurting their feelings. And longer still since he'd cared if he did. Yet for some reason this woman had breached the defenses he'd constructed around his heart. Perhaps because she seemed so…solitary. So alone and isolated. Not just in a geographic sense, but at a deeper, more fundamental level. As if she lived in the world but wasn't part of it.

For the past two years, Keith had felt as alone as he'd thought a person could feel. Angry and lost, he'd turned his back on a world and a God that had betrayed him. Yet he had a feeling that this woman, living in this isolated place apart from society, was even lonelier than he was. He also sensed at some intuitive level that she had accepted her solitary existence, knowing that her physical scars would never heal, shunning a world that looked on her with morbid curiosity and pity—much as he had done moments ago.

That was the difference between them, he mused. When Keith had set out on his trek, he'd hoped his travels would help him discover a way to pick up the pieces and start over, healed and made new again. Although that hadn't happened yet, deep inside he held on to the hope that it would. It was the only thing that kept him going. The notion of spending his remaining years in a vacuum devoid of all the things that had once made his life rich and full and satisfying was too terrifying. Yet he had a feeling the woman inside this house didn't have that hope. But how in the world did she go on, day after day, without it?

She wasn't his problem, of course. He was just passing through, a stranger who knew nothing about her except her last name and marital status. And given her reticence, he doubted whether he'd learn any more. He ought to forget about her.

Yet, as he picked up the hammer, climbed the ladder and set to work on the errant piece of siding, he felt a need to apologize. Trouble was, he didn't have a clue how to do that without calling more attention to her scar and making the whole thing worse.

Years ago, he would have prayed for guidance in a situation like this. But he didn't have that option anymore. Instead, all Keith had to rely on were his own instincts. And considering how they'd failed him two years before, he had no confidence that they would help him rectify this situation.

But as an image of the woman's shattered face flashed once again across his mind, he knew he had to at least try.

Inside the house, Jill stirred the simmering pot of soup she'd made at the crack of dawn, struggling to contain the tears that threatened to leak out the corners of her eyes. *Don't cry!* she admonished herself fiercely. As her sister, Deb, used to say, she'd already cried enough tears to sink a ship. Too bad Deb wasn't here now. In her no-nonsense way, she'd always helped Jill regain her balance when the world began to tilt. She'd done that a lot during the weeks and months after the fire, through the surgeries and treatments and rehab, always an anchor to hold on to when the pain and the grief became unbearable. If it hadn't been for her older sister, Jill was sure she'd have given up and let the suffocating sense of loss overwhelm and destroy her.

She tried to imagine what Deb would say if she *were* here. "Get a grip," no doubt. She'd point out that the man's shock had been a normal, human reaction, and that he hadn't intended to hurt her. That once he got to know her, he'd forget about the scars that served as a constant reminder of the tragic night that had forever changed her world.

Yeah, right.

Although Deb meant well, Jill knew better. Oh, sure, people tried to act nonchalant once their initial shock passed. But they were never able to get past the scars. Even here, after two years. The islanders she saw on her trips to church or into the villages were nice. Too nice. That was the problem. They smiled too much, kept up a stream of chatter about inconsequential things, wished her a good day with bright smiles. They tried to act as if they enjoyed seeing her, but in truth they were glad when she left. She made them uncomfortable.

That was just the way it was. The way it would always be. Jill thought she'd accepted that. Thought she'd learned to deal with it. Nowadays, when people stared at her, she felt nothing beyond a twinge somewhere deep in the recesses of her heart. It had been a very long time since anyone had managed to evoke even the hint of tears. Yet this man, a stranger who would soon slip out of her life as suddenly as he had slipped in, had managed to awaken a sadness that she'd long ago subdued. And she had no idea why.

Yes, you do, a little voice whispered at the edges of her consciousness.

Startled, she stopped stirring the soup and grasped the edge of the counter with her free hand, trying to suppress the answer that kept bubbling to the surface much as the herbs in her soup pot were doing. But the little voice wouldn't be stilled.

Because he's a man.

It was a truth Jill couldn't dispute. Her tenant's reaction disturbed her because he was a man. A scruffy one, no question. Not the kind of man she'd ever have looked at twice in years past. But he was close to her age. And his expression of shock, horror, pity and revulsion had clarified for her, if she'd ever harbored any secret hopes otherwise, that no man could ever look at her again as a desirable woman.

Nevertheless, the strength of her response shook her. Jill had assumed that any romantic yearnings had died along with Sam. After all, she hadn't thought about love once since then, not on a conscious level. Yet, if the reaction of an unkempt stranger could reduce her to tears....

Taking herself in hand, Jill resumed stirring the pot with vigor and swiped the tears out of her eyes. This was just an aberration. Brought on by too little sleep during the storm-tossed night, she rationalized. As soon as he finished repairing her siding, the man would be gone. Peace would once more descend on her world. She'd have a little breakfast, pay a few bills, then spend the next few hours painting in her sunny studio upstairs. It would be a typical, quiet morning. The kind she always enjoyed and looked forward to.

Except for some odd reason, thinking about her solitary plans didn't lift her spirits at all. Instead, it depressed her.

The aromas wafting through the kitchen window were driving him mad.

As Keith banged the final nail into the siding, his salivary glands went into overdrive. Chicken soup. That's what it smelled like. Homemade chicken soup. The kind his mother used to make, its enticing aroma greeting him when he came home from school. To this day, that simple meal always evoked happy memories of home and love and security.

Too bad he'd botched the conversation with his landlady this morning, Keith thought, finding yet another reason to regret his rudeness. He'd have loved to wrangle a sample of whatever was cooking in that pot. But given the woman's reaction to his insensitive gawking, the odds of that happening were slim to none. Even after the apology he still planned to offer.

Once he double-checked the board to ensure it was secure, Keith descended the ladder, then headed toward the front door and knocked. As he waited for her to answer, he tried to think of how to frame his apology. But when she cracked the door open, he hadn't yet found the words.

"I'm finished. Where would you like the ladder?"

"Just leave it. I'll put it away later." She started to close the door.

"I'd rather finish the job. That means putting away the tools."

Hesitating, she gave him an uncertain look. "There's a shed around back. It goes in there."

Before he could say another word, she shut the door.

So much for the apology, he thought, as he headed back around the house, located the surprisingly well-equipped toolshed and slid the ladder into a slot inside. Someone around here knew tools. And since the woman at the house seemed to be the sole occupant, it must be her. Impressive.

When he stepped outside, a curtain fluttered at the back window. She was continuing to keep tabs on him, it seemed. Not that he blamed her, considering his disreputable appearance. For all she knew, he was some derelict who was up to no good. What surprised him was his reaction. It bothered him that she might consider him dangerous or unsavory. In light of the fact that for the past couple of years he hadn't cared a lick what people thought about him, his reaction was odd. But for whatever reason he didn't want this woman to think ill of him—or to regret her kindness to a stranger. All of which brought him back to his apology. It was time.

Combing his fingers through his too-long hair in a futile effort to tidy it, he strode toward the house, stepped up onto the back porch and knocked on that door.

When she eased it open, the delicious aroma that wafted out almost did him in. But he did his best to focus on the reason he'd come to the door instead of listening to the pleas of his stomach.

"I'll be heading out now, ma'am. I wanted to thank you again for your kindness last night. I don't know what—" A flicker of movement across the field caught his eye, and he turned just as a small boy darted behind a boulder. "Looks like you have a visitor."

Curious, Jill opened the door wider, enough to peer in the direction Keith was looking. "Where?"

"Over there, behind the rocks. A little boy. He moved back when he saw me. Is he a friend of yours?"

Leaning farther out, Jill scanned the boulders. It was the same place she'd spotted the boy. "I don't know who he is. I saw him for the first time yesterday."

She continued to look toward the rocks as Keith shifted his gaze back to her. She still wore the floppy hat, but he could see the concern etched on her shadowed face.

"Maybe he'll come out when I leave."

"No. It's not you that's holding him back. He ran away when I tried to talk to him, too." Her attention remained fixed on the far edge of the field.

This was the time, Keith thought, taking a deep breath. "Before I go, I'd like to apologize for staring earlier. It was a rude thing to do, and I'm sorry if I upset you."

Startled, Jill turned back to him. Then did a double take. The man was doing something no one except her family—and her doctors—had ever done. He was looking right at her scar, without flinching, without skittering past it. He didn't try to ignore it, as most people did. Instead, he traced it from end to end—at least what he could see of it beneath the wide, protective brim of her hat. She wanted to turn away, wanted to hide her face. But there was a compelling expression in his eyes that held her motionless.

"I also want you to know that I'm sorry for whatever happened to cause that." His voice was gentle, his eyes kind. "And that I'm sorry for whatever trauma you've had to endure since then. If I added to your pain in any way, I ask your forgiveness."

The man's direct approach, along with his sincere remorse, left Jill speechless. Not only was he looking at her scar, he was talking about it! She had no idea how to respond.

When the silence between them lengthened, he shifted from one foot to the other. "Well, I better be off. I wonder if you could direct me to the nearest place to get some breakfast?"

Food. The man was asking about food. It took Jill a few moments to collect her thoughts, but when she did it occurred to her that he must be starving. He'd had no dinner that she was aware of, and there wasn't a dry cracker to be found in the cabin. She started to open her mouth to direct him to Olga, the closest village, when that persistent little voice in the back of her mind spoke once more.

You could feed him instead.

Again, though she tried to suppress it, she met with little success. The man had fixed her siding, after all. And from the looks of him, he could use a good meal. His jeans sat low on his lean hips. Too low. And she didn't think it was a fashion statement. Rather, she suspected his spare frame was the result of too many missed meals. It wouldn't hurt her to give him some food before sending him on his way. It was the hospitable thing to do. The Christian thing. Didn't the Lord feed the multitudes with loaves and fishes when they were in need?

Besides, there was something about him that drew her, that made her want to find out more about what made him tick. To discover why this stranger seemed able to look past her scars, past the brokenness, and see the whole person underneath. And giving him a meal would buy her a little time to do that.

Taking a step back until she hovered on the edges of the interior shadows, her fingers tightened around the door. "I can give you some breakfast."

Now it was Keith's turn to be shocked. The last thing he'd expected from this woman was an invitation to dine. But if the aromas that continued to waft through the door were any indication of her culinary abilities, he was in for a treat. That alone would compel him to accept.

Beyond that, though, he knew that her invitation also meant she'd accepted his apology. And that fact, even more than the thought of a good meal, lightened his heart.

"Thank you. I'd like that very much."

"Come back in twenty minutes. I'll have it ready by then."

As Jill shut the door, cutting her off from the man on the other side, she drew a long, shaky breath. Already she was having second thoughts. Why on earth had she impulsively offered a stranger breakfast? It could be a huge mistake. One she might very well live to regret.

Yet even as that dire warning flashed across her mind, in her heart she somehow felt that she'd made the right decision.

Chapter Three

What in the world was she going to feed the man?

Hands on her hips, Jill scanned the contents of her refrigerator. Too bad she hadn't gone to Olga two days ago, as she'd planned, to stock up on perishables. She was down to her last two eggs, and there was no breakfast meat of any kind. Nor much of anything else. At one time, she'd enjoyed cooking. But solo meals held little appeal. These days she got by on cold cereal, sandwiches, dairy products and fruit. Homemade soup represented her sole foray into the culinary arts, and she almost always had some on hand—like the pot of chicken-rice soup now simmering on the stove, flavored with the herbs she'd plucked from the pots on her kitchen windowsill. But even though it had once earned rave reviews from family and friends, it didn't qualify as breakfast fare.

Closing the refrigerator, she turned her attention to the cabinets. At least she had all the basics on hand—flour, sugar, salt, spices. When a bottle of maple syrup—a leftover from her sister's last visit—caught her eye, she thought of the blackberries she'd picked last season at their peak of juicy sweetness, preserved in her freezer. Inspiration hit…black-berry pancakes!

In no time, Jill was whipping up a batch of batter. Though she seldom made pancakes anymore, the recipe was etched in her mind. Sam and Emily had loved them so much they'd become a Saturday-morning tradition.

Her hand slowed. Funny. She hadn't thought about that once-a-week ritual for months. Hadn't *let* herself think about it. Like so much of her previous life that was gone forever, it was too painful to remember. And now wasn't the time to start, she reminded herself, resuming her measuring and stirring.

Once the batter was ready and she'd poured three generous circles on the griddle, Jill set a single place at the small table on the back porch, adding a glass of orange juice and a cup of coffee. Then she returned to the house to flip the fluffy pancakes. When her unexpected guest reappeared at the far end of the meadow, she transferred the pancakes to a plate. After dusting them with powdered sugar, she tilted the maple syrup that had been warming on the stove into a small crockery pitcher and arranged everything on the table. By the time he arrived, she was back inside, working at the sink where she could catch a glimpse of him through the large window in front of her.

In the past hour, the morning had warmed quite a bit, and the northeast-facing back porch was bathed in sunlight as Keith ascended the two steps. In spite of his hunger, he stopped when he saw the carefully set table and the appetiz-ing plate of food waiting for him. It had been a long while since anyone but a fast-food worker or a short-order cook in some diner had prepared a meal for him. Longer still since anyone had cared to provide him with any of the niceties of dining. Like a cloth napkin, with crisp, precise folds. Or a woven placemat. Or the cushion on the wooden chair, added since his earlier visit. Not to mention the small vase of wild-flowers that now graced the center of the table.

All of those touches registered in a flash as Keith scanned the setting. So did the single place setting. But it was the plate of mouthwatering pancakes that caught and held his attention.

"Go ahead and eat before they get cold."

The woman's husky voice came through the open window in the kitchen, and Keith moved forward. He didn't need a second invitation. "Thanks."

Seating himself at the small wooden table, he dived in, making liberal use of the maple syrup and washing down the feather-light pancakes with long swigs of strong, black coffee. In minutes, the plate was empty.

"Would you like some more?"

Glancing up, Keith saw his hostess hovering at the back door. A smile tried to lift the corners of his mouth but his lips balked at the unaccustomed tug, as stiff and resistant as a painter's brush that had gone too-long unused. "Do I look that hungry?"

"I expect you could manage another serving."

"You're right. Thanks."

While Keith waited, he sipped his coffee, noting that the little boy had returned, still hiding behind the boulders on the other side of the field. When the woman reappeared a few minutes later with another overflowing plate and hesitated at the back door, he figured she wanted him to come and get his food. That way, she could stay in the shadows. Instead, he inclined his head toward the rocks. "Your friend is still here."

That caught her attention. Jamming her hat farther down on her head, she pushed through the door. As she focused on the far side of the field, she gave him a shaded view of her classic profile. "I don't see him."

"He was there a minute ago. I have a feeling he's been watching the house for some time."

Frowning, she deposited Keith's plate on the table and refilled his mug from the pot she carried in her other hand, keeping one eye on the distant boulders. "When I saw him yesterday, he didn't look very well cared for. He might even be hungry. If I could figure out a way to coax him closer, I'm sure I could find out. I used to be pretty good with kids."

Her concern for the little boy had overridden her self-consciousness and reticence, and Keith marveled at the change in her. For a brief moment he had an intriguing glimpse of the engaged, self-assured woman she must once have been.

But that window into her past closed the instant she realized he was watching her. Turning abruptly, she started back to the house.

"Aren't you having any?"

His question stopped her, and she half turned. "I don't eat much breakfast."

He wasn't surprised. Now that she'd ditched the bulky jacket, there was no question about her gender. Her lithe figure was rounded in all the right places. A soft chambray shirt hinted at the curves beneath, and her unpretentious jeans encased her long legs like a second skin.

It had been a long while since Keith had noticed a woman's physical attributes, and years since he'd taken such a detailed inventory. He had no idea what had possessed him to do so now. And he wasn't inclined to analyze it. Better to move on to another—safer—topic.

"If you won't join me, at least let me introduce myself." He rose and extended his hand. "My name is Keith Michaels."

He wasn't sure she would respond, but after a brief hesitation, she dipped her head, stepped toward him and took his fingers in a grip that displayed surprising strength. "Jill Whelan."

As the stranger held Jill's hand, he also held her captive with his compelling blue eyes. They seemed to delve into her heart, searching, seeing things she had never given voice to. Of course, such fanciful thoughts were no more than the product of an overactive imagination, she chided herself. But it was an odd sensation nonetheless.

The sudden ringing of the phone broke the spell, and with a slight tug, she reclaimed her hand and turned toward the house. "You'd better eat those while they're warm. Some things taste just as good cold, but pancakes aren't one of them."

Hurrying toward the phone, Jill left the back door ajar instead of closing and locking it, as she had up until now. There was something in the man's face—character and integrity, certainly, but also a distant sadness as if he, too, had suffered some terrible tragedy—that told her she had nothing to fear from him. Nothing physical, anyway. Her emotions were another story. He'd disrupted those already. But she had a feeling no wooden door would protect her from that kind of danger, anyway.

When she answered the phone, she was a bit out of breath—which didn't escape her sister's notice.

"Is everything okay? Did I catch you at a bad time?" Deb queried.

"No, no. I'm fine. I was outside."

"At this hour? You're always eating your yogurt and reading the paper now."

Goodness, was she that predictable? But the resounding answer was: yes! Deb called like clockwork at nine-thirty every Saturday morning, and like clockwork Jill would be reading the local weekly paper, which she saved for that occasion in order to differentiate the weekend from the workweek. Except today she'd forgotten all about the paper and her yogurt and even Deb's call—thanks to one Keith Michaels, now ensconced on her back porch eating her blackberry pancakes.

"We had a storm last night and a piece of siding got ripped off the side of the house," Jill explained, redirecting her attention to the conversation.

"I hope you weren't climbing on ladders."

"There's not much choice when the problem is on the second floor."

"But you hate ladders. Look, I know you're handy, but can't you get someone to fix it for you?"

"It's already done, Deb."

"That figures." Her sister gave a long-suffering sigh. "You know, I ought to send my husband out there to take a few lessons from you. Tony is a wonderful provider, but when it comes to home maintenance he's as useless as a cell phone with a dead battery. You must have been at it at the crack of dawn."

Before she could respond, the back screen door opened and Keith came in far enough to deposit his plate and juice glass on the counter. Then he retreated to the porch, the screen door banging behind him.

"Jill? What was that?"

Typical Deb. She didn't miss a thing, Jill thought with a wry shake of her head. "The back door."

"Who came in? Is everything okay?"

"Everything's fine. Look, it's kind of a long story."

"I've got all day."

"It's no big deal, Deb."

"Then why don't you just tell me?"

Shaking her head, Jill let out a resigned sigh. "Did anyone ever tell you you're pushy?"

"Yeah. You do. All the time. But hey, that's what sisters are for. Now spill it. If you have a visitor, I want to hear all about it. This doesn't happen every day."

Knowing Deb wouldn't let up until she got the information she wanted, Jill gave her a shorthand version. "I let a guy use the cottage last night. They sent him out from town because there isn't a room to be had over the holiday weekend, and it was raining cats and dogs. Turns out he's a carpenter, and he offered to put the siding back up for me. I gave him breakfast on the back porch as a thank-you. He just brought in his empty plate."

Silence greeted her narration. When it lengthened, Jill spoke again. "Deb? Are you still there?"

"Yeah. Yeah, I'm here. You took in a boarder? And you're letting him wander around your house?"

"He's not a boarder. He stayed for one night. And he's not wandering around my house."

"Who is this guy?"

"I have no idea."

"What does he look like?"

"What difference does that make?"

"Just answer the question."

"I don't know." She turned to look out the door. Keith was standing by the porch railing sipping his coffee, his strong profile thrown into sharp relief by the morning sun. Angling away from the door, she lowered her voice. "He's a little shaggy around the edges and a bit road-weary. But he looks honest."

"How old is he?"

"What is this, the third degree?"

"Look, when some guy shows up on my sister's doorstep—my sister who avoids people like the plague, especially men—and she lets him wander around her house, I have reason to be concerned. So how old is he?"

Letting her sister's remark about avoiding people pass, Jill answered the question. "Fortyish, maybe."

Another few beats of silence passed. "I'm not sure I like this, Jill. I love your place, but it's very isolated. I worry about you alone out there."

"I'm fine, Deb. There's no need for concern. I was just being a Good Samaritan. He's been very polite and grateful. And he's leaving in a few minutes. End of story."

"Hmm." She didn't sound convinced. "Call me after he's gone, okay?"

"Deb."

"Just call me, okay? Otherwise I'll worry about you. More than I already do."

"Fine. I'll call. Now let's talk about more important things. Like your visit in two weeks. I can't wait to see you and Dominic."

"We're looking forward to it, too. Dominic can't talk about anything else. It's Aunt Jill this and Aunt Jill that, and can we collect rocks at the beach again and go watch whales and climb that mountain, yada, yada, yada."

"Tell him the answer to all of those questions is yes. Now let's talk logistics." As they worked out the details, Jill realized that she was as excited about the annual visit as her sister and nephew were. Much as she loved her life on her little corner of Orcas Island, it did get lonely on occasion. More so at some times than others.

Turning toward the porch again, her gaze once more sought

Keith. He was standing with his back to her now as he looked toward Mount Constitution. In a few minutes, he would be gone, as she'd told Deb. And even though she knew nothing about him, even though his visit had been brief, she had the oddest feeling that his departure would initiate one of those "more so" times.

Only snatches of conversation drifted through the open screen door to Keith. But he heard enough to realize that Jill was discussing plans with a woman named Deb for a visit. And that pleased him. It meant there was someone who cared about her and gave her an occasional reprieve from her solitary existence.

He drew in a long, cleansing breath of the fresh morning air, enjoying the warmth of the sun against his face. To his surprise, the sense of peace he'd awakened with was still with him. He'd expected it to dissipate along with the wisps of mist that had hung over the field earlier in the morning as he'd trekked across. The feeling was so welcome, so calming, that he was loath to drive away and risk leaving it behind. But he had no excuse to stay. The woman in Eastsound had told him that Jill didn't lease her cottage. Besides, he didn't have enough money to pay rent for very long, anyway.

Yet, he wanted to stay. For a few days, at least. Long enough, perhaps, for the peace to soothe his soul and give him a chance to figure out where he was going to go from here. His finances could handle a short extension of his visit. The trick would be convincing his reluctant landlady to prolong her hospitality.

When Jill reappeared, Keith's mug was almost empty. "Sorry for the interruption. Would you like some more coffee?" she offered, keeping her distance.

"No, thanks. The breakfast was great. I haven't had a meal like that in ages."

She acknowledged the compliment with a slight tip of her head. "Thank you for fixing the siding."

"It was the least I could do after you took pity on me in the storm. I don't know what I would have done otherwise."

"The holiday weekend is always crowded here. I doubt there's a vacancy anywhere on the island."

She'd given him the perfect opening. His grip on the mug tightened and the muscles in his shoulders tensed even as he tried to keep his tone casual. "I found that out the hard way. The truth is, I'd hoped to spend a few days here, but every place will be booked at least for a couple more days. The woman in Eastsound told me you don't rent out the cottage as a rule, but is there any way I could convince you to let me stay a bit longer? Not free, of course."

His request surprised her. And at some elemental level, it also pleased her. She wasn't sure why. Perhaps because her less-than-welcoming manner and damaged face hadn't scared him off. Of course, she was silly to read anything personal into his request. It was based on practicalities, after all. She had a cabin; he needed a place to stay; everywhere else was booked. It was as simple and straightforward as that.

Her spirits deflated a bit. She must be more starved for human companionship than she'd realized. If that was the case, she needed to figure out how to deal with it. Because she didn't anticipate any changes to her solitary existence anytime soon. Even if this man extended his stay, he'd be gone in a few days. But Deb and Dominic would follow in a couple of weeks, she reminded herself. She should be counting her blessings for having such a loving, supportive family instead of griping about the life she'd chosen for herself.

In the meantime, this man needed a place to stay and she was in a position to provide it. There was no logical reason to refuse his request.

"You can use the cottage for a few days. It's sitting there empty, anyway." She started to gather up the condiments from the table.

"Just let me know what you think is a fair price."

"There's no charge. You're not getting any great bargain out there. It's pretty bare bones."

"It's far better than camping, which is what I do most of the time. I wouldn't feel right about staying if you won't let me pay."

Straightening, she sent him a sideways look. "I don't need the money, Mr. Michaels."

"Keith. And that's beside the point. I prefer to pay my way."

From the stubborn set of his jaw beneath the stubble and the resolve in his eyes, Jill could see that her unexpected guest wasn't about to budge on this issue. Shrugging, she resumed her work. "Fine. Let me think for a minute." Silence ensued as she gathered up the tablecloth, and when she finally threw out a number, Keith frowned.

"You can't even get a cheap motel for that rate," he protested.

The barest hint of a smile played at the corners of her mouth. "I think there's something wrong with this picture. Isn't the buyer supposed to try and negotiate a lower price, not a higher one?"

An answering grin tugged at his mouth. This time his lips cooperated, twitching up a fraction. "I want to be fair."

"I consider the price I quoted more than fair, since I offered the cabin to you free."

Her point was hard to dispute. With a gesture of capitulation, he gave in. "Then I accept. With thanks." He took the last swig of his coffee and handed her the mug. When his firm, strong fingers brushed hers, she tried not to notice. "I think I'll head out and do a little exploring, stock up on some provisions. Thanks again, Jill."

He turned and struck out across the field. As Jill watched him recede into the distance, focusing on his broad back, she tried to figure out why she'd agreed to rent her cabin to this stranger. Considering how she guarded her privacy, it was an odd thing to do. She should be sending him on his way, not inviting him to share her space. It made no sense.

And if she couldn't explain her behavior to herself, how in the world was she going to explain it to Deb?

Chapter Four

The place was a pigsty.

Hot color crept up Jill's neck to her cheeks as she surveyed the cluttered, dirty cabin where Keith had spent last night. The dust was deep enough to write in, bits of debris clung to the woven rugs, and the thick grime on the windows was as effective as shades in diffusing the sunlight. On top of all that, the whole place smelled musty, half of the lightbulbs were burned out and cobwebs had staked a claim on the corners of the ceiling.

Yet her unexpected visitor not only wanted to pay to stay here, he considered it a bargain!

Well, Jill knew better. The place was more suited to its current role as a storage shed than to human habitation. Of course, at one time it had been much more livable. Jill had spent the first six months of her stay here while she rehabbed the decrepit main house. But since moving out, she'd done little to maintain the interior. Now that she had a paying guest, however, she needed to make up for lost time.

Unsure how long Keith would be gone, Jill went into high

gear. She dusted, vacuumed, mopped, scoured the kitchen and bathroom, stripped the bed and remade it with clean sheets and washed all the windows. Then she gathered up the baskets on the counter, carried the boxes of kitchen odds and ends outside, and collected her art supplies, wedging them into her car for a trip across the field to the house. As a final touch, she put a vase of fresh wildflowers in the center of the small oak dining table, propping a note beside it that directed Keith to the refrigerator.

Finished, she stepped back to assess the results of her two hours of intensive labor. The windows sparkled, the polished surface of the table glistened, every bit of dust and debris had been vanquished, the bathroom and kitchen were spick-and-span, and the light fixtures gleamed. With a satisfied nod, she packed up her supplies and headed home.

As she crossed the field, she couldn't help but wonder what her temporary tenant would think about the transformation in his accommodations. She hoped he'd be pleased. After all, if he was willing to pay for the privilege of occupying her modest cabin, the least she could do was give it a thorough cleaning. Of course, if he was like a lot of men, he wouldn't notice the care she'd taken to make him feel welcome.

But already Jill was getting the distinct feeling that Keith Michaels wasn't like a lot of men.

Not even close.

For a fleeting second, Keith wasn't sure he was in the right cabin.

As he stepped across the threshold, arms laden with grocery bags and laundry, he came to an abrupt stop. The cabin was immaculate. Every vestige of grime and neglect had been removed. The place was so clean is almost glowed.

Stunned, Keith did a slow inventory. Crisp curtains hung at the spotless windows. When he dropped the laundry onto the couch, no dust cloud engulfed him. A peek into the bedroom revealed a neatly made bed, with decorative pillows fluffed against the headboard. The bathroom floor looked clean enough to eat off, and the kitchen was pristine.

Completing his circuit in the dining alcove, he spotted the flowers and note. Reaching for the single sheet of paper, he scanned the simple message, which was written in a flowing, graceful script.

"Sorry for the mess you found when you arrived. Hope the homemade soup in the fridge helps make up for it!"

Somehow, the fact that Jill had scoured the place didn't surprise him. But the soup was an added—and touching—bonus. With an eagerness he couldn't have suppressed if he tried, he returned to the kitchen and opened the fridge. Sure enough, a large container stood in the otherwise empty interior. Lifting the lid, he inhaled. Ambrosia! Memories of better times, of home and comfort and love, washed over him in a cleansing wave, and for a second it was like a taste of heaven.

Though the impression was fleeting, it was a balm to Keith's ravaged soul. That brief glimpse of happiness, of joy and contentment and rightness, was the first such moment he'd had since his world began to fall apart. And if he could have one such moment, perhaps others would follow, he realized, his spirits notching up another peg.

Odd. Just when his hope was running on fumes, it had been given a boost by his reluctant landlady. A woman who had suffered her own trauma, who had lost a man Keith assumed she loved, who had suffered a terrible injury, and who now lived alone with her memories, secluded in this beautiful but remote place. A woman who had chosen a solitary life, but had nevertheless reached out to him in his need. Her unselfish kindness touched him in a way nothing else had for two years.

A long time ago, Keith would have paused to thank the Lord for leading him to this place when his soul most needed replenishing. And maybe, somehow, the Lord's hand was in this. But he wasn't sure. About that…and about so many of the things he'd once believed with such fervor and absolute conviction. That uncertainty was, in fact, the root cause of his problem.

But what did God expect, after the crippling blow life had dealt him? He'd tried to remain upright in the torrent that raged around and within him, but in the end he'd lost his balance and fallen. And kept falling, until he was sucked so far down into the swirling vortex, so shrouded in darkness, that he wondered whether he would ever find his way out. God knew, he'd tried! But without his faith to sustain him, the quest had been futile. Where once he'd found strength and courage and fortitude in his beliefs, there was now a black void.

Part of him still yearned to turn to God, to plead for help. But God had been deaf to all his entreaties, refusing to answer even a man who had dedicated his life to spreading His good news, to gathering His flock. The bitterness already on Keith's tongue had grown more acrid as the silence lengthened, distancing him further from the One who had once guided his every step. The chasm had deepened, widened. Until now, Keith felt as isolated spiritually as Jill was geographically.

Yet deep in the recesses of his heart, he wanted to believe. Wanted to trust once more in the Lord's goodness. To put his life in God's hands, as he'd often counseled others to do. To rely with confidence on the Lord's guiding presence even

when the powers of darkness loomed and threatened. Without
that trust, without that belief, he was floundering, seeking
answers where none were to be found. But how did he reconnect? How did he find his way back to the Source, to the
spring of life that had once refreshed his parched soul?

For the past year he'd been seeking the truth, searching for
answers, looking for release. But nowhere in his travels had
he found these elusive quarries. Nor had he come close to
finding a hint of the infinite peace bestowed only by God.

Until he'd come here.

As he'd walked across the tranquil meadow this morning,
Keith had attributed his heightened sense of hope to the place
itself. And there was something special about this rocky piece
of land, with its soaring mountains and verdant forests and
shimmering, crystalline seas. But it wasn't just the place.

It was also the woman.

Despite their brief acquaintance, Keith had already been
touched by Jill in ways he couldn't begin to articulate. Though
marred by tragedy, and sensitive about her scars, she had a
serenity about her that he envied. As if she'd made her peace
with the horrendous injury that had forever changed the way
the world looked at her. And considering her reclusive lifestyle,
the kindness and generosity she'd shown to a stranger at her
door had been remarkable—as well as humbling. She'd asked
nothing from him in return for her benevolence. Instead, she'd
continued to give, living the golden rule he'd often preached.

Once more Keith scanned the cabin, drawing in a deep,
contented breath. There was order here. And peace. The room
was filled with sunshine and warmth, the aura of caring so
potent that it seeped into the very marrow of his bones. It felt
good in this place. And right. Like this was where he'd been
heading all along, through his months of aimless wandering.

As he stood in the sunlit room, the restless urgency that had plagued him, driving him on and on, abated. He wasn't sure why. After all, he still had no answers. He still felt adrift, far from land, at the mercy of the relentless surf. But for the first time, he caught sight of a light in the distance, as when a boat crests a storm-tossed wave, offering a glimpse of the distant shore. And that little glimmer of light gave him hope that perhaps, at long last, he was approaching solid land once more.

There was no doubt in his mind that the comforting aroma of the chicken soup he held in his hands was contributing to his more upbeat mood. But as Keith glanced out the window of the cabin and spied Jill at the far edge of the field, he knew she could claim the lion's share of credit for the sudden lightening of his spirits. This woman's simple goodness and kindness had renewed and uplifted him, chasing away the despair that had clung to him like a wet garment after the rain. For that unexpected blessing, he gave thanks. Whether God was in the mood to listen or not.

And then he set out to thank someone he knew *would* listen.

The baby bird was in trouble.

Dropping to her knees in the field, Jill stroked a gentle finger over the downy fluff that would, in time, give way to feathers as the hatchling matured. But without immediate care, this victim of last night's storm was destined never to see adulthood.

Her expression softened in sympathy as the pitiful creature stared up at her with wide eyes, too weak to lift its head. Its heart thumped heavily in its scrawny chest, each beat a desperate plea for life. It was an entreaty that Jill had never been able to ignore. That was why her home had always been a temporary refuge for critters of all sorts. Animal Care Central, as Sam had often teased her, she recalled with a pang.

Scooping the tiny creature up with tender care, she cupped the limp bird in her hand, the thump of its heart pulsating against her palm. It couldn't be more than a couple of days old. And it was in dire need of warmth and nourishment. With conscientious care, though, she was sure it could not only survive, but thrive. She'd rescued enough sick and injured birds and animals in her life to know that TLC often did the trick. For all of God's creatures—including humans.

Just as she started to rise, a flicker of movement in the nearby forest caught her eye. Without even turning in that direction, she knew her young visitor had returned. She also knew better than to look his way, since scrutiny seemed to spook him. If she wanted to build his trust, it would have to be in small, nonthreatening increments.

Angling her body a bit more in his direction, she spoke loudly enough for him to hear her, keeping her gaze fixed on the bird in her hand.

"Looks like this baby bird was a victim of last night's storm. Goodness, he's a tiny thing! But his beak is huge. That's so he can get enough food to help him grow, I suppose. I wonder what he is? A flicker, maybe. Or a Steller's jay. If he's a jay, he'll have a beautiful blue chest when he grows up."

As Jill spoke, she sensed the boy creeping closer, cautious but curious. She extended her hand a bit to give him a glimpse of the tiny bird, hoping he would come near enough to let her get a good look at him. His ragtag state concerned her, and she wanted to know more about him—who he was, where he lived, if he had enough to eat. But before she could engage him in conversation, she had to convince him that she posed no threat.

With cautious steps he approached her, until only a few yards separated them. Jill continued to speak in a gentle, soothing voice, directing her comments to the little bird. But the reassuring words were meant more for her young visitor, designed to put him at ease and build his comfort level.

When he was half a dozen feet away, Jill shifted and risked a quick glance in his direction, holding out her hand at the same time. "Would you like to see him?"

The boy stopped, and alarm flashed across his face.

She smiled at him and extended her hand farther. "It's okay if you take a look. He won't hurt you." *And neither will I.*

His wary eyes regarded her, uncertainty in their depths. She held her breath, hoping her unspoken message had registered. He took a tentative step closer. Then he took another. And…

All at once, his head jerked up and he stared over her shoulder. Panic tightened his features, and before Jill could say a word he turned and ran back toward the woods as fast as his short legs could carry him. In seconds he'd disappeared into the shadows.

Her shoulders slumped with disappointment, and Jill turned to see what had frightened her young guest—only to discover her other guest striding across the field toward her. And he *was* a somewhat formidable figure, she acknowledged. Although he seemed a bit underfed, he still had a powerful, athletic build. Throw in his height advantage over the youngster, not to mention his scruffy appearance, and she couldn't fault the little boy for being uneasy. Keith Michaels had the same effect on her. For different reasons.

In one lithe movement she stood and turned to face him.

"I'm sorry. It looks like I chased off your visitor." He stopped a few feet in front of her and planted his fists on his hips, twin furrows creasing his brow as he stared into the woods.

"It doesn't take much. He's as skittish as the deer I sometimes surprise nosing around my garden. I thought I might pique his curiosity with this and coax him a bit closer."

The wide-brimmed hat shaded her features, and when she dipped her chin to look down her face was hidden from his view. Following her line of sight, he realized she was holding a newly hatched baby bird.

He took a step closer. "Where did you find him?"

"Here. Lying in the field. A victim of last night's storm, I guess." She cocooned her hands around the bird, hoping some of their warmth would seep into the tiny creature. "I need to get him inside, out of the breeze. And feed him."

Doubt clouded Keith's eyes. "He's pretty little. I don't think his odds are too great."

Once more Jill looked up, and he didn't miss the stubborn tilt of her chin. "I don't plan to give up without a fight. And I bet this little guy won't, either. My record with baby birds is pretty good."

Without waiting for him to respond, she set off across the field. As Keith fell into step beside her, a sudden chuckle rumbled deep in his chest.

At the unexpected sound she came to an abrupt stop and stared at him. "What's so funny?"

A wry grin pulled at the corners of his mouth. "The woman at the shop in Eastsound told me that you liked to take in strays, and I had this image in my mind of an eccentric spinster lady with dozens of cats roaming all over her house. Not a young woman who rescues baby birds. I guess that shows how wrong preconceptions can be."

For several moments she continued to look at him, her expression solemn. "You were wrong about the cats, anyway." She struck off again toward the house.

His grin faded. He'd meant the comment as a compliment; instead, he'd upset her. Again. In half a dozen long strides he caught up to her.

"I'm sorry. I didn't mean to offend you." She didn't slow her pace. Nor did she respond. "Look, the reason I came over was to say thank you for all the work you did at the cottage. It doesn't even look like the same place. And the soup was a bonus. It brought back a lot of happy memories. My mom used to make chicken soup, and back when times were simpler, it was the solution to a lot of life's problems. One bowl, and everything was right with the world again."

Her pace slowed a bit, and she looked down to stroke the baby bird's head. "I wish it were that easy." Her voice was so soft he had to lean close to catch her comment.

They'd reached the back porch and he stopped at the bottom of the steps as she ascended. There was a world of meaning in her simple remark. A profound sadness that touched his soul. "Is there anything I can do to help?" he asked. When his husky tone brought a startled look to her face, he cleared his throat and gestured toward the bird. "I could build you a little box to keep it in."

Dipping her head, she shielded her eyes from his view. "That's okay. I've got one in the kitchen that will do. But thank you."

With that she retreated to the house and closed the door.

Long after she'd disappeared inside, Keith remained at the bottom of the steps, his expression pensive. The woman in the store had been right. His landlady did take in strays. She'd adopted an abandoned baby bird, determined to nurse it back to health. She wanted to help the ragtag little boy. She'd given him shelter when he had nowhere else to go. But while she tended to those in need, who tended to her?

Shoving his fists into his pockets, Keith turned and set out across the meadow. His distraction blinded him to the flowers all around him, which were struggling upright again after the storm, and to the spruce trees that were shaking the weight of the rain off their boughs and once more lifting them to the heavens.

Nor did he see the woman peering from behind a curtain in the upper window, who watched him go.

Chapter Five

For the first few days, Keith didn't stray far from Rainbow's End. He hiked a little in Moran State Park, spent hours watching the sea from a nearby rocky beach, took long naps and prepared simple meals from the provisions he'd bought at the general store a few miles down the road. For the most part, he was content to let the peace and quiet of the place seep into his soul.

He saw no further evidence of the mysterious little boy who stayed on the fringes of the property. Nor did he see much of his landlady. Once he happened to catch a glimpse of her when she ventured out to the toolshed. Another time he saw a light burning in an upstairs window late into the night. Beyond that, there was no sign of life at the house.

Only when his supplies began to dwindle did Keith decide it was time for another trip into town. Besides, he owed his father a call, and his cell phone didn't work here. He'd left a message on his father's machine the day after the storm, when he'd gone into town for groceries, but it had been cryptic. He owed his dad more than that, after all the support and love he'd provided when Keith's world had collapsed.

As he headed out the door, his camera caught his eye, and on impulse he reached for the case. He hadn't had much interest in taking photos in quite a while, but this island was special in a way he couldn't quite define. He might see something that would pique his interest enough to motivate him to get the camera out of the case.

Two hours later, after exploring a bit in Eastsound and stocking up on provisions, he found a pay phone and placed a call to his dad's cell number. When his father picked up, Keith could hear the sound of a saw in the background. He pictured the older man, solid and hearty, dressed in his typical work attire of worn jeans and a cotton shirt, his bristly white hair standing at attention in the crew cut style he'd always favored, a stubby pencil stuck behind his ear.

"Dad, it's Keith. Is this a good time?"

"It's always a good time to hear from you, son." The warmth in the older man's voice soothed Keith like a healing balm. "I got your message the other night, but it was scratchy. Did you say you were in San Juan? I thought you were heading west, not south."

A smile lifted the corners of Keith's mouth. "I'm in the San Juan Islands, Dad. Off the coast of Washington State. A beautiful little spot called Orcas Island."

There was a moment of silence as Bob Michaels tried to recall when his son had last noticed beauty. He couldn't even remember. Perhaps this, finally, was the turning point he'd been praying for since Keith had walked away from the traumatic memories that had distorted and darkened his vision of the world. *Thank you, Lord,* he whispered in the silence of his heart.

"And what's so special about Orcas Island?" Bob asked, after swallowing past the lump in his throat.

"It's quiet here. And peaceful. Not like anywhere I've ever been. I don't know quite how to describe it, except that it feels like a place apart from the world, where you can regroup and make a fresh start." Keith didn't mention that his unique landlady added to the specialness of the place.

"Sounds mighty fine. Where are you staying?"

"A little cottage. There are very few people for miles around. It's just the forest and the mountains and the sea."

"Staying there for a spell might do you good. How are you fixed for cash?"

Leave it to his dad to home right in on a looming problem. "I'm okay for now. I might try to pick up some carpentry work if I decide to hang around for a while."

"You need a few dollars to tide you over, son?"

"No. I'm okay. But thanks for asking. How are you doing?"

"Can't complain."

That was his father's standard response. Keith couldn't remember one occasion when Bob Michaels had grumbled or griped about anything, even though he'd had his share of sorrow. His first son stillborn. A wife who died far too young, when Keith was only twelve, of a congenital heart defect. All the challenges of single parenthood. Watching a beloved father who suffered from the debilitating effects of Alzheimer's slowly slip away. Yet he'd never become disheartened. Nor had his faith ever wavered. Keith wished he'd inherited his dad's ability to stand firm through the storms of life.

"I'll call again soon," Keith promised. "My cell doesn't work here, so I have to go into town and use a public phone. I don't know the phone number of the woman who owns the cottage, but I'll get it and give it to you next time I call in case you need to reach me."

"That would be great. In the meantime, I'm going to look

up those San Juan Islands in my Rand McNally. Sounds like a spot I might want to visit one of these days."

"You'd like it here, dad. Lots of good fishing, I bet."

"My kind of place for sure, then. You take care now, son. And God be with you."

That was how his father always ended their conversations, Keith mused as he replaced the receiver. Asking God to walk with his son. Funny. In his old life, he'd always been the one to invoke that blessing on his father, who would respond in kind. Now the roles were reversed. Except Keith never returned the sentiment. Why bother, when God and he weren't on the same wavelength anymore? Still, it gave Keith some sense of comfort to hear the words from his father. And who knew? Maybe God would listen to him.

Jill didn't know any young child who could resist homemade chocolate chip cookies, still warm from the oven and washed down with a tall glass of cold milk. She'd whipped up a batch of dough three days ago, and it had been sitting in the refrigerator waiting for the little boy to appear at the edge of the woods. But her young friend didn't seem inclined to make his presence known when Keith was around.

However, she'd heard the crunch of gravel on her driveway a couple of hours ago, meaning Keith had gone out. She'd been watching the woods ever since from the window of her spare-bedroom-turned-studio. So far, though, she'd seen no sign of her young caller. If he didn't come soon, she'd have to bake the cookies and either eat them or send them over to Keith.

At the thought of her paying guest, Jill combed her fingers through her hair and tried to still the nervous flutter in her stomach. Although he seemed nice enough, she felt edgy and tense in his presence. A feeling prompted, she suspected, by the deliberate way he'd looked at her scar that first day, then commented about it instead of ignoring it. She wasn't used to that kind of blatant, almost matter-of-fact perusal. And she wasn't sure she wanted to *get* used to it. For reasons she wasn't inclined to consider.

As she daubed bright color on the canvas in front of her, she wondered what the island people thought of her reclusive life. She supposed most would attribute it to vanity, but she knew better. Any vanity she might once have had had been expunged long ago. No, she'd withdrawn from the world for other reasons. Weariness, for one. She'd grown tired of dealing with the questioning looks, the averted glances, the expressions of pity. Tired and sad. It grieved her that no one could see past her scars to the woman she'd once been. Or was even willing to try.

Then Keith Michaels had walked into her life, and for the first time a stranger had looked at her as a person. Yes, he'd been shocked initially. As Deb would say, that was just human nature. The scars were horrendous. But once he'd recovered, he'd looked at her in a way no one, except her family, had since the accident. Like he could accept her disfigurement, could see past it to the tender heart that still beat within her. In his eyes she'd detected compassion and kindness and acceptance. It had been the kind of look that could engender friendship.

But if she opened the door to friendship, she'd have to talk about what had happened. And she wasn't ready to do that yet. Maybe she never would be. The hurt went too deep, the loss was too grievous. Burying those emotions had been her best coping mechanism, and she was afraid to upset the delicate balance she'd created in her life. Talking about them would be as painful as ripping the crust off a newly formed scab.

That's why she'd kept herself scarce over the past few days. She didn't want to run into her tenant again. Besides, she had plenty of work to do in the studio—even if she was starting to go stir-crazy. Her pattern had been to spend part of every day outside, walking to the shore, working in her garden, painting in the early-morning and late-afternoon light. Being cooped up didn't suit her for extended periods. She'd spent way too much time in sterile environments, confined to antiseptic-smelling hospitals, sequestered in darkened rooms. She needed fresh air and sunlight like she needed water and food.

As a result, she wasn't sorry to hear Keith drive off that morning. Nor was she surprised when she spotted the young boy at the edge of the field half an hour later.

Moving into high gear, she cleaned her brushes. Then she headed for the kitchen to scoop out dough for the first tray of cookies, her foot tapping out an impatient rhythm as they baked. How could ten minutes seem like forever? *Please, Lord, let the boy stay around long enough for me to make contact,* she prayed.

When at last the cookies were done, she put eight on a plate and poured a tall glass of milk. Tucking a copy of *Tom Sawyer*—retrieved from a long-packed box of books—under her arm, she pulled on her hat and headed out, forcing herself to walk at a slow pace that wouldn't frighten him away.

As she approached, he ducked behind a boulder, peeking out as she deposited the plate and milk on a rock. He remained motionless as she moved off a bit to sit in the shade of an old apple tree gone wild, her back against the trunk as she munched on a cookie.

"I brought some cookies and milk for you, too, in case you're hungry," she called out. "And I thought you might like to know how our little bird is faring. He's eating, and he's starting to get a few feathers. I named him Homer." She kept up a steady stream of banter, and as she talked the young boy eased closer, casting furtive looks into the woods over his shoulder. When he reached the treat she'd set out, he gobbled up the cookies, downed the milk in one long gulp, then retreated to his place behind the boulders.

Reaching for the book, Jill opened it to the first page. "I found one of my favorite books the other day. It's a story about a young boy who has some great adventures. I thought I'd read it again." Pitching her voice to a volume he could hear, she began to speak the words she recalled from her childhood.

For a long time, only the sound of her voice broke the stillness in the meadow. She noticed that her young friend settled into a more comfortable position beside the rocks instead of crouching, poised to flee, as was his typical stance. A good sign, she concluded. He seemed to be more relaxed around her today.

Or at least he was until the scrunch of tires on the gravel announced her tenant's return.

One thing Jill didn't have to worry about was her young visitor's hearing. The second the sound registered he was on his feet. When a quick glance confirmed that a car was coming up the drive, he took off at a run, disappearing into the woods in a flash.

Sighing, Jill rose and gathered up the remnants of his snack. Not a crumb remained on the plate, causing her to wonder yet again if he got enough to eat at home—wherever that might be. She'd also noticed that he'd been wearing the same clothes today as on other occasions, suggesting a life of either extreme poverty or neglect. Like the baby bird she was tending, her young visitor looked like he could use some TLC.

As she started back toward the house, she was surprised to

see Keith's car slowing by her front porch. She supposed he might be stopping by to tell her that he was moving on. A sudden pang in the pit of her stomach caught her unaware, and she frowned. She'd known that he was only planning to stay a few days. And she'd seen very little of him during his visit. In fact, she'd gone to great lengths to avoid him. In light of that, why should the thought of his departure produce such an empty feeling deep inside?

Before she could analyze her reaction, Keith got out of the car and headed her way, balancing a large pizza box in his hands. When he drew close the savory aroma wafted her way, setting off a rumble in her stomach that reminded her she hadn't yet had lunch.

A furrow creased his brow when he saw the empty plate and glass in her hand, and his step faltered. "Did you eat lunch already? I was hoping you'd join me. I picked this up in town and it's way too much for one person. Besides, I owe you a meal after that great soup you left for me."

Surprised by the unexpected invitation, Jill eyed the box as she searched for her voice. She hadn't had pizza in ages. Once, in a long-ago life, it had been a menu staple for her family on Friday night as they celebrated the end of the workweek by indulging in their favorite take-out food. Since the accident, however, pizza had held little appeal. But all at once she was ravenous. Still, Keith didn't owe her a thing. And spending time in his company didn't seem like a good idea.

Shaking her head, she made a move to continue toward the house. "Thanks, but there's no obligation."

Instead of stepping aside to let her pass, as she expected, Keith remained in place. Tipping back her head, she sent him a puzzled look from under the rim of her wide-brimmed hat.

"I can't eat all this myself." He grinned at her and waved the box under her nose. "There's plenty for two."

"Unlike pancakes, pizza is good left over. You can finish it tomorrow."

"Ah, tomorrow. That's a topic I want to discuss with you. We could talk over lunch."

The man wasn't giving up, Jill realized. And the pizza did smell good. What harm could it do to share a meal with him? He'd be gone soon, anyway. In fact, that could be what he wanted to talk about. No sense putting off the inevitable.

"Okay. We can eat on the back porch. I'll heat up the pizza and get some drinks."

"Great. I'll run down to the cottage and put a few perishables away." After handing over the box, he turned and strode back toward his car.

For a few seconds, Jill stared after him. Then she continued toward the house, still not sure this impromptu lunch was wise. And still not sure how Keith had convinced her to accept. But he did have an engaging grin. And she did find him intriguing. Who was he, really? He didn't strike her as the drifter type by nature. Yet it sounded as if that was what he'd been doing for quite a while. Why? What was the source of the restlessness she sensed in his soul? Those questions had kept her awake late into the night way too often since his arrival. Of course, her curiosity might be nothing more than a reflection of her isolated existence. A long-stifled hunger for simple human interaction.

Yet that didn't ring quite true. There was something about this man that gave her a sense of…*connectedness* was the word that came to mind. As if they were linked by some common thread she couldn't quite identify.

Now there was a far-fetched, fanciful notion if ever she'd

heard one, she chided herself. What could she possibly have in common with this stranger, a refugee from a storm who had appeared on her doorstep by pure chance?

Pushing through the screen door, Jill took the pizza out of the box, set the oven temperature and slid it inside. Pure chance. She mulled over her choice of words, thinking about the verse from Jeremiah. "For I know well the plans I have in mind for you... plans for your welfare not for woe, plans to give you a future full of hope." Could Keith's unexpected visit be part of God's plan for her, rather than chance? If he hadn't arrived on the Fourth of July weekend, if he hadn't stopped at the market, if the checker hadn't thought of her cottage, he would never have come her way. It was hard to believe that coincidence could account for all those pieces falling into place.

But perhaps she was overanalyzing. Once they shared their lunch, he'd probably settle his bill, pack up his car and leave, closing out this odd chapter in her life.

She'd know soon enough, she supposed. In the meantime, she might as well bake the rest of the cookies for dessert. She had a feeling her temporary tenant would enjoy them just as much as the mysterious little boy.

As Keith splashed some water on his face and toweled it dry, the terry cloth scratching against the rough stubble on his chin, he tried to figure out what had prompted him to invite his landlady to share his lunch. He hadn't intended to. The idea hadn't even occurred to him until he'd driven up the driveway and seen her walking across the field, her face shaded by her ever-present hat. She'd seemed so alone, and once more he'd been struck by her isolation. It didn't feel right for such a young woman to be cut off from the world, even if the isolation was self-imposed. Didn't she yearn for human interaction? If once she had loved, didn't she miss that physical connectedness, as he did? The entwined hands, the comforting hugs, the soft smiles and warm gazes that said "you matter to me"?

But all those things had been stolen from him. As had the calling that had once been the center of his life. Stolen through spite and retribution, leaving him with a legacy of such deep hatred and disillusionment that he'd been barely able to function for months. He'd hoped, in time, that those destructive feelings would dissipate. He wanted his life back. Wanted to rid himself of the debilitating emotions that held him hostage. That was why he'd set off on his cross-country quest. He hadn't made much progress yet, but at least he was still trying.

And that was the difference between him and his landlady, he suspected. She'd stopped trying to get past whatever it was that held her captive in her self-imposed isolation. What he'd first attributed to acceptance, he now recognized more as resignation. And there was a world of difference between the two. Perhaps that's why he'd issued his impromptu lunch invitation. She'd given him new reason to hope; maybe, on some subconscious level, he'd felt obliged to try and return the favor.

Whatever the motive, he found himself looking forward to sharing a meal with her. He'd already seen evidence of her kind, compassionate, caring nature. What other surprises did his reclusive hostess have to offer, hidden behind the wall she'd built around herself?

Breaching that wall wouldn't be easy, of course. She didn't seem to let anyone through. But difficult as it would be to break through her defenses, he knew that the real challenge today would be getting her to go along with the plan he'd formulated on his way back from town.

Chapter Six

Jill peered out the window as Keith approached across the field, wiped her damp palms on her jeans and reached for her oven mitts. It was ridiculous to be nervous about sharing a meal with someone. So she was a little bit out of practice. Well, maybe more than a little, considering she hadn't broken bread with another living soul since Deb and Dominic had visited the year before. But she'd shared plenty of meals with people in her old life. She and Sam had given some great dinner parties, filled with laughter and spirited conversation that ebbed and flowed with a natural, easy grace. She knew how to make small talk. It would come back to her. Like riding a bicycle. She was sure of it.

Sort of.

As she carried the pizza out to the table, already set with plates, forks and water glasses, Keith came up the stairs. She sat and motioned him to the chair across from her. "I always say grace before meals. I hope you don't mind." Without waiting for him to respond, she bowed her head, the floppy brim of her hat obscuring her features. Though it felt awkward, Keith was left with no option but to follow her example as she began to speak. "Lord, we thank You for this meal and for the many blessings You bestow on us. Keep us always in Your care, deepen our faith, and grant us the light of Your hope even on our darkest days. Amen."

Keith's throat tightened at the simple, heartfelt prayer. How had Jill known to ask for the very things he most needed? Or did she need them, too? Raising his head, he looked across at her, his eyes searching, probing. She met his gaze for the briefest second, then lowered her chin and reached for a piece of pizza. Once more, the wide brim hid her face from his view.

"Do you always wear that hat?" he asked, his tone conversational.

For an instant, her hand stilled as she weighed her response to the unexpected question. "I need to protect my skin from the sun."

Her cautious, just-drop-it inflection wasn't lost on Keith. But something impelled him to press on. "It's not sunny up here."

A knot formed in Jill's stomach. So much for small talk. While she'd been trying to think of inane, surface things to discuss, like the weather and sightseeing, he was diving right into deep water.

"The pizza's getting cold," she responded.

Silence greeted her comment. She could feel his scrutiny as she rearranged the pepperoni on top of her slice. She could sense that he wanted to say more, and she held her breath. Only when he helped himself to a piece of pizza did she exhale, assuming he was going to drop the subject.

She was wrong. The breath caught in her throat at his next remark. "I've already seen your face, Jill."

Startled, she stared at him, unsure how to respond. Most people danced around the subject of her appearance. He seemed to prefer addressing it head-on, in an easy, straightforward manner. And it rattled her.

Color stole up her neck and she looked down, playing with her checkered napkin. "I always wear the hat around people."

"Why?"

This was getting way too personal. "Why do you want to know?" She turned his question around on him, her tone wary, stalling as she tried to think of some response that would deflect his inquiry.

"You have lovely hair. And your eyes are the color of autumn. It's a shame to keep all that beauty hidden away."

Whatever Jill had been expecting him to say, that wasn't it. She could only stare at him, speechless.

If Jill was surprised by his comment, Keith was even more stunned. Where in the world had that come from? He wasn't a smooth talker, not when it came to women. Never had been. And in the past two years he'd gone out of his way to walk a wide circle around females in general, to give no indication that he'd noticed them, let alone found them attractive. Yet he'd paid the woman across from him a direct compliment, going against all the rules he'd written for himself. But Jill seemed so in need of tender care, just like the baby bird she continued to nurture. The words had come out before he'd had a chance to consider their ramification.

As he watched, soft color spilled onto her left cheek, confirming his suspicion that she was unaccustomed to flattery about her physical appearance. He waited, not sure if she would ignore him or reply. A few seconds ticked by, and all at once he saw the sudden sheen of tears in her eyes. His gut tightened, and his immediate instinct was to reach over and wrap her long, tapering fingers in a comforting grip. Instead, he dropped his hands to his lap and balled his fists around his napkin before he did anything inappropriate.

Just as he prepared to change the subject, she surprised him by answering his question about the hat.

"My scars make people uncomfortable. It's easier if they don't have to look at my face. So I do what I can to camouflage them," she told him in a subdued voice. His simple, sincere compliment had shattered her defenses and compelled her to respond.

"They don't make me uncomfortable."

Curious, she studied his features, finding only honesty in his eyes. "Why not?"

"Why should they? What counts is the person inside. And I've seen enough since I've been here to know you're kind, caring and compassionate. Your willingness to take me in during the storm is proof enough of that, let alone everything else you've done to make me feel welcome. And I've seen your concern about that young boy, not to mention the way you rescued the baby bird. All those things tell me you have a good heart. A beautiful heart."

His words warmed her, but they didn't change the reality. "In a not-so-pretty package."

"Is that why you hide out here, away from everybody?"

"I'm not hiding." Her response was swift. Too swift. And to her surprise, defensive. Confused, and suddenly uncertain, she frowned. Why should she be defensive? After all, Keith was dead wrong. She wasn't hiding. People only hid when they were afraid of something, when they felt threatened by imminent danger and were seeking safety. Her reasons for withdrawing from the world had nothing to do with fear or safety. Absolutely none. She took a deep breath and tried again. "Look, this is just…easier. For a lot of reasons."

His eyes narrowed in speculation. "Like vanity?"

"No!" Her denial was instant—and vehement. This, at least, she was sure about.

"Then take off the hat."

Startled by the challenge, she stared at him. Her hat was her security blanket, her protection from the eyes of the world—in a figurative sense, if nothing else. Without it, she'd feel exposed and vulnerable. Only around family and her doctors did she take it off. Yet…she now found herself giving serious consideration to picking up the gauntlet Keith had tossed down. But why?

As she grappled to find that elusive answer, she searched his face. He continued to regard her across the table, his gaze steady, supportive and sure. Matter-of-fact, even. As if her disfigurement, when fully exposed, wouldn't have any effect on the way he looked at her or treated her.

And in fact, she already had evidence to support that. He'd seen her without her hat once, for a brief instant. And later, when her hat was back in place, he'd looked right at her shadowed scars and commented about them. In their subsequent conversations, she'd seen no indication that they made him uncomfortable, nothing to suggest that he was morbidly curious about them. It was as if he'd accepted that her scars were just part of her, the same way her hair and eyes were, a physical feature that had nothing to do with who she was as a person. Removing her hat wouldn't shock him. She suspected he wouldn't even blink. That was why she felt safe enough to consider his challenge.

Besides, she didn't want him to think she wore the hat out of vanity. For some reason, it was important to her to set the record straight on that.

With trembling fingers, she reached up and slowly pulled the hat off, letting her hair tumble around her shoulders in soft waves. As she did so, she found strength in a familiar Bible verse that had often replayed in her mind, like a mantra, during difficult encounters. She spoke it now in a quiet, not-quite-steady voice. "'Not as man sees does God see, because man sees the appearance, but the Lord looks into the heart.'"

"Samuel."

A flicker of surprise scuttled across her face. She wouldn't have expected her guest to be well versed in scripture. "Most people have a hard time seeing past the scars."

"That's their loss."

He rested his elbows on the table and linked his fingers. She managed to endure his scrutiny without flinching, but it was one of the hardest things she'd ever done. Her whole body was quivering, like it had been the day she'd left home for college. Although eager to step into the larger world, she'd also been anxious about the unknown that lay ahead. And certain that things would never be quite the same again. She felt like that now.

As Keith looked at the woman across from him, he did his best to maintain a passive expression. But it was difficult. Now he better understood what she meant about the way people looked at her. His brief glimpse of her scars that first morning when he'd repaired the siding hadn't prepared him for the extent of her injury, fully exposed now in the midday light. And it was a hard thing to get past. A good portion of the right side of her face was discolored, a mottled red intermixed with shiny, taut skin that wasn't quite normal in texture or color, parts of the surface uneven and ridged. Nothing less than a severe burn could produce a scar like that.

The edge of the scar touched the outside of Jill's eye, and he focused there, trying to regulate his breathing as he grappled with the severity of her injury. "Is your eye okay?" It was all he could do to maintain a conversational tone.

"Yes. I was lucky. I could have lost my sight."

"It's a burn, right?"

"Yes."

"How long ago?"

"Three and a half years."

He took another few seconds to examine her face, his perusal unhurried. She expected his next question to be, "What happened?" and she tried to prepare for it. To figure out how she could deflect it. She wasn't ready for that discussion. Taking off the hat had been traumatic enough for one day.

But he surprised her. Instead of probing further, he just repeated a comment he'd made that first day. "I'm sorry, Jill. I can't even begin to imagine the horror of a burn like that. But it doesn't change my impression of you. Now let's eat our pizza before it gets cold."

Although he took a hearty bite of his slice, Jill didn't think she'd be able to swallow anything. Her emotions were too chaotic. But somehow Keith managed to calm her down. He told her about his trip into Eastsound, asked about the climate on the island, spoke of her mysterious young visitor, inquired about the baby bird. In other words, he made small talk.

Odd. That was how Jill had expected to *start* the meal. Instead, he'd reversed things. But it worked. By getting the awkwardness out of the way at the beginning, he'd made it possible for her to relax for the rest of the meal instead of worrying about if or when he'd broach the subject of her appearance.

On top of that, he paid no special attention to her scar. When he spoke to her, he looked into her eyes, not at her disfigured face. By the end of the meal, she was more at ease than she would ever have imagined possible. For a brief few minutes, she even forgot about the scars.

When they were done, she collected their plates, then went to retrieve the plate of still-warm chocolate chip cookies. Keith's face lit up when she carried them through the door, and she couldn't help smiling.

"I think these had the same effect on my young visitor this morning. It must be a male thing." She deposited the plate on the table, along with a mug of coffee, strong and black, the way he'd taken it that first morning at breakfast.

An appreciative smile curved his lips as he picked it up, and he gave her a mock toast. "Just the way I like it. Thanks for remembering."

His compliment brought a warm glow to her heart, and she took her place across from him, reaching for a cookie. "When you got back earlier, you said you wanted to talk about your plans." They'd had a nice meal, and she'd enjoyed the brief interlude very much, but if he was going to leave tomorrow there was no sense putting off that discussion. Even if raising the subject did cause that odd, empty feeling to reappear in the pit of her stomach. Instead of eating her cookie she broke it into pieces as she waited for him to respond.

To buy himself a little time, Keith took a long, slow sip of his coffee. All the plans he'd formulated on the drive back from town rested on one big contingency: whether or not he could stay on at Rainbow's End. The peace and serenity he'd found here was the real attraction of this island. Without that, there was no reason to linger. So the first trick was convincing her to let him remain. If he succeeded at that, his next challenge would be to find a way to fund an extended visit. And he hoped she could help him with that, too.

Withdrawing an envelope from his pocket, he laid it on the table next to her plate. "This should settle up my bill through tonight."

The knot in Jill's stomach tightened, and she clenched her hands in her lap, fixing her attention on the plate in front of her.

"I've enjoyed my visit here. In fact, I'd like to stay on for a while, if you'll let me," he continued. Her chin jerked up, and Keith didn't quite know how to interpret the look in her eyes. He'd almost call it relief, but that didn't make any sense.

"You want to stay?" Jill was having a hard time digesting that, since she'd already reconciled herself to his imminent departure.

"Yes. I do."

An almost euphoric feeling welled up inside her. "Okay."

Now it was his turn to stare. "Okay?"

A warning light flashed in her heart, telling her to proceed with caution, but she ignored it. "Yeah. Okay." ·

He'd never expected it to be this easy. "That's great. Thank you. But the thing is, I do have a little cash flow problem. I've been on the road for almost a year and my funds are running pretty low. Despite the great rates you charge, I can't stay a whole lot longer unless I find work. I was hoping you'd be able to point me to some area contractors or carpenters who might be interested in taking on a temporary employee."

"You don't need to worry about the money. I told you, the cabin is just sitting there vacant. You're welcome to use it as long as you like."

"I won't stay without paying my way."

"I don't need the money, Keith. I told you that when you first brought this up."

"Maybe not. But I need to pay."

Ah. It was a pride thing, Jill realized, backing off. "Okay. Fine. The rate's less for an extended stay."

"It can't get much less."

"Yes, it can." When the weekly rate she quoted brought a frown to his face, she crossed her hands over her chest. "And I won't consider a penny more. Take it or leave it."

At first she thought he was going to argue, but once again he surprised her by chuckling instead. "You drive a hard bargain, lady."

A smile twitched at the corners of her mouth. "Does that mean we have a deal?"

"Yeah." He held out his hand, and after a brief hesitation she took it. His fingers closed around hers, warm and strong and firm, and she was sorry when he let go. "But I still need to find work. Can you direct me to anyone?"

"I'm afraid not. I don't know many of the island people." Suddenly an inspiration began to take shape in her mind, and her expression grew thoughtful. "But I have an idea. I've been wanting to build a studio ever since I got here. The upstairs room I use now isn't ideal. I've even drawn up a design."

Leaning back in his chair, he wrapped his hands around his mug. "So you're the artist. I saw all the equipment in the cabin the night I arrived." The irony wasn't lost on him. What a cruel twist of fate that a woman who created beauty should have her own so disfigured.

"I try, anyway. I used the cabin as a studio at first, but there's not enough light there. The ideal spot would be over there." She indicated an empty stretch of ground behind the left side of the house. "How about this? I'll supply the materials and the design, you build me the studio, and we'll call it even. A barter arrangement."

The idea appealed to Keith. If he built a studio for Jill, he could spend most of his time at Rainbow's End. What could be more perfect? But as he prepared to accept, he saw indecision cloud her eyes. "What's wrong?"

Her guest was observant, she'd give him that. "It just occurred to me that you'll be getting the short end of this deal. You'd come out ahead financially by working for someone else and paying me rent. Besides, a project this size would take weeks, and I…you haven't said how long you plan to stay." She played with her cookie, which had now been reduced to crumbs.

The tension on his face eased. "Forget about the money. I'm not here to get rich. And as for the construction schedule, it could take anywhere from three or four weeks to three or fourth months to complete, depending on how grandiose your plans are. But I'm in no hurry to leave. And the arrangement sounds fine to me. If you'll throw in a hot meal every day, that is. And that's my counteroffer. Take it or leave it."

He grinned at her, and an ember of happiness ignited deep in Jill's heart. It was tiny, but it was there. She told herself it was because at long last she would get the studio she'd always wanted. But it was more than that, and she knew it. Her happiness had also been fueled by the man who sat across from her. Keith Michaels, with his direct manner and his ability to coax her out of the solitary world she'd created for herself, had brought a refreshing newness to a life that had begun to grow stale. Until he'd knocked at her door, she hadn't even realized that at some point over the past couple of years her life had gone from comfortable to confining.

Once more, the verse from Jeremiah replayed in her mind. And as it did, she sensed that Keith Michaels was part of whatever plan God had in mind for her. Now she just needed to put her trust in the Lord and see where He led her.

Chapter Seven

"Gracious! You weren't kidding when you said your house was a construction zone!"

Shooting her sister a quick look, Jill maneuvered the car around several piles of lumber and pulled up by her back door. "Keith doesn't waste any time."

"When is the dump truck coming, Aunt Jill?"

Seven-year-old Dominic had ditched his seat belt the instant the house came into view and was now bouncing around in the back, trying to take it all in.

"Tomorrow. I hope you weren't planning to sleep in."

"I like to get up early," he assured her.

Deb rolled her eyes. "Why couldn't I have a normal kid who sleeps till noon in the summer?"

"Hey, I'm a normal kid," Dominic protested.

"Above normal, I'd say," Jill added.

"Except when it comes to sleeping in." Deb stifled a yawn. "Sorry. It's been a long day. You could have picked somewhere to live that was easier to get to, you know."

"I didn't want a place that was easy to get to. And stop complaining. Tourists pay a lot of money to come to this island. You're lucky you have a free place to stay."

"Yeah. A construction site."

Setting the brake, Jill poked her sister in the ribs. "Too bad Keith's in the cabin, or I'd put you out there."

A mock shudder passed through Deb. "No, thank you. Once was enough. I still remember waking up that first night to find a deer staring at me through the window. Talk about freaking out! As a city girl, I prefer to view my wildlife from a distance. A long distance. Like on the TV screen."

"Tell Keith that when you see him. When he heard you were coming, he wanted to move out so you'd have a place to stay. It was all I could do to convince him that you preferred the house, cramped as it is."

"Hey, I'm used to sharing a bed. Besides, you take up less room than Tony—and you don't snore. But don't ever tell him I said that."

Chuckling, Jill looked back at Dominic. "I hate relegating Dominic to a sleeping bag on the floor, though."

"Are you kidding? He loves it. He thinks it's an adventure. Right, Dominic?"

The youngster was already opening the door, oblivious to the adult conversation. "Can I look at all that stuff, Aunt Jill?"

"Sure. But don't touch anything until Keith is around."

"Where is your tenant, anyway?" Deb dropped her sunglasses into her purse.

"In the cabin, I expect. You'll see him tomorrow." Jill opened the door and stepped out.

"I'm looking forward to meeting him."

"Why?"

"Curious, I guess. Any man who could convince you to take him in has to be special."

Lifting the trunk, Jill ignored Deb's comment and hefted out one of her suitcases. "What did you bring, anyway? The kitchen sink?"

"That's what Dad said when he dropped us off at the airport," Dominic chimed in with a grin.

"Very funny. I only brought the absolute necessities." Deb turned back to Jill. "You're avoiding the question."

"I didn't hear one." Jill handed Deb one of the bags. She should have figured her sister wouldn't drop the subject.

"What makes this guy special?"

"I didn't say he was."

"You didn't have to. His mere presence is proof enough. Is he one of those hunky construction types, all muscles and hard hat?"

Planting her hands on her hips, Jill gave her sister an annoyed look. "He's just a nice guy, okay? A bit scruffy, but nice."

"Uh-huh."

"Okay, fine." Jill threw up her hands. "You can check him out for yourself tomorrow."

"Oh, I intend to, dear sister. First thing tomorrow, after a good night's sleep."

As it happened, "first thing tomorrow" turned out to be seven o'clock, when the rumble of a dump truck straining to ascend the drive broke the early-morning stillness.

Jill was up, of course. She'd always been an early riser. And Dominic hadn't been too far behind. He was already in the shower. Last time she'd looked, Deb had still been dead to the world. Her slumber wouldn't last long with the racket that was coming from outside, though.

Since she saw no sign of Keith, Jill stepped onto the back

porch, pulling her hat low over her face as she moved to the edge of the railing. A burly man was surveying the wooden forms Keith had built for the foundation and footing. "I'm afraid my construction manager isn't here yet," Jill called to him from the shadows.

Shading his eyes, he peered up at her. "That's okay. I'm a little early. Keith said seven-thirty, but I thought it would take me longer to get here than it did. I don't come out this way much. Mighty pretty spot, though."

"Thanks. Would you like a cup of coffee while you wait?"

"No thanks. Always bring my own java." The man held up a thermos and grinned. "Nobody brews it as strong as I like. Pure grounds, the wife says."

With a wave and a smile, Jill headed back inside. Deb was just walking into the kitchen, bleary-eyed, her short blond hair sticking out in all directions, her skin wiped clean of makeup. She wore faded jeans and a long, shapeless T-shirt that helped disguise the few extra pounds she'd been trying to lose for the past five years.

"You weren't kidding about an early morning, were you?" she groused good-naturedly.

"Nope. But look on the bright side. Since the concrete has to cure for a few days, it shouldn't be too noisy during the rest of your stay. Want some coffee?"

"I could be talked into it."

As Jill poured a hearty cup and added a healthy dose of cream and sugar, she glimpsed Keith through the window, on the far side of the meadow. "Well, you're about to get your first look at my tenant," she told Deb, handing her the coffee.

That perked up her sister. Wrapping her hands around the mug, she moved to the window. "Where? Oh, I see him. Sort of. The sun's shining right in my eyes. Besides, I don't have my contacts in yet." She squinted, then shook her head. "No good. I'll have to wait until he gets out of the glare and comes closer."

A few minutes later, when the sound of male voices drifted in the open window on the other side of the kitchen, Deb made a move in that direction. Jill grabbed her arm and gave her a stern look. "It's not polite to eavesdrop."

"I just want to get a look at him."

"I'll introduce you as soon as he's done talking to the cement guy. Be patient."

Making a face, Deb opened the refrigerator and began scrounging around. "So what's for breakfast? How about pancakes? The ones we had on our last visit were fabulous. I dreamed about them for weeks after we went home. I told Tony that I wasn't even going to worry about my diet while I was out here. I mean, what good is a vacation if you can't…"

A sharp rap at the back door interrupted her, and she straightened up. Jill flashed her a grin. "See? Everything comes to those who wait."

As she pulled open the door to usher Keith in, Jill turned to Deb, planning to introduce her. But at her sister's incredulous expression the words died in her throat. Deb's mouth had dropped open, and the hand holding her mug was frozen halfway to her mouth. The way she was gaping at Keith was downright embarrassing, and hot color suffused Jill's cheeks. It wasn't like her sister to be rude. Even if her tenant was a little scruffy and rough around the edges. But his appearance didn't call for the kind of reaction Deb was having.

Struggling to find some words to smooth over her sister's impoliteness, Jill turned to Keith—and had exactly the same response as she stared in shock at the man beside her. A man transformed.

Gone was the shaggy mane. His medium brown hair was now cut in a short, fashionable style. The stubble had disappeared, too, revealing a strong, clean-shaven jaw with an endearing cleft in the center that reminded her of Cary Grant. In the two weeks he'd been on the island, he'd also filled out a bit, and the angular bone structure of his face had softened. His jeans fit as if they'd been designed for him, and his snug T-shirt called attention to his broad chest and impressive biceps. A flicker of amusement deepened the cobalt blue of his eyes as he took in the reaction of the two women.

When the silence lengthened, he took the initiative. "Good morning, ladies. You must be Deb. I'm Keith Michaels." He moved over to Deb and extended his hand.

For once, her sister seemed at a loss for words. She took his hand, then cleared her throat. "Hello."

Grinning, Keith turned to Jill. "Sorry for the early start. I didn't expect the cement to arrive for at least another half hour. But he won't be here long. I hope we didn't disturb anyone."

All Jill could manage was a shake of her head.

Still grinning, he disappeared through the door, leaving shocked silence in his wake.

"I thought you said he looked scruffy?" Deb croaked when she located her voice.

"He did."

"You could have warned me, you know," her sister continued, as if she hadn't heard Jill's reply.

"About what?"

Propping her hands on her hips, Deb shook her head. "Jill, I know you've been out of circulation for a while, but surely you can still recognize good looks when you see them." Staring down at her clothes, Deb groaned and ran a hand through her hair. "I'm a mess! Talk about bad first impressions."

"You look fine. And what does it matter, anyway? You're happily married. It's not like you're trying to attract a guy."

"My dear sister, a woman always likes to be noticed by a handsome man. It's good for the ego." She moved over to the window and peeked through the curtain. "Who is this guy, anyway? The way you described him, I thought he was some down-on-his-luck drifter. Now that I've seen him—no way."

"I don't know anything about him, except that he's been on the road for a while."

Turning back, Deb gave her sister a skeptical look. "The man's been living on your property for two weeks and that's all you've found out?"

"I didn't want to pry."

"Prying and showing interest are two different things." Deb's face grew thoughtful. "I see my work is cut out for me."

"Deb." The warning note in Jill's voice was clear. "He seems like a very private person. Don't push."

"When have I ever pushed?" Deb gave her an innocent look.

"Deb."

"Okay, okay, I promise to behave. Or at least try to behave."

That was as good as she was going to get, and Jill knew it. Unfortunately, it left plenty of wiggle room.

"So what brought you to Orcas Island, Keith?"

Jill kicked Deb under the table. They'd only been eating a few minutes, and already her sister was edging into private territory. Deb ignored her, keeping her attention fixed on Keith as she smoothed one stray strand of her perfectly coiffed hair.

"Would you like some more lemonade, Keith?" Jill offered.

"Yes. Thanks."

As she picked up the pitcher, Jill suspected that Keith was already sorry he'd agreed to have lunch with them. Since the two of them had reached their barter agreement, they'd been sharing a hot lunch every day. But he'd insisted that they suspend that arrangement during Deb's visit, claiming he didn't want to intrude on family time. However, when Deb found out about it, she'd put her foot down, saying she didn't want anyone to alter their routine because she and Dominic were visiting. After Keith had continued to demur, she'd threatened to go into town for meals. In the end, he'd capitulated. A decision he was now regretting, Jill suspected.

When she finished pouring the lemonade, Jill was tempted to "spill" some on her sister's fashionable capri pants and matching top. Enough that she'd have to excuse herself to clean up. Of course, that wouldn't be nice. But it would get her off Keith's back for a few minutes. Her hand hovered for a brief second—long enough for Deb to shoot her a suspicious look. In the end, Jill returned the pitcher to its spot on the table, relying on prayer to keep her sister in check.

Too bad God wasn't listening.

"We were talking about your visit here, Keith," Deb prompted.

"I've been doing some traveling, and this area sounded interesting."

"Where's your home base?"

Keith hesitated, causing Jill to wonder if he was just reluctant to share that information—or if he didn't have one. "I left on my travels from Missouri."

"Well, isn't that a coincidence! Jill lived in Kansas before she came out here. You were almost neighbors."

"Have some turkey, Deb." Jill shoved the platter at her.

"I think I will." She helped herself, looking at the food

instead of her sister. "I always eat way too much when I come out here. Jill's such a good cook. I used to tell her she should open a restaurant. But she loved being an art teacher. Besides, those hours were hard enough to manage with a family, let alone trying to run a restaurant. Do you have a family, Keith?"

The volleys were coming so fast Keith was having difficulty keeping up. Not just because he was dodging the questions, but because he was also trying to assimilate the new information he was getting about Jill. He'd known she was a widow, but he'd known nothing of a family—as in children. The news startled him, and he shifted his attention to her even as he tried to frame a response to Deb's question. Her gaze met his, and he saw apology in her eyes. He wished he could assure her that her sister's queries didn't bother him, but that would be a lie. Still, if the reward for revealing a little about himself was additional background on Jill, he considered it a fair trade.

"No. My wife died a couple of years ago, and we didn't have children."

As Jill tried to process that bombshell, compassion softened Deb's features. "I'm so sorry."

"Thank you."

"Have you always been a carpenter, Keith?" Until now, Dominic had been too busy eating to pay much attention to the adult conversation. But as he started on his second helping of turkey, his pace slowed. He'd been following Keith around all morning, awed by the man's deft handling of tools and lumber. Now, it seemed, he was Deb's ally in the interrogation. Except his interest was innocent.

Turning his attention to the youngster, Keith smiled. "Not always."

"How did you learn to do all that stuff?"

"My dad's a carpenter. He was a great teacher."

"My dad's a lawyer. He works in an office and goes to court to talk to judges and help people who are in trouble."

"Good for him."

"Jill sure could have used your help when she first moved out here," Deb joined in, directing her comment to Keith. "Rehabbing this house was no small job."

"You rehabbed the house?" Keith angled his head toward Jill.

"The whole place, top to bottom," Deb answered for her. "It was a wreck. She stripped wallpaper and woodwork, re-finished the floors, replaced siding, painted. She did an amazing job."

Impressed, Keith looked over at her. No wonder she had such a well-equipped toolshed. "I agree."

A flush rose on Jill's cheeks. "It was mostly cosmetic."

"It was a lot more than that. You couldn't have gotten me to tackle this for all the tea in China," Deb declared.

"This is really good, Aunt Jill." Her nephew was buttering his third roll.

"Thanks, Dominic. And we have brownie sundaes for dessert."

"Awesome!" He tilted his head and inspected her as he chewed, then gave her a gap-toothed grin. "Hey, you know what? Your face looks better this year."

"Dominic!"

Deb's reproving tone had little impact on the youngster. "Well, it does." There was a stubborn tilt to his chin as he responded to his mother before turning back to Jill. "And your eyes are happier, too."

At the sudden speculative look on Deb's face, Jill decided to clear the table. "Okay, on to dessert."

Rising, Keith reached for Dominic's plate. "Let me help."

"You don't need to do that."

"I want to."

Rather than argue, Jill gathered up a stack of dishes and headed for the kitchen, Keith close on her heels. When she'd deposited her load on the counter, she took a deep breath and faced him. "I'm sorry about that."

A grin teased his lips. "Your sister missed her calling. I think the FBI or CIA could use her for interrogation work."

"She can be a little pushy."

"At least the trait doesn't seem to run in the family."

An answering smile played at the corners of her mouth. "I think I inherited my mom's diplomacy. Deb got my dad's inquisitiveness." Then her expression grew earnest. "But she's a wonderful person. I couldn't have survived without her after the…" Her voice choked, and she clamped her lips shut.

"Hey, I like your sister." He laid a reassuring hand on Jill's slender shoulder. "I wasn't offended."

The warmth of his fingers seeped through the fabric of her blouse, and her heart skipped a beat. "I'm glad. But I think I also owe you an apology for this morning. I'm sorry we both…that we stared. You just looked…different."

This time he gave her a full-fledged grin. "It's okay. I'm flattered…assuming different means better." Without giving her a chance to confirm or deny, he rubbed a hand over his clean-shaven jaw and spoke again. "I have to admit I feel more human again since I ditched the refugee look."

"Why did you do it?"

He considered her question. "I suppose I didn't want your sister to think you'd taken in a derelict. And it was time." Before she could ask him to clarify that ambiguous comment, he glanced over her shoulder and changed the subject. "Nice glassware collection, by the way. I've been meaning to compliment you on it. The pieces really catch the light."

Half turning, Jill surveyed the rainbow-colored vases and bowls that were displayed on the shelves above the half wall that separated the kitchen from the living room. "I rescued them from garage sales when…when I was first married. It was inexpensive entertainment, and I found some great buys. They're all flawed or damaged, but I could see their beauty, even if the owners couldn't. I figured they'd be relegated to the garbage heap if no one rescued them."

"Sort of like that baby bird." *And the mysterious little boy. And me.* But Keith left the latter thoughts unspoken.

His soft comment, and the warmth in his eyes, played havoc with Jill's equilibrium and her voice deserted her. But he didn't seem to expect a response. Instead, he headed for the door. "I'll gather up another load of dishes," he called over his shoulder.

Forcing thoughts about her reaction aside, Jill returned to the table. She needed all her wits about her to deal with Deb's barrage of questions. But to her relief, the conversation stayed on impersonal subjects for the remainder of the meal. Nevertheless, by the time Keith went back to work, Dominic trotting along behind him, Jill was exhausted. She hoped this wasn't a preview of meals during the rest of Deb's stay. She couldn't handle the tension.

The dishwasher was almost loaded when Deb wandered in from the table, nursing the last of her coffee. Jill gave her a quick look, then went back to work.

"You're mad at me, aren't you?"

"I asked you not to push."

"I didn't push. I just asked a few questions."

"You pushed. And why did you have to bring up the rehabbing? And my family?"

"I figured he knew at least some of that already. You eat lunch with him every day. Don't you ever talk about yourselves?"

"No. I'm not nosy—unlike some people I know." Jill gave her a pointed look.

"The word is interested. And all Italians are like that."

"You're not Italian."

"After twelve years of being married to Tony, I'm Italian by osmosis. But I have to admit that I didn't do very well today. Your guest was quite adept at sidestepping most of my questions. We found out he's a widower, but not much else. How did his wife die? What did he do before he was a carpenter? And did you notice how evasive he was when I asked where he was from? That Missouri answer was vague."

Shaking her head, Jill shut the dishwasher and turned it on. Then she faced her sister, folding her arms across her chest. "Leave it be, Deb. If he wants to talk, he will."

"Sometimes people need a little coaxing."

"If you keep on 'coaxing' he may stop coming for lunch."

A faint furrow appeared on Deb's brow as she mulled that over. "You may have a point. Okay, I'll back off a little."

"A lot."

"Yeah, yeah. By the way, Dominic was right about how you look, you know." She dumped the dregs of her coffee in the sink and rinsed the cup.

A melancholy look stole over Jill's face as she reached up to touch her cheek. "My face is never going to look even close to normal, Deb. We both know that."

"I wasn't talking about your face. I was talking about your eyes. They do look happier. I wonder why?"

Without waiting for a response, Deb deposited her cup on the counter and headed upstairs. It was clear she already had her own theory. One that involved Jill's unexpected visitor.

In all honesty, Jill couldn't dispute her. Since Keith had walked into her life, she'd felt more alive than she had in three and a half long, lonely years. Of course, it might not be him so much as the fact that she was simply hungry for human contact. Perhaps anyone would have had the same effect.

But if she said that to Deb, she suspected her sister would laugh and tell her to stop kidding herself.

And deep in her heart, Jill knew that Deb was right. Keith Michaels was special. And for as long as he inhabited her world, whether it be four weeks or four months, she was determined to savor every moment.

As for when it came time to say goodbye…she wouldn't think about that just yet. Nor would she analyze why the very thought of his departure made her feel empty and sad.

Chapter Eight

He was back.

Since Deb and Dominic's arrival, Jill had seen nothing of the mysterious little boy. But now, two days into their visit, he was hovering at the edge of the field, watching as Dominic searched for insects to feed Homer. She'd turned over the baby bird's care to her nephew, who had taken on the responsibility with conscientious diligence.

As she watched, Dominic spotted the boy. She'd told him and Deb about her young visitor, so Dominic didn't seem surprised. Though he was too far away for her to hear, she could tell he was talking to the youngster. When he walked toward him, Jill prepared herself for the inevitable fast exit.

But much to her surprise, the little boy didn't run. In fact, as Dominic drew closer, he came out from behind the boulders and took a few tentative steps toward him. Well, well, she mused. So that was the secret to coaxing her mystery visitor into the open—another child his age! *Praise the Lord,* Jill rejoiced in the silence of her heart, confident that Dominic could draw him out. Like his mother, he was a people person with the gift of gab. If her nephew couldn't earn the little boy's friendship, she doubted anyone could.

Side by side, the contrast between the boys was telling. Dominic wore casual but clean clothes, sized to his frame. The other boy was still dressed in grimy, mismatched attire that hung on his slight physique. Where Dominic looked robust and nurtured, the mystery boy seemed underfed and neglected. It was hard to judge his age, but Jill considered Dominic to be about the normal size for a seven-year-old, leading her to speculate that her shorter, more delicate-looking young visitor was about a year younger.

Dominic held out the jar of bugs to his new friend, and the boy leaned close to examine it. Then, with a nod toward the toolshed, Dominic took off. After he'd gone several steps, he turned and gestured for the boy to follow. Jill could sense his indecision—as well as his yearning to accept Dominic's invitation. Finally, with a furtive glance over his shoulder toward the woods, he trotted after him.

The two boys had to pass Keith, who was laying out some of the framework for the studio walls flat on the ground while the cement cured. Dominic didn't even slow down as he passed, but the other boy hesitated, walking a wide circle around Keith.

Jill could see Keith's surprise as he straightened up to stare after the duo. He looked toward the house, almost as if he was wondering whether she'd noticed. When he caught sight of her in the doorway, he smiled. Though he didn't say a word, Jill interpreted his expression to mean, "Looks like there's been a breakthrough. And I'm happy for you, because I know how concerned you've been about the boy."

Then she chided herself for reading far too much into his look. For all she knew, Keith was just glad that Dominic had found a friend who would keep him out from underfoot.

But in her heart, she knew that her interpretation was correct. And that made her feel good. Too good. She didn't want to start relying on other people to stoke her happiness. Especially transient people. For two years, since the day she'd stepped onto Orcas Island, she'd been self-contained, content with her seclusion, finding satisfaction in her painting and comfort in her faith. She didn't want that to change.

Yet it was. For whatever reason, Keith's arrival had disturbed her placid, secluded world. Stirred up emotions that were best left undisturbed. Awakened in her a restlessness, a sense that some essential component was missing in her life. The feeling was not only unsettling, but growing.

And there didn't seem to be a thing she could do to stop it.

When they gathered for their noon meal, Deb had to call Dominic three times before he appeared at the door of the toolshed.

"Lunch is ready!" She motioned for him to join them on the porch.

Ducking back inside, he reappeared a few seconds later, tugging on the arm of the reluctant young boy.

"Hey, Mom, can George eat with us?" he called.

Just then Jill stepped out on the porch, carrying a large platter of poached, fresh-caught salmon that Deb had brought back from the market after a morning foray into town. "Of course," she responded. "We have plenty."

Indecision flickered across the boy's face, and Jill held her breath. When the youngster took a step in their direction, her heart soared with hope.

But it was short-lived. When Keith appeared around the corner of the house, the boy pulled his arm free and took off across the field without a backward look.

His shoulders drooping with disappointment, Dominic trudged toward the porch, arriving at the same time as Keith.

"Hey, buddy, what happened to your friend?"

"He doesn't like grown-ups much, I guess."

As they settled into their places, Jill offered a blessing before turning her attention to Dominic. "Did you say your friend's name is George?"

"That's what I call him." Dominic helped himself to a generous serving of Jill's oven-fried potatoes. Keith wasn't too far behind, she noticed.

"Didn't he tell you his name?"

"Nope. He doesn't talk."

Deb cocked her head as she speared a bite of salmon. "What do you mean, he doesn't talk?"

Shrugging, Dominic dipped a potato in ketchup. "Like I said. He doesn't talk. But he was real good with Homer. He got him to eat a bunch more bugs than I did."

"Are you saying he didn't say one word?" Jill stopped eating and looked at Dominic.

"Nope."

"That's odd," Deb remarked. "Usually you can't get kids to *stop* talking."

"I guess he just didn't have anything to say," Dominic reasoned in a matter-of-fact tone.

So much for her hopes of learning any more about her mysterious visitor, Jill thought. If anything, his interaction with Dominic had raised more questions. Why didn't he talk? Was it because he couldn't—or wouldn't? Why was he afraid to get close to adults? Why did Keith in particular frighten him?

No answers were forthcoming. But Jill was determined to find them—sooner or later.

* * *

In between whale-watching outings and hikes in Moran State Park, Dominic spent every spare minute with George while Deb relaxed on the back porch, catching up on her reading while keeping an eye on the two boys. Though Dominic tried every day to coax his new friend to stay for lunch, the invitation was always rebuffed.

Then Jill had an inspiration. If the little boy wouldn't come to them at the house, they could go to him on territory where he felt more comfortable. "How about a picnic in the meadow today?" she suggested to Deb and Dominic at breakfast. "Since you'll be leaving tomorrow morning, we should make our last lunch special."

"Cool!" Dominic enthused.

"Okay by me," Deb seconded. "As long as we don't have to sit on the ground. My sacroiliac can't take that."

"Don't tell me you're getting old," Jill teased.

"Mom's already old," Dominic offered.

"Thanks a lot!" Deb gave Jill a disgruntled look. "Let me tell you, there's no hiding from the truth when you have kids around."

"Well, I think we can accommodate your old bones," Jill assured her, stifling a smile.

And so, at twelve-thirty, Jill and Deb carried the fixings of a gourmet picnic out to the field, near the boulders where Jill had first seen George. They enlisted Keith's help in setting up a portable table and chairs, and while Deb began unpacking the food, Jill spread a checkered cloth on the ground a dozen yards away.

"What's that for?" Deb queried.

"I thought Dominic might be able to convince George to join us if they kept their distance."

"It might help even more if I made myself scarce. I could eat at the house," Keith offered, his gaze fixed on Jill.

She gave him an appreciative smile but shook her head. "No. Let's see if this works."

"Okay, we're set." Deb surveyed the table, cupped her hands around her mouth and called Dominic.

"I'll be right there, Mom!" He poked his head around the side of the toolshed and waved. Keith had given Dominic some scrap lumber and shown him how to sand and hammer and measure, and Dominic in turn had shared his new knowledge with George. The two boys had been occupied all morning on the far side of the shed, building a display shelf for Jill's new studio.

A couple of minutes later he appeared, with George close on his heels. Since Jill had positioned the picnic near the spot in the woods where George entered and exited, he had to walk near them in order to leave. She hoped, when he saw the cloth set apart on the ground and got a good look at the food, he'd be tempted to stay.

When they drew close enough to talk without shouting, Jill spoke. "I set a place for you and your friend over there, if he'd like to stay." She gestured toward the checkered cloth on the ground. "We have plenty of fried chicken and potato salad and biscuits. And I baked brownies for dessert."

"Aunt Jill cooks real good," Dominic told George, tugging him along behind him. "Come on! After we eat we can feed Homer and work on the shelf some more."

When the boy hesitated, Keith moved to the portable table, choosing a chair that put his back to the young boys. Touched by his sensitivity, Jill sent him a grateful look. The smile he gave her in return warmed her heart.

Once Keith was seated, George seemed more inclined to

stay for lunch, though his posture was in marked contrast to Dominic's. While her nephew flopped down and reached for a chicken leg, his focus on a V of Canada geese high above, George kept a close eye on Keith, crouching more than sitting, as if he was prepared to bolt at the slightest provocation.

His nervousness did diminish during the meal, however. The tense line of his shoulders eased a bit, and once he started eating, Jill was amazed at the quantity of food he consumed. Dominic had to come to the main table to replenish their supply more than once, and Jill's biscuits disappeared as fast as ice on a hot summer day.

Although she was grateful that the boy had ventured closer, the trick would be to sustain his comfort level once Dominic and Deb left tomorrow. Perhaps Homer was the key, she speculated. If George was still willing to come and care for the abandoned bird, then maybe…

"Kyle! I been lookin' everywhere for you, boy. Git back to the house. Now!"

Startled out of her reverie by a voice as rough as the heavy-duty sandpaper she'd used in her rehab project, Jill turned. A grizzled, older man stood at the edge of the woods, his ill-fitting clothes grimy and tattered on his burly frame. His eyes were hard and angry, the stubble on his chin coarse, his gray hair uncombed and greasy. He wore a dirty felt hat that looked as if it had been punched and shaken and slapped so often that all the stiffness had come out.

In the few beats of silence it took for Jill to assess the man, the mystery boy sprang to his feet. She transferred her gaze to him at once, noting the sudden fear in his eyes before they went flat. His expression reminded her of a cowed animal. One that had been beaten into submission and expected to be

punished for any transgression—or perceived transgression—
and left with no choice but to comply with its keeper's wishes,

As the boy darted toward the woods, his half-eaten brownie
forgotten, Jill started to rise. But Keith laid a hand on her
shoulder, pressing her back into her seat. Then he stood
instead and faced the man, his posture daring him to lay a hand
on the boy as he scurried past.

Whether the man had intended to touch the boy or not was
uncertain. But if he had been entertaining such thoughts,
Keith's look stopped him. After giving the younger man a
defiant stare, he turned without another word and clumped off
into the woods.

For a few moments, stunned silence hung over the small
group in the meadow. Dominic scooted toward the adults, his
own brownie compressed in his hand, squeezed almost
beyond recognition. "W-who was that?"

Deb pulled him close, enfolding him in a warm, comforting hug. "I don't know, sweetie. But he's gone now. You can
sit here by me while we finish our lunch."

Except no one felt much like eating, Keith noted in one dis-
cerning sweep. The brownies lay untouched on the plates, and
a heavy silence hung over the table. Dominic was upset, Deb
was concerned and Jill's distress was almost palpable.
Someone needed to try and salvage the situation, and it looked
like the task fell to him.

Doing his best to smile, he tousled Dominic's hair. "Why
don't you go show your mom that great shelf you're building
while your aunt and I clean up the picnic?"

Relief flooded Deb's features. "That's a great idea,
Dominic."

She rose, but Dominic held back, his face troubled. "Is
George going to be okay?"

"I think his name is Kyle, honey. And that might be his grandpa. He was probably just late for lunch and his grandpa came to find him." Deb's explanation was weak, but Jill hoped Dominic would buy it. She didn't want her nephew to be distressed by the encounter. She was upset enough for both of them.

"He looked mad." Dominic cast a worried glance toward the woods. "And he didn't look like a grandpa."

Picturing Tony's gregarious, nurturing, jolly parents, Jill saw Dominic's point.

"You can't always judge people by the way they look," Keith interjected. When Jill turned to him, she was disconcerted to find him looking at her, not Dominic. "He might be a very nice man."

"Yeah. Maybe." Dominic didn't sound convinced, but neither did he seem as upset.

"So are you going to show me that shelf?" Deb prodded.

"Sure. Come on. Keith showed me how to put the nails in straight, and he said Aunt Jill could use it to hold her supplies, or she could put a picture of me on it to remember our visit and…"

As his voice receded, Jill drew a shaky breath and turned to find Keith watching her.

"I didn't especially like the looks of that." His voice was quiet, his eyes steely.

"Me, neither."

"You said you just started noticing the boy the day I arrived?"

"Yes. That afternoon. I've never seen the older man until today, although the owner of the neighborhood grocery store did tell me that an 'old hermit,' as she described him, lived on the adjacent property."

"But no mention of a child?"

"No."

"He must be a new arrival, then."

Tears blurred Jill's vision, and she blinked them away. "I think he needs help, but I'm not sure what we can do."

"It's difficult to do much unless there's evidence of abuse of some kind." Keith had had to intervene in a few of these situations in his prior life, and it had never been easy. Or pretty.

"We don't have that."

"I know."

"What do you think we should do?"

He almost said *pray,* but stopped himself. "Let's see if the boy comes back again. Now that the ice is broken, he may warm up to you and start to talk. If he does, he might tell us something that would give us grounds to go to the authorities."

"If Dominic couldn't get him to talk, I doubt I'll have any better luck." She turned and looked into the shadowy woods. "But I'll pray about it, ask God to give me some guidance."

Her comment didn't surprise Keith. He already knew that Jill had a strong faith. He'd seen the worn Bible she kept in her kitchen. She quoted scripture, prayed before meals, led a godly life. At one time, he, too, would have turned to God in a situation like this. Except, God had stopped listening to him long ago. But maybe He'd listen to Jill.

Keith hoped so. Because he suspected that Kyle needed all the help he could get.

Chapter Nine

For two days after Deb and Dominic left, Jill saw no trace of her young visitor. And the longer he was absent, the more worried she became. Was he being mistreated by the gruff older man who had summoned him from the picnic? The question gnawed at her, but she had no idea how to find the answer.

Then, on the third morning, as she turned from putting away her gardening tools in the shadowy shed, she found Kyle hovering in the doorway. A swift perusal confirmed that, at least on the visible parts of his body, he bore no ill effects of the older man's anger. Relief flooded through her.

"I'm glad you came back, Kyle." She smiled, gesturing toward the small, insect-filled jar clutched in his hands. "Did you come to feed Homer? I think he misses all the attention you and Dominic gave him."

His only response was a hesitant nod.

"Good. I'm happy to turn the job over to you again. He's grown quite a bit in just the past two days. Pretty soon I think he'll be ready to test his wings. Go ahead, take a look. I have to go back to the house anyway."

As she moved toward the door, he stepped inside, then edged away from her toward the bird.

"I'll be painting, and Keith is gone to Friday Harbor, over on the next island. He won't be back until late tonight. Spend as much time as you like with Homer."

With a lighter heart, Jill headed back to the house and retrieved her painting supplies. Now that Kyle was back, she could implement the next step in her campaign to win his confidence.

Forty-five minutes later, when Kyle emerged from the shed, she waved at him from her easel in the middle of the meadow. "Would you like to see what I'm working on?" she called.

When a swift survey of the field and woods confirmed that they were alone, Kyle edged closer.

"I wanted to paint the meadow with all these yellow and orange poppies," Jill told him when he drew near. "Isn't it bright and cheerful?"

He seemed interested, but he kept his distance.

"I thought you might like to paint a picture," Jill continued. "I set up an easel over there for you, and put out some brushes and paints. Would you like to give it a try?"

His gaze flickered to the small easel about twenty feet away from Jill's, and his eyes lit up. She held her breath while he considered the invitation, letting it out slowly when he moved toward the blank canvas. Success! He'd taken the bait.

Although she made a pretense of working on her own painting, Jill's focus was on her young visitor. She watched as he picked up a brush, examined it and studied the paint she'd squeezed out on a palette for him. His first few dabs at the canvas were tentative, but after a few minutes he became absorbed in the task, the furrows on his brow evidence of his absolute concentration. It was almost as if he'd forgotten Jill's presence.

And that was good. It gave her a chance to scrutinize the little boy without having to be concerned about spooking him. His ragtag clothes and dirty face confirmed once again that there was a lack of TLC in his life. But what caught—and held—her attention was the way he leaned very, very close to the canvas as he painted, as if he was having trouble seeing at a distance of more than a few inches.

That, too, spoke of neglect, Jill reasoned. If he had vision problems, why wasn't someone taking care of them? And since they weren't, would the authorities consider that reason enough to check out his situation? But even if they did, she could offer them little information. All she had was the boy's first name; she had no idea where he lived.

But she could find out, Jill realized. All she had to do was follow Kyle home today. She'd have to take care that he didn't see her, but considering the shadows in the forest and the carpet of pine needles that would deaden her steps—not to mention his apparent vision problems—she was sure she could remain undetected. Once she had a location, she could direct the authorities to his home. Assuming, of course, that she could convince them he needed help. She prayed that his worn clothing, grimy appearance and unaddressed vision problems would be enough to justify a visit.

The painting project occupied Kyle for well over an hour. But when Jill mentioned lunch, he shot her a startled look and cast a furtive glance toward the woods, as if the older man had told him to be back by a certain time. With reluctance, he laid his brush down and looked at her.

"You can eat here if you like, Kyle. But if you need to go, I'll put your painting away and you can finish it tomorrow."

Once more, he acknowledged her comment with a brief

nod. Then he stuck his hands in his pockets, lowered his head and trudged toward the woods.

Jill waited until he'd entered the forest before she went into action. Laying aside her own brush, she rose and walked across the meadow, toward the large boulders where she'd first seen Kyle. She forced herself to adopt a leisurely pace, just in case he was watching. When she reached the edge of the field, she turned, angling her body so that it would appear she was surveying the meadow when in fact she was surreptitiously scanning the woods.

It was clear at once that she didn't have to worry about Kyle watching her. She could see him in the distance, weaving in and out among the trees, his back to her as he maintained his slow, plodding pace. If she kept low and stayed in the shadows, this ought to be a piece of cake.

A quarter of a mile later, her back aching from her crouched position, her knees protesting from the constant up and down as she dived behind rocks and darted from tree to tree, Jill hit pay dirt. A ramshackle structure—more lean-to than house—appeared. In front of the hovel stood a rusted, older-model pickup truck, and the ground around the place was littered with garbage and decaying machinery. When Kyle reached the door, he hesitated. Then, his shoulders drooping, he went inside.

After waiting a good fifteen minutes, Jill saw no further evidence of life. Nor any indication that harm had befallen her young friend for a tardy return It was time to go.

On her trek back through the woods, Jill considered her next move. It was clear to her that Kyle was in desperate need of nurturing. The challenge would be to convince the authorities of that. But to do so, she'd have to lodge an official concern—which would require her to reconnect with the world, at least for a while.

Oddly enough, while that possibility would once have made her feel sick, it now caused no more than a flutter in her stomach. In part, because her concern for Kyle was stronger than her dislike of the curious, pitying stares of strangers. As to whether she could convince the authorities to investigate Kyle's situation…that was a bigger challenge. When she got back to the house, she'd jot down a few notes, put some thoughts together. In the morning, she'd run it by Keith. She wanted a second opinion, and she'd come to respect his sound thinking. Besides, two heads were always better than one. She'd have just one chance to present her argument, and she didn't want to blow it. Not when a little boy's future hung in the balance.

And in the meantime, she prayed that the Lord would keep Kyle safe.

"Jill? Sorry to disturb you so early, but I think there's something wrong with Kyle."

Cradling a mug of coffee in her hands, Jill stared bleary-eyed out the screen door at Keith, noting the faint creases in his brow. Although she'd gone to bed at her normal hour, she'd still been awake when the crunch of gravel announced his return late in the evening. She'd also been awake two hours later, when the moon had appeared in her bedroom window. And at six in the morning, she'd watched the dawn paint the sky a faint pink. In all, she doubted whether she'd clocked more than three hours of intermittent sleep. Her concern for Kyle had been too deep and disturbing to permit a restful night. When sleep had finally come at dawn, she'd given in to it, staying in bed an extra hour. Even so, she felt sluggish— and in desperate need of coffee to chase away the cobwebs from her brain.

But Keith's announcement had the same effect as a high-octane jolt of caffeine. Her heart began to bang against her rib cage, and when she spoke a tremor ran through her voice. "What do you mean?"

"He's in the toolshed. I noticed him as I walked by. He's sitting on the floor, and I think he's crying. My first instinct was to go in, but I was afraid he'd run off if I got too close."

Her alarm escalating, Jill set her mug on the counter and crossed the room. "I'll take a look."

"I won't be far if you need me." Keith opened the door for her as she approached.

She acknowledged his comment with a quick dip of her head, then almost ran to the shed, slowing her pace only when she was steps away.

Once she reached the doorway, a quick survey confirmed Keith's assessment. Kyle was sitting on the floor, hunched over Homer's box, which rested in his lap. His shoulders were heaving as silent tears coursed down his cheeks.

"Kyle?"

At the sound of her gentle voice, he looked up at her with stricken eyes. Slowly, his arms trembling, he held out the box. Homer lay still and quiet in one corner.

With an aching heart, Jill moved beside him and dropped to her knees. She wanted to comfort him, to give him reasons for what had happened. But what could she say? Sometimes there was no explanation for the death of cherished living things—be they birds or people.

Knowing words wouldn't ease his sadness or sense of loss, she did the next best thing. She gathered him in her arms and just held him.

At first, Kyle stiffened, as if unaccustomed to such displays of affection. But in increments his posture changed from resistance to a desperate hunger for consolation, and he clung to her, weeping against her shoulder with deep, wrenching sobs. Shocked at the sounds coming from a child who had always been mute, she stroked his back and murmured soothing words of comfort.

When at last his crying subsided, Jill drew back to study the tear-streaked face he turned up to her. As he looked at her, the grief in his eyes suddenly became tempered by another emotion. Surprise, perhaps. Or curiosity. His attention was riveted on the right side of her face, as if he'd never noticed her scars. And perhaps he hadn't, she realized with a jolt. If his vision was as poor as she suspected, he may never have discerned them from the distance he'd always kept. But at this proximity, he couldn't miss them.

All at once a memory came rushing back to Jill, of the first time she'd ventured out in public after her final skin graft. Deb had invited her to lunch to celebrate and wouldn't take no for an answer. Although Jill hadn't been keen on the idea, it had seemed important to Deb. And after all her sister had done for her, she hadn't wanted to refuse.

Things had gone okay at first. Of course, her appearance had attracted a lot of attention. Discreet glances, whispered comments as she passed, skittering gazes if she turned and happened to find another diner watching her. Even the waitress had refused to establish eye contact with her. She hadn't been surprised. That had been the typical reaction ever since the accident. Nevertheless, she'd resolved to put her discomfort and self-consciousness aside for that one day and enjoy the lunch with Deb.

And she had. Until a mother, engaged in conversation with another woman, had walked by with her young daughter in tow. The child couldn't have been more than four or five, a beautiful little girl with golden-blond hair and an angelic countenance. Much like Emily, Jill had thought with a pang that had produced an almost physical pain. The girl had smiled at Deb, but the smile had been replaced by a look of horror when she'd transferred her attention to Jill. She'd started to cry, emitting a panicked wail of fear as she grabbed her mother's leg and hid behind her.

The scene that had ensued, played out before a packed house of diners, was forever etched on Jill's mind. The mother had reached for her daughter in confusion, then turned to Jill and Deb, seeking the cause of her child's terror. When she looked at Jill, her initial revulsion had quickly morphed into recrimination. As if Jill had frightened her daughter on purpose. As if she'd *chosen* to look like something from a freak show.

The little girl had been inconsolable, and the two women had exited the restaurant—leaving an awkward, unnatural hush in their wake. It took almost a full minute before the clink of silver indicated that people had once again resumed their meals. Too numb to react, Jill had been unable to eat a bite of the lunch she'd ordered, despite Deb's best efforts to cheer her up.

Now, as Kyle stared at her, she tensed, preparing herself for a similar reaction. But instead, he did something that shocked her. With a tentative, gentle hand he reached up and touched her scars.

Jill's instinctive reaction was to jerk back and turn aside from his scrutiny. But she forced herself to remain motionless. For some reason, Kyle wasn't repelled by her appearance. Nor was he afraid. His expression couldn't quite be described as curious, either. Yet her appearance seemed to…intrigue him. But why?

Seconds later, she had her answer when he pulled back his sleeve to reveal a series of similar scars on his arm. Except his were round and symmetrical. Like hers, they'd faded a bit, but she could tell they were of more recent vintage. And there was no question that they were from burns.

Only once before had Jill seen scars like that—on an abused child in one of her art classes. Kyle's burns weren't from an accident. They'd been inflicted in a purposeful way by a smoldering cigarette, designed to punish and hurt and control.

As rage surged inside her, it took every ounce of her self-control to maintain a surface calm when she spoke. "Who did that to you, Kyle?"

Instead of responding, he pushed his sleeve back down and bowed his head.

Lord, help me get through to him! Jill prayed. *After hearing him cry, I'm sure he has the ability, if not the inclination, to speak. Help him to trust me, to tell me about his situation so that I can help him.*

"Kyle, who did that to your arm?" she tried again, her voice soft.

Once more tears welled in his eyes, but he remained silent.

A shadow fell across the doorway, and they both looked up to find Keith standing there. "Can I help?"

Though his tone was caring and kind, Kyle tensed in her arms as he stared up at the man, his whole body quivering.

"Come down to our level," Jill suggested quietly.

A flash of understanding dawned in Keith's eyes, and he dropped down to balance on the balls of his feet. "What's going on?"

"We lost Homer." Jill gestured toward the box, her gaze meeting Keith's.

After taking a quick glance at the dead bird, Keith gave her a quizzical look, as if to say, "Is that it?" But before he could speak, a familiar voice floated across the meadow, muffled by the walls of the shed but still distinct.

"You here, boy?"

Kyle stiffened, and before Jill could stop him he jumped up and ran for the door, almost knocking Keith over as he shot past.

"Should I go after him?" Keith steadied himself, his fingertips brushing the ground.

Swallowing past the lump in her throat, Jill shook her head. When she spoke, her voice was raspier than usual. "No. But I think it's time to call the authorities."

"You found some grounds to suspect abuse?"

"Yes. Of recent enough vintage that it should be sufficient to compel someone to investigate his situation." She drew a steadying breath and rose, trying to control her anger. "Kyle has cigarette burns on his arm."

A beat of silence ticked by as Keith slowly stood. "I take it you mean deliberate burns." His tone was grim, and his eyes grew flat and hard.

"Yes."

A muscle twitched in his jaw. "You're sure?"

"I saw this once before, when I was teaching. And I know what burns look like."

"Then we need to call the state division of Children and Family Services…or Social Services, whatever they call it here. That's the agency that's designed to protect abused and neglected children."

His quick and knowledgeable response surprised her. It was almost as if he'd been down this road.

"I dealt with a couple of abuse situations in a past life," he said in response to the unasked question in her eyes.

So he hadn't always been a carpenter, after all. Deb had surmised as much. Then what *had* he been? Jill wondered. But now wasn't the time to speculate about her tenant. Her first priority was to ensure Kyle's safety. Considering that the studio was only about thirty percent done, Jill figured she had a few more weeks to satisfy her curiosity about Keith. Except she wasn't very good at ferreting out information.

Too bad Deb wouldn't be back for another year.

"Jill Whelan? Cindy Howard, Division of Family Services. We spoke on the phone. Since I was in the neighborhood, I thought I'd stop by. May I come in?"

Although Jill recognized the voice of the woman who stood on the other side of her front door, the social worker didn't fit the image she'd constructed in her mind of a motherly, middle-aged type. With her flaming red hair, slight build and fashionable attire, Cindy looked to be in her early thirties at the most. But more important, why was she here? Jill hadn't expected to have to talk with anyone in person. Still, if she had new information…

"Have you had a chance to check on Kyle?"

"Yes. That's what I wanted to talk with you about."

So much for her self-imposed isolation, Jill reflected, steeling herself for the woman's reaction as she stepped back and motioned her in. Cindy did seem a bit taken aback for a brief second, but Jill's disfigurement didn't distract her from the purpose of her visit. After seating herself on the couch Jill waved her to, she got down to business.

"Thank you for bringing this situation to our attention," she told Jill.

"Can you tell me what you found out?"

The woman consulted a notepad. "Some. The little boy's

name is Kyle Corbett, and the older man is his grandfather. Who was not too happy to see me, by the way."

"I'm sorry."

"Goes with the job." Cindy shrugged. "Anyway, even though Mr. Corbett was reluctant to share information, I managed to find out that the boy has been living with him for the past six weeks. Kyle's mother died a few months ago, and it seems that Kyle was cramping his father's style. I also suspect from a few of the grandfather's comments that Kyle's father was abusive to both his 'partner'—he wasn't married to Kyle's mother—and to his son."

"What about the vision problem? And the fact that he doesn't speak?"

"Mr. Corbett confirmed that the boy hasn't spoken since he's been living with him, but indicated that he can speak. And I concur with your assessment that Kyle needs glasses. I recommended that he have a vision test, and provided some information to his grandfather about a free clinic in town. But to be honest, I don't have a lot of hope that he'll follow through."

A frown creased Jill's brow. "So what happens next?"

"I'll continue to monitor the situation. For one thing, I suspect Kyle should be starting school this fall. His grandfather wouldn't confirm his age, but I can check birth records. Beyond that, however, there's little we can do. There was food in the house, and I saw no evidence of present abuse." Cindy closed her notebook.

"But—but he's still suffering from the effects of past abuse! He doesn't even speak. That has to be a result of trauma. And he's in desperate need of love and care."

A soft look stole into Cindy's eyes. "I can see how much you care about him, Jill—if I may call you that?" At Jill's nod, she continued. "I wish we could do more. But I can't find any immediate grounds to take him out of his present environment. For now, the best I can do is continue to make periodic visits."

Clasping her hands in front of her, Jill leaned forward, her posture taut and tense. "Is there anything else *I* can do?"

"Just continue what you've been doing. Based on our phone conversation a couple of days ago, it sounds like Kyle has been a regular visitor. And after meeting you, I can see why. I suspect he finds the kind of nurturing here that has long been absent from his life—if he ever had any."

"It's not enough." Jill's voice was a mere whisper.

"For now, it will have to be." Cindy tucked her notebook into her purse. "If you see anything else that looks suspicious, please call me. At any time." She dug in her purse and handed Jill a card. "My office, home and cell phone numbers are on there. Don't hesitate to use them if you need to. And keep caring about Kyle. He needs someone like you."

Long after Cindy left, Jill remained in the living room, her shoulders slumped. How could people be indifferent to children? Or, in Kyle's case, not only indifferent, but abusive? She thought of the circle of love she and Sam and Emily had shared. Emily had thrived in that nurturing environment, laughter coming as easily to her as breathing. On the other hand, Jill had never heard Kyle laugh. Or even seen him smile. No matter what Cindy said, it wasn't right. Maybe his grandfather gave him food and shelter and clothing, but he needed more. Much more. He needed nourishment and shelter for his heart and his soul, as well as for his body.

She was still sitting there when a knock sounded at her back door. Turning, she saw Keith framed in the doorway. With a weary sigh, she rose and joined him on the porch.

One look at her face, and Keith knew something bad had

happened while he'd run into town to order additional supplies. His stomach tightened into a knot. "What's wrong?"

Shoving her hands in the pockets of her jeans, she moved to the railing and stared into the dark woods at the edge of the meadow. "I had a visit from the social worker who looked into Kyle's situation."

"And?"

"There's nothing they can do." She gave him a quick recap of Cindy's report. "It seems our hands are tied."

The dejected slump of Jill's shoulders tugged at Keith's heart, and it took all of his willpower to squelch a powerful— and unexpected—urge to walk up behind her and wrap his arms around her in a comforting, caring hug. Instead, he jammed his hands in his pockets and moved beside her, angling his body to give him a view of her profile.

"You tried, Jill."

"It didn't do any good." She choked back a sob.

"You never know. Sometimes the smallest action can have repercussions we could never imagine. You did your best, and God knows that. Now you just have to put this situation in His hands and trust that all things will work to His good." He wasn't sure where those words had come from.

His comments touched her, and she blinked back tears. "Thanks for reminding me of that." Then she gave him a tremulous smile. "You know, maybe you missed your calling, Keith. I have a feeling you would have made a good minister."

The unexpected comment jolted him, and he reared back almost as if someone had delivered a hard right to his jaw. "Yeah, well, I need to get back to work. We'll talk later."

With that, he turned and strode away.

Shocked by his reaction, Jill could only stare at his stiff back as he made a hasty retreat. She'd intended her comment to be a compliment, had hoped it would bring an answering smile to his lips. Instead, the color had drained from his face, and in the instant before he shuttered his eyes a flash of pain had ricocheted through them. What in the world had that been all about? Why was he upset? Questions zipped through her mind, all of them unanswered.

Where was Deb when she needed her?

Chapter Ten

A short time after Keith's abrupt departure, he took off for town, saying he had to talk to the electrical contractor. Jill had a nagging feeling that she owed him an apology, but for the life of her she couldn't figure out why.

Although she tried to paint, her thoughts were too distracting. She finally gave up and went out to tend her garden, hoping physical labor would dispel her troubled musings. When that didn't work, either, she put her tools away and decided she needed a Deb fix. Her sister always had a way of putting things in perspective.

"So how's the studio coming along?" Deb greeted her.

"Great. Keith is making a lot of progress."

"And how is Keith?"

"Fine. I guess."

"What does that mean?"

"I think I offended him earlier today. But I have no idea why."

"Ask him."

"Easier said than done."

"That's what I'd do if I was there."

Jill didn't doubt it. "Since you aren't, that doesn't solve my problem."

"Okay…try reconstructing the conversation. That might help you figure out why he's upset. What were you talking about?"

"Kyle." She filled Deb in on her discovery of Kyle's burns and her subsequent call to the authorities. "A social worker paid his grandfather a visit, but couldn't find any current grounds to take action."

"What happens next?"

"She said she'd keep the situation on her radar screen, and she's going to do some digging to figure out if Kyle should be in school this year."

"Sounds like she's doing all she can."

"I suppose so. She was very nice. And she hardly glanced at my face. I guess in her job, she's seen it all."

"Or it could be that you're less sensitive about it. I told you all along, Jill. You need to give people a chance. Once they get past the initial shock a lot of them would be able to put your scars aside and treat you like the normal person you are. You don't give them enough credit. Keith doesn't even seem to notice them."

"He's different."

A couple of beats of silence ticked by. "Yeah. I think he is, too. Look, about this misunderstanding. Give it a little time. He might end up telling you what's bothering him without any prompting."

Three hours later, when Jill saw a light bobbing across the field toward the house, her earlier conversation with Deb came to mind. Perhaps Keith was coming to explain his odd behavior and to offer some answers to the questions that had been swirling around in her mind. And if that wasn't the purpose of his visit, perhaps she could find the courage to follow Deb's advice and flat out ask him what she'd said to upset him.

Wiping her hands on a dish towel, she stepped out onto the back porch and moved to the railing. But when the figure grew close, she realized it wasn't Keith after all, but Kyle's grandfather. In the flickering lantern light, the grim set of his features was thrown into stark—and menacing—relief.

Before she could retreat to the safety of the house, he stepped up onto the porch, moving with an agility that surprised her, to plant himself between her and the back door.

"All right, missy. You and me have some talking to do."

Summoning up her courage, Jill straightened her shoulders and stared him down, keeping a nervous eye on the flickering lantern in his hand. "No, I don't think we do."

He took a step closer, and continued as if she hadn't spoken. "I don't like do-gooders sticking their nose into my life. How I raise the boy is nobody's business but mine, you hear? Sending the state to check up on me wasn't smart. It's hard enough taking on a snot-nosed kid without having the authorities butting in and asking a lot of nosy questions. You want what's best for the boy? Then you back off. Got it?"

"Is that a threat, Mr. Corbett?" Jill tried to sound assertive, but she couldn't control the quiver that ran through her voice.

"Call it what you like." He lifted the lantern a bit higher and peered at her in the flickering light. "Say, what's wrong with your face?"

"That's none of your business."

"Not exactly Miss America, are you?" he sneered. "I've heard stories about you, the widow-lady recluse. Now I see why you hide out here. Can't be much of a life, though. Maybe that's why you figure you got to mess in other people's."

His vile words sent a shiver down her spine. "Get off my property, Mr. Corbett."

He took another step in her direction and waved the lantern

in front of her. It was so close that Jill could feel the heat, and she gasped and shrank back against the railing, lifting her hands to shield herself as the thick bile of fear rose in her throat. "I don't take orders from women."

"Then you can take them from me."

At the sound of Keith's voice, the older man's head whipped around. But he didn't budge.

"Like the lady said, get off this property," Keith told him in a curt, authoritative tone that Jill had never heard before. "Now. Or *I'll* call the authorities."

For a few seconds, the man seemed to be weighing his options. At last, without another word, he brushed past Keith, descended the steps and retraced his route across the meadow until his lantern was a mere speck of light in the distance.

Only when it was clear that the man was gone did Keith turn his attention back to Jill. She was slumped against the railing, and though her features were masked in the dim light, he could feel the tension emanating from her body. "Are you all right?"

The husky, concerned timbre of his voice chased away the last of her composure. She dropped her head into her hands, and despite her attempts to stifle it, a ragged sob escaped from her throat.

Earlier in the day, Keith had found the strength to resist the strong impulse to touch her, to console her. This time, he didn't. Without stopping to consider her reaction—or the consequences—he followed his heart. In two long strides he was beside her. Pulling her close, he wrapped his arms around her in a protective, comforting hug.

His cheek resting against her soft hair, Keith held her until the shudders rippling through her body at last abated and she relaxed in his arms. It had been a long time since he'd touched a woman. Longer still since doing so had evoked feelings other than simple caring support. That was all Ellen had needed from him in the end. For the final few months of her life, he'd become more caretaker than husband. And after she died, after his world disintegrated, he'd been so filled with hate that he'd never again expected to experience the gentler emotions.

Well, he was experiencing them now. Big-time. His intent had been merely to comfort and protect Jill, but all at once he felt more. Much more. Her soft, slender body made him yearn for things he'd almost given up hope of ever experiencing again. And reminded him that despite all that had happened, he was still a man. A man capable of responding to a special woman. This woman.

That revelation rocked Keith's world. When he'd arrived on Orcas Island, he'd been hoping to find many things. Answers. A way back to God. Hope. A new life. He hadn't been looking for romance. In fact, that hadn't even been on his radar screen. But now he realized that during the past few weeks, thanks to the woman he held in his arms, he'd begun to take the first steps toward the resolutions he'd been seeking. That here, at the literal end of the road on his journey, he was finding a new beginning. And along the way, Jill had become far more than a landlady.

Although he was stunned by that insight, this wasn't the time to reflect on it. Right now, Jill needed the comfort and strength of his arms. Later, he could try and figure out when his feelings toward her had begun to deepen. And, more importantly, how he was going to deal with that.

As they stood on the dark porch, the stillness of the night surrounding them, Jill wasn't quite sure how she'd ended up in Keith's arms, her cheek pressed against the soft flannel of his shirt, his heart beating a steady, strong, reassuring tempo beneath her ear. All she knew was that it felt right. And good.

A few weeks before, the very notion that she'd ever again find herself in a man's arms would have seemed ludicrous, Jill reflected. As would the suggestion that her private hideaway would be visited by a whole new cast of characters—Keith, Kyle, Mr. Corbett, Cindy. That was more callers than she'd had in the entire previous twelve months. After years of seclusion she was rejoining the world instead of watching it from the sidelines. And it was exhilarating. But it was also a bit unsettling. Yet Jill wouldn't change a thing about the past month. Or this moment. Or this man.

For as long as she dared, she stayed in the circle of Keith's strong arms, relishing the soothing way his hand was stroking her back, enjoying the feel of his chin nuzzling her hair. But when suddenly she found herself wondering what it would be like to kiss him, she gave a startled gasp and backed off.

Instead of letting her go, Keith gripped her upper arms and scanned her face in alarm. "Jill? Are you okay?"

"Y-yes. I'm f-fine." She could barely choke out the words.

"You don't sound fine." His eyes narrowed, and his lips settled into a thin, hard line as he scrutinized her. "He didn't touch you before I got here, did he?" His question was quiet. Too quiet.

"No. My white knight appeared just in time." She tried to laugh but couldn't quite pull it off. "How did you know that I…that there was a problem?"

"I saw the light from the cabin. Since you aren't exactly overrun with visitors here, and considering the direction the light was coming from, I put two and two together." His back was to the dim light in the kitchen, his expression shadowed and unreadable. "Will you be okay here by yourself tonight?

I don't think he's coming back, but I could camp out on the porch if it would make you feel safer. I have a sleeping bag."

The temptation to accept his offer was so strong that it took every ounce of Jill's self-discipline to subdue it. Knowing he was close by would give her a feeling of safety sure to be absent once he trekked back across the field. But she couldn't do that to him. Not when he had a nice, comfortable bed at the cabin.

"No, I'll be fine. But…would you like to come in for some coffee before you leave?" She owed him that, at least. Not to mention the fact that it would delay his departure a bit.

Did he hesitate, or was it her imagination? "Sure. I could use a cup."

Leading the way in, she bolted the door behind them and gestured to the kitchen table. "Make yourself comfortable. It will just take a minute."

As she busied herself at the sink, it occurred to Jill that this was the first time Keith had been in the house for any reason other than to deliver dirty dishes or give her a progress report on the studio. Their noon meal was always taken outside. Somehow, having him sit at her kitchen table introduced a new feeling of closeness to their relationship. Not good, considering the inappropriate direction of her thoughts on the porch.

"Can I help?"

His voice at her ear, so close she could feel the warmth of his breath on her neck, startled her. Her hand jerked, sending water sloshing out of the coffeepot.

"Let me do this. Why don't you sit down?"

Since she couldn't seem to speak, she relinquished the coffeepot and did as he suggested.

When he joined her a couple of minutes later, she'd managed to get her breathing under control. Sort of.

"I'm sorry about tonight," he said.

Now what did that mean? she wondered, staring at him in silence. Sorry that he'd held her? Or sorry that she'd been frightened?

"He's a pretty scary character. When I saw that light in the meadow I didn't want to take any chances."

He was still talking about Kyle's grandfather. Okay. Good. She could handle that. She laced her fingers together and set them on the table. "I'm glad you came over. I don't know if he's dangerous or not, but on an intimidation scale he's close to a ten. I was holding my own, though, until he started waving that lantern in my f-face."

Her voice broke and a shudder rippled through her. Keith's first instinct was to reach for her hand, but he stifled it and rose abruptly instead. "I'll get our coffee."

When he returned a couple of minutes later, he set her mug on the table. Then he wrapped his hands around his own and took his seat. Her pinched features and the tremor in her fingers as she reached for her mug told him that her close encounter with the lantern tonight had been far more traumatic than he'd first realized. "I'm sorry he upset you, Jill. I remember the night I arrived you told me you don't even keep candles in the house."

"I don't use the fireplace, either."

"I can understand that."

She played with her cup, staring into the dark depths as she traced a fingertip around the rim. "You've never asked me what happened."

"I figured you'd tell me if you wanted to."

Did she want to? Jill wasn't sure. She hadn't talked about that terrible night with anyone in three and a half years. She'd answered the questions of the authorities as best she could,

when her condition had allowed. And she'd done one hysteri-
cal, almost incoherent retelling of the story for Deb during a
hospital stay when drugs for the excruciating pain had
loosened her tongue. But that had been it. She'd buried the
horror of that night deep inside, just as she'd buried the family
she loved. Her life, like the home she'd created with such joy,
had been reduced to ashes. Talking about it wouldn't bring
anything back.

Refusing to put the horror into words hadn't stopped the
nightmares, however. But even they had been beaten into submission, rearing their ugly head on rare occasions these days.
She'd dealt with the trauma in the only way she could and
moved on, building a new, solitary life for herself. And over
the years, the rawness of her grief had diminished. Why let
this man trespass into that off-limits territory by sharing her
painful past with him?

The answer wasn't long in coming. Keith Michaels had not
only earned her trust, he had the ability to make her forget that
the scars left by the tragedy marred her face as well as her
heart—just as Deb had implied. When he looked at her, he
looked at *her*—not her battered face. And in his eyes, she felt
whole again. Almost like the woman she'd been so very long
ago.

More than that, she sensed that the hurts she'd suffered
mattered to him. That he cared. Truly cared. And if he did,
didn't he deserve to know the secrets she held close to her
heart?

The debate taking place in Jill's mind was reflected in her
eyes, giving Keith a window to her soul. He watched her battle
the demons that had held her captive and apart from others for
years, hoping that she would find the courage to risk stepping
out of her safety zone. At the same time, he suspected that her

story could rock his world. Change him in ways he wasn't sure he was ready to deal with. Yet at some intuitive level, he knew they'd been brought together, and to this place tonight, for a reason. He also knew that he, too, needed courage to see this through. *Please, Lord, be with me.* The prayer echoed in his heart before he could call it back.

"It's not exactly a bedtime story." Jill's uncertain tone, her watchful eyes, snapped him back to the present.

"I'm not planning to go to bed for hours." His gaze held hers, steady and sure.

Lifting her mug, she took a fortifying sip of coffee, set it back on the table and rose. "I'll be right back."

Had she changed her mind? Keith watched as she moved into the living room and stopped at a long table that stood against the wall below the stairs. After a brief hesitation, she opened a drawer and withdrew a picture frame. Returning to the kitchen, she put it on the table in front of him and took her place in silence.

Keith picked up the frame and studied the photo. It was a family picture. A smiling blond-haired man, dressed in a red sweater and wearing a Santa cap, sat on the floor, one knee drawn up. One hand rested on the shoulder of a little blond girl with merry eyes who sat at his feet, a reindeer-ear headband holding back her long, wavy blond hair. His other arm was draped around the woman who sat at his side, also wearing a Santa cap. Jill.

But it wasn't a Jill that Keith had ever known. Not because her face was whole and lovely, so perfect it took his breath away. No, it was her luminous eyes that captured and held his attention. Filled with life and love and exuberant happiness, they reflected a joy that had not yet been tempered by tragedy and loss. Seeing her like this, radiant and content, tightened his throat with raw emotion. Unable to speak, he simply looked over at her.

The compassion and sorrow on Keith's face touched a place deep inside Jill, refreshing parched soil long barren. It was as if he understood the depth of her pain and loss even before she'd uttered a word of explanation. As if, somehow, he'd walked in her shoes and knew the road had been long and difficult and fraught with danger. She wondered why he seemed to have such insights, but she couldn't dwell on that now. He was waiting for her to speak, and she needed to focus on the story she had set herself up to tell.

"That was the last picture we ever had taken. We used it on our Christmas cards." Her words came out more hoarse than usual, and she cleared her throat. "That's my husband, Sam, and my daughter, Emily."

"You all look happy." Keith continued to hold the photo, but his attention was riveted on the woman across from him.

"We were. Blissfully so. It never occurred to me that things could change in the blink of an eye. Or a spark." Her grip on the mug tightened, whitening her knuckles. "I had the flu and a bad cough that holiday season. I was sleeping in the guest room, because Sam had been working long hours and needed his rest. My cough medicine had codeine in it, which knocked me out. That's probably why it took me such a long time to realize something was wrong."

She started to raise the cup to her lips, but her hands were so shaky that some of the liquid sloshed out, leaving a dark splotch on the oak table. She set the cup back down with the exaggerated care of a drunk. "Anyway, when I woke up and smelled something burning I panicked. I was running a high fever and my thinking was fuzzy, so the whole sequence of events has always been as hazy as the smoke that was filling our house. I remember running down the hall. I woke Sam. He told me to go to a neighbor's. To have them call 911. He said he'd get Emily."

She drew a shuddering breath, and when she continued her words were choppy, her voice unsteady. "I alerted a neighbor and ran back to the house. Sam and Emily should have been out by then, but there was no sign of them. I ran toward the door. My neighbor grabbed my arm and tried to stop me. He said the fire department was coming. I heard the sirens. But I couldn't wait. I jerked free. When I got to the front door, all I could see was a wall of fire. I didn't care. I ran in anyway. But I only got as far as the stairs before a falling beam knocked me down. I was pinned to the floor, and the smoldering wood was…was angled against my face and…across the front of my left shoulder. I could hear…" She choked on the words, closing her eyes as a spasm of pain contorted her features. "I could hear sizzling…and I realized it was my…my skin burning. The pain came next. Agonizing pain. I thought I was dying. Later, I…I wished I had."

The last words were whispered, and so wrought with anguish that Keith was left with no option but to take her hand, enfolding her cold fingers in the warmth and strength of his clasp. She didn't even seem to notice, so focused was she on the past. When she continued, her voice was flat and emotionless, her eyes glazed.

"I found out later that our Christmas tree had ignited. I'd always insisted on a real tree and those big old-fashioned colored lightbulbs. Sam was in the insurance business, and he said it wasn't safe. But I badgered him until he let me have my way. A hot bulb against dried-up needles was the most common theory of how the fire started. Anyway, it went up in a flash. The fire spread with incredible speed, but the smoke was worse. That's what…that's how Sam and Emily died. Smoke inhalation. The flames never touched them, thank God."

"But they touched you." Keith's voice was ragged, and he reached out to caress her scarred cheek, much as Kyle had done, his fingers gentle.

Startled by his touch, she nodded. "S-second- and third-degree burns on my face and shoulder. And my vocal cords were irreparably damaged. I went through extensive treatment, including multiple skin grafts, for a year and a half. Deb took me in during that whole time. I'll never be able to repay her for that."

"I expect you would have done the same for her."

That was true. They were family, and that's what families did. But that didn't diminish her gratitude. "She was a rock. And she got answers for me that I was too injured to seek on my own. Like, why hadn't the fire alarm gone off? Turns out, the battery was dead. We always changed it the first of the year. But for some reason, this one had run out way too soon.

"And she handled all of the paperwork for me, too. Being in insurance, Sam had taken out large policies on both of us. He'd seen too many cases where a spouse was left with nothing after a tragedy because the couple was young and didn't think insurance was necessary. Deb dealt with the insurance company and made sure all the *t*'s were crossed and the *i*'s dotted. She was determined that at least I'd have no financial worries. She got me all the money I was entitled to. But she couldn't get me the only thing I really wanted."

Once more, Jill's voice choked and she bowed her head. Keith's grip tightened, and she squeezed back a thank-you. She hadn't cried once during the recitation, but when she looked at him, her eyes were brimming with tears. "You…

you're the first person I've ever shared that story with, except for family."

Jolted, Keith stared at her. He wanted to ask why, then thought better of it, not sure he was ready for the answer.

When he didn't respond, Jill sent him an uncertain look. "It was more than you wanted to know, wasn't it?"

"No." His reply was swift and sure. "I've been wondering what happened ever since Deb mentioned your family. I'm glad you felt comfortable enough to tell me. And it makes me look at these in a whole new light." Once again he ran a gentle finger down the scars on her face.

"W-what do you mean?"

"They're a badge of honor, Jill. You got these trying to save your family. They represent courage and love and sacrifice. All those noble qualities we're called to display, but often don't." He didn't give her time to dwell on that comment, moving on to another question instead. "How did you end up here?"

It took her a few beats to change gears. "When…when I was growing up, my family vacationed here one summer, and I always remembered it as a magical place…a place apart. It was the last vacation we had together before cancer took my dad. Mom and I came back once, before she died ten years ago. All my memories of this place were happy. I thought they could be again."

"And are they?"

His quiet question gave her pause, and she chose her words with care. "In a different way. I've had a chance to pursue my art, which I'd always dreamed of doing."

"But don't you get lonely, Jill?" His voice was gentle, but his expression was intent.

Yes, Jill reflected. Of course she got lonely. Especially

since a certain carpenter had come into her life, reminding her of the simple joy of shared meals and lighthearted conversation and just knowing another person was nearby. But she chose to answer in a different way. "I'm not really alone. God has been by my side every day."

That raised a whole new set of questions for Keith. Ones that hit even closer to home. "How did you manage to hold on to your faith after such loss?"

There was an undertone to Keith's question, a nuance, that told Jill the answer was important to him. A quick check of his eyes confirmed that impression. In their depths she saw a yearning so intense that she forgot her own anguish and sought to ease his. "It wasn't easy at first," she said slowly, struggling to put into words the turbulent faith journey of those first months after the accident. "I'd always believed that God would be there to sustain me if I was ever given a heavy cross to bear. But in the beginning, I felt alone. And abandoned. The God in whom I'd put my trust seemed to have vanished, along with all my hopes and dreams for the future. I called out to Him over and over again, asking for comfort and guidance. Asking why. Yet He seemed deaf to my pleading. Finally I got angry and turned away from Him."

It was almost as if Jill had looked into his heart and told his own story, Keith realized with a start. The process she'd described was the same one he'd gone through. Except he still felt alone and abandoned, while Jill had found her way back to her faith. How? "What happened next?" he prompted.

"I stopped searching for answers."

Confused, he stared at her. "What do you mean?"

"I stopped asking why."

"That's it?"

"Yes."

"I don't understand."

She leaned forward, earnest and certain. "Neither did I. And in the end I realized I never would. That's my point. The thing is, Keith, God's ways aren't our ways. His plans surpass all our understanding. Seeking a logical explanation for what happened to me…it doesn't make sense to even try. There is no logical, human answer. Only God knows why I was given that cross. Someday, when He and I are face-to-face, I might be given the wisdom to understand. But for now, it's beyond me. I had to learn to accept without understanding."

She sat back, and there was a sense of peace about her when she continued. "Once I did that, I started to hear His voice again. I suspect it was there all along, but the clamor of my questions—demands, even—was drowning it out. And my anger was blinding me to His presence. You can't reconnect with a loving God when your heart is filled with rage. So I let it go. And when I did, when I replaced it with love instead, God was waiting to welcome me back. That doesn't mean it was always smooth sailing after that. Some days were rougher than others. Despair resurfaced on occasion. But over time, it got better. The sorrow over my loss will always be with me. But at least it's easier to bear with God by my side."

The silence in the room was broken only by the distant, plaintive call of a loon. Keith was awed—and humbled—by Jill's deep, abiding faith. A faith she'd struggled to hold on to despite God's apparent absence, while he had turned his back on the Almighty. And he'd done so with what he now recognized as arrogance—a sense of entitlement that he, of all people, should have God's ear during a crisis. That God should give him the answers denied to others. As if he was somehow better. Or more worthy.

Well, if anyone was worthy of God's special grace, it was

the woman sitting across from him, whose hand continued to rest in his. A woman who had recognized that love wasn't something to be grasped at, or demanded, but given. Only then could it be returned. Only then could the voice of the beloved be heard with the heart.

As he glanced at their entwined hands, Jill looked down, as well—and seemed surprised to discover that her fingers were still engulfed in his clasp. A flush of color suffused her cheeks, and she gave her hand a gentle tug. But Keith's grip tightened. He didn't want to let go. Not yet. Her hand was like a lifeline, her goodness and kindness flowing through her fingertips directly into his soul.

Surprised, she looked back at him, a question in her eyes. But he had no answers. Yet. With one more gentle squeeze, he forced himself to release her slender fingers and stand. "Thank you for sharing all of that with me." He moved toward the door, pausing on the threshold. "Lock this after me."

"Okay." She rose and joined him at the door, expecting him to exit at once. Instead he stood there, looking down at her with an expression that was hard to read. She saw gratitude in his eyes. Colored with some other emotion she couldn't quite identify. But it was deep and rich and full, and it reached inside her heart, nudging to life a flame she'd thought had long ago died. Her own eyes widened in surprise as their gazes locked—and held. Mesmerized, she watched him swallow. Hard.

Several eternal beats of silence ticked by as a storm of emotion swirled in the still air. Then all at once he turned and fumbled for the door. "Sleep well, Jill. I'll see you tomorrow."

His voice was as rough as the outer layer of bark on the madrone trees that thrived on the island. As unsteady as a newborn black-tailed deer. As confused as a sailor set adrift on the open sea without a compass.

Her hands trembling, Jill shut the door behind him and slid the lock into place, leaning against the hard wood as she closed her eyes. She knew that Keith Michaels had been tempted to kiss her—for reasons neither of them seemed to understand. Sympathy, maybe. Or pity. Or perhaps to comfort her after the story she'd just told him. Whatever the motivation, she was convinced he'd considered it.

And she was even more convinced that she'd have let him.

Another surge of longing rippled through her, and she struggled to subdue it. She couldn't let herself get carried away. Okay, so maybe Keith liked her. Even cared about her as a friend. Enough to kiss her out of compassion or consolation. But she didn't want kisses motivated by pity.

Unfortunately, since those were the only kind she was ever likely to get, she'd best learn to do without. Even from a man who touched her heart in a very special way.

Chapter Eleven

"Keith! It's good to hear from you, son."

The affection in Bob Michaels's voice was unmistakable, and Keith smiled. "Thanks, Dad. Sorry it's been a whole week. I've been busy with the studio."

"How's it coming?"

"Great. Things move a little slower on the island, though, so it takes a while to get some of the other crafts people out to the property. But we're about halfway there."

"Glad to hear it. Everything else okay?"

"Yeah. Yeah, I think so."

Two beats of silence ticked by. "Want to tell me about it, son?"

The man had an uncanny ability to pick up on the most subtle vibes, Keith acknowledged with a shake of his head. In fact, there were times when he was sure his father was a mind reader. This was one of them. And, in all honesty, hadn't he hoped for such a question? His father had always been a good sounding board, and Keith could use some feedback about now.

"I never could get anything past you, could I, Dad?"

The older man chuckled. "Oh, I expect you managed to slip a few things by me through the years."

A grin lifted the corners of Keith's mouth. "Not many. And not this time." He stopped, trying to figure out how to put into words the jumble of emotions he was feeling. In the end, he decided to start with God. "I've been…I've started to pray again, Dad."

On the other end of the line, Bob Michaels closed his eyes. *Thank you, Lord.* "Tell me about it."

"Well, it's not really prayer. At least not in a formal sense. Nor is it even a conscious decision. It's just that I've started…I don't know…I guess *talking* to God is the way to describe it. Sort of a spontaneous thing."

"That's the best kind of prayer, in my book. Is He talking back?"

"Not yet. But I…I'm starting to think that He might be listening."

"Then it won't be long before you hear His voice, son."

"That's how it worked for Jill."

Interesting. It seemed his landlady had had a hand in Keith's change of heart, Bob reflected. Even better. *Another thank you, Lord.* "She sounds like a godly woman."

"She is. Someday I'll tell you all about her." But not today, Keith suddenly decided. He needed to sort through his feelings first.

"I'd like that."

"I'll call again soon. God be with you, Dad."

"And with you."

As Keith hung up the phone, he realized that he'd reverted to their traditional sign-off, with him initiating the blessing. And he realized something else, as well.

It felt good.

* * *

"Keith! Wait up!"

Still deep in thought from his conversation with his father, Keith didn't realize at first that he'd been hailed. But when the voice at last registered, he halted his trek toward the East-sound side street where he'd parked his car. Turning, he saw Larry Miller heading his way. With his long, graying hair tied back in a ponytail and his propensity for tie-dyed T-shirts, the electrician always reminded Keith of a hippie. But despite his laid-back manner, the man knew his stuff. He'd been out to the studio twice already, and was scheduled for one more visit to do a final hookup.

"Hi, Larry. What's up?"

"Listen, I was talking to some folks over in Deer Harbor yesterday. They're getting ready to put an addition on their house and asked me to recommend a good carpenter. I thought of you right away. You interested in the work? They aren't going to start until November or December, and I figure you'll be done with the studio long before that."

A job. He was being offered a paying job. But Keith hadn't thought that far ahead yet. Would he still be here in November? Did he still *want* to be here in November?

"I'm not sure what my plans are yet," he told the man.

"That's cool. Just think about it. They won't be deciding on contractors for a while. Let me know when you need me to come out to the Whelan place to finish up."

With a wave, the man sauntered off down the street.

Was this a sign? Keith wondered. Was there a message in this unexpected job offer? And if so, what was it?

No answers presented themselves. But instead of feeling overwhelmed or panicked, as he had so often during these past two years when uncertainty plagued him, Keith followed Jill's example. He took a deep breath and put the issue in the Lord's hands. Perhaps, in His time, the answers would come.

"Morning, Jill. I was passing by and thought I'd drop in to check on the progress of your studio. It's looking good."

At the sound of Madeleine DeWitt's voice, Jill turned away from the forest. She'd taken to scanning it several times a day from the back porch, hoping to spot Kyle. But since his grandfather's visit the week before, there'd been no sign of him. And she was worried.

"Hello, Madeleine." As always, the gallery owner-artist rep's attire was stylish, with an unmistakable flair that Jill had always admired. Today, her jet-black hair was caught at the nape of her neck with a beaded clasp that Jill was sure reflected the hand of a local jewelry designer. Black slacks and a black turtleneck were offset by a fuchsia-pink blazer, while the hand-painted scarf draped around her neck added an elegant touch.

"Sorry to drop in unannounced, but I brought some cinnamon rolls from Café Olga to make amends." She lifted a large white bag.

It was the same conversation they always had. Madeleine never called. Not even for her first visit, when she'd followed up on a letter Jill had sent with some photos of her paintings. Madeleine had been interested in displaying them in her gallery in Eastsound, but Jill had declined her invitation to come into town to discuss it. Nor had she invited Madeleine to her home. So the woman had just shown up one day, with apologies—and Olga's cinnamon rolls.

Never once had Jill invited her inside. They'd always chatted on the porch, Jill's hat pulled low. But today she'd been caught without it. More and more, she was forgetting to wear it around the house. Suddenly self-conscious, her hand fluttered to her cheek and she angled her body away from the woman.

When Jill didn't respond, Madeleine lowered the bag to her side. "Are you working on anything interesting?" Her tone remained bright and friendly.

Jill risked a glance at her. The woman wasn't paying a bit of attention to her scars. In fact, now that she thought about it, other than a brief flicker of surprise when they'd met, Madeleine had never given any indication that she noticed them. Her reaction had been much like Keith's. And Cindy's.

Perhaps Deb had been right, Jill conceded. Maybe some people could get past her disfigurement and treat her as a normal person if she gave them a chance instead of shutting them out by retreating behind a wall of aloofness.

For years, she'd told herself she'd withdrawn from the world because she was weary of being treated differently. But all at once, with jarring insight, she realized that wasn't her only motivation. Or even the main one. In truth, it was just safer when people felt ill at ease around her. Their discomfort ensured that she never had to talk to them long enough to reveal anything about her past. That, in turn, allowed her to keep all her grief and traumatic memories buried deep in her subconscious, surrounded by thick, impenetrable walls.

In other words, for the price of isolation, she got insulation.

It seemed Deb wasn't the only one whose insight was sound, she acknowledged, as a second truth hit home. Keith's comment over pizza that day had been on the mark, too. She *had* been hiding.

But now that she'd shared some of her memories with him—and survived—they seemed to have lost their power to trigger the wrenching anguish that had once twisted her stomach into knots. Armed with that knowledge, she had the courage to risk breaking down the protective walls a little further.

"Yes, I've got a few new pieces in the works," Jill responded. "Would you like to come up and see them?"

Surprise flashed across Madeleine's face, followed by a warm smile. "I'd love to."

As they passed through the kitchen, Madeleine deposited the white bag on the counter.

"Maybe we could…if you have time…it might be nice to have a cup of coffee and sample those before you leave," Jill offered in a halting voice.

Madeleine's smile widened. "Now that's an offer I can't refuse. It's impossible to say no to Olga's cinnamon rolls."

A few minutes later, after Madeleine had silently perused Jill's in-progress works wearing her serious "art expert" expression, she turned to her client. As always, Jill's nerves kicked in as she waited for the woman's evaluation. She'd come to respect Madeleine's judgment, and she knew the gallery owner would be honest and fair in her assessment.

"I have only one word for these new pieces…wow!" Crinkles appeared at the corners of Madeleine's eyes as she smiled.

Relaxing, Jill smiled back. "Thanks."

"Your seascapes and landscapes are always great, Jill." Madeleine turned back to examine again the three works in progress. "But I'm glad you're starting to include people in your paintings. I love this one of the little boy looking straight at us, half in and half out of the shadows. It's evocative, and it raises questions—as all great portraits should. And this one…" She gestured toward a canvas showing two young boys intent on their task of feeding a baby bird. "This one speaks of friendship and childhood innocence and nurturing. I love it. And even this landscape…it would work without the man in the far distance, looking toward the heavens. But the inclusion of that figure gives it humanity. And hope, somehow. This is stellar work."

Flushed with pleasure, Jill smiled. She'd thought the pieces were good, too. But it was nice to hear her own assessment confirmed by an expert. "Thank you."

"I'm just being honest. Now how about that coffee?"

Ten minutes later, after both were seated at the kitchen table—which, it seemed, was fast becoming a gathering place—Madeleine took a bite of her cinnamon roll and closed her eyes. "Ah. Fabulous."

"I agree," Jill seconded.

When she finished chewing, Madeleine leaned forward and rested her elbows on the table, tapping one perfectly manicured nail—in the exact shade of pink as her blazer—against the mug she held in her hands. "I have some good news. A rep from a very prestigious gallery in Seattle stopped by a few weeks ago. He was quite taken with your work and bought a couple of pieces. Both have been sold, and he's interested in more. Not only that, he'd like to host a show of your work at his gallery in December. And he'd like you to attend the opening."

Up until the last sentence, Jill had been excited. But a public appearance? No way. She opened her mouth to decline, but Madeleine spoke first.

"I know you don't get out a lot, Jill. In fact, I almost didn't bring it up. But when you asked me in today…I don't know, I had a feeling things might have changed. In any case, please think about it, at least. It would be great promotion and a real boost for your career."

Torn, Jill stared at the woman. She hadn't gone into

painting to become famous. The insurance settlement had been substantial, and it was invested wisely, ensuring her a good living for a very long time. Still, it would be nice to have her work receive some recognition. For self-satisfaction, if nothing else. But appearing in public, being the center of attention at a gallery opening…it was too much of a stretch. She hadn't even ventured off the island in two years.

"I appreciate the opportunity, Madeleine. And your support. But I don't think…"

The sound of footsteps on the wooden back porch interrupted them, and Jill turned to find Keith framed in the doorway.

"Oh. Sorry. I didn't realize you had company."

He started to turn away, but Jill rose. "It's okay. Come on in. I'd like you to meet Madeleine."

The other woman also rose, extending her hand as Keith stepped inside and Jill made the introductions.

"So you're the man who's building that great studio," Madeleine commented.

"Guilty."

Tilting her head, she studied him. "I've been around here long enough to know most of the faces, and I don't recognize yours. You must be new to the island."

"Yes. I came in July. Jill took me in during the storm, when there wasn't a room to be had over the holiday weekend, and I ended up staying to build the studio."

"You're staying here?" Madeleine's eyebrows rose, and she shot Jill a speculative look.

"In the cabin," Jill interjected quickly as her neck grew warm.

"Of course. Well, Keith, I want you to know you're supporting the work of a very talented artist. Who would be on her way to fame if she'd accept an offer from a gallery in Seattle for a show. But I'm not having any luck convincing her."

It was as if Madeleine had sensed an ally in Keith, Jill thought, giving her a shrewd glance. But the other woman's expression remained innocent.

"A gallery in Seattle wants to feature your work?" Now it was Keith's turn to look at her. There was no wondering about *his* expression. It was genuine pleasure. "That's great! How come you don't want to do it?"

"They want me to come to the opening."

"Okay." For an instant he seemed puzzled. As if he'd forgotten about the way she looked and couldn't figure out why a personal appearance was a stumbling block. Then comprehension dawned. "Oh."

Reaching for her purse, Madeleine took that as her cue to exit. "See what you can do to convince her, Keith. We have a star in the making here. Jill, I'll be in touch. Let me know when those paintings you're working on are finished and I'll swing by and pick them up. Or you could deliver them to the gallery and we'll go to lunch." Without waiting for a reply, she waved and pushed through the screen door.

Though she knew Keith was watching her, Jill busied herself at the sink. But she wasn't surprised when he pursued the subject.

"Maybe you should consider doing the show, Jill. I've only seen the half-finished pieces you're working on outside, and I'm no artist, but even I can tell that you have talent."

"I can't, Keith."

The silence in the room was broken only by the clink of cutlery as she tidied up from her impromptu coffee break. *Please, Lord, let him drop the subject,* she prayed. *I'm not ready for anything like that.*

"Would you consider it…I mean, I know it would be tough to do that alone. But if you had friends with you…Madeleine would be there, I'm sure. And if it would help, I could…well, I'd be happy to go with you. Honored, in fact."

Her hands stilled, and a sudden rush of tenderness tightened her throat. This man's caring and compassion had done more to brighten her life in the past few weeks than all of the accolades she'd received for her work since launching her new career. But there was one piece of information he didn't know. And she had to share it—even though she was afraid to hear his response. She spoke without turning toward him.

"The show wouldn't be until December, Keith."

The silence that greeted her comment was more telling than words. No quick reassurances that the timing didn't matter, that he'd be around. Not that she'd expected him to be, of course. All along, she'd known this was a temporary arrangement. That as soon as the studio was finished, he'd move on. But she hadn't had to confront it directly until now.

"I didn't realize that." Keith wanted to tell her that he'd still be on the island in December. But in truth, he didn't know where he'd be by then.

"Of course not. It's okay. I appreciate the thought anyway."

"Well…I guess I'll get back to work."

The screen door opened, then closed, behind her. She listened as his steps echoed across the back porch and down the stairs, finally disappearing in the distance. Leaving her alone.

The way she would be again in the not too distant future.

He was back. Jill stopped sweeping and stared. For a second, she almost didn't believe her eyes when she saw Kyle emerge from the woods in the fading light. It had been almost two weeks since the upsetting visit from his grandfather. Two weeks with worry as her constant companion. On more than one occasion she'd picked up the phone to call Cindy, to plead with her to do a follow-up visit. But the woman seemed conscientious, and Jill felt confident she was already doing everything she could. Now, it didn't matter. Kyle was here!

She set the broom aside and took the steps at a run, calling over her shoulder to Keith, who was working late on the studio. "Kyle's here!"

But Jill's elation evaporated once she was close enough to get a good look at the little boy. Panic etched his features, and given his labored breathing, she suspected that he'd been running at full speed since leaving his house. There was a long scratch on his cheek, and his hands were scraped and bloody. Her protective instincts kicked in and she pulled him into the shelter of her arms, scanning the dark woods over his shoulder with trepidation as her heart kicked into double time.

"It's okay, Kyle. It's okay. You don't have to be afraid. You're safe here." His thin chest was heaving, and she stroked his back, trying to calm him.

With surprising force, he pulled out of her embrace and clutched her arms, his grip loosening and tightening convulsively. His panic hadn't abated one iota. If anything, it had ratcheted up a notch. His mouth worked, as if he was trying to speak, and Jill smoothed his tousled hair back from his forehead, trying to control her own accelerating alarm. "What is it, Kyle? Can you tell me?"

His attention shifted over her shoulder, and Jill half turned to see Keith approaching. But this time the man's presence didn't seem to phase the boy. Kyle didn't budge, though his whole body was trembling.

"What's wrong?" Keith stopped a couple of feet away and dropped to their level, resting on the balls of his feet.

"I don't know." Jill tried to figure out what could have caused such panic in the boy, but came up with only one explanation. "Is your grandfather following you, Kyle?"

He shook his head, then reached for her hand and tugged, urging her toward the woods.

Surprised, Jill turned to Keith. "I think he wants us to follow him."

"I don't like that idea, considering our encounter with a certain gentlemen a couple of weeks ago. Why don't I…"

"Help!"

The single word came out in a croak, like a rusty hinge on a long-unused gate. Startled, Jill and Keith turned to Kyle in unison. When neither reacted at once, he tugged again. "Truck…fell."

At last Jill found her voice. "Is your grandfather hurt, Kyle?"

At his vigorous nod, Keith rose. "Is he near the cabin, Kyle?" Again, the boy nodded. "Jill, where's the cabin from here?"

"Northwest. About a quarter of a mile."

Keith took off toward the woods at a jog. "Call 911," he called over his shoulder.

"Wait! It might be better if we…"

But he was already fifty feet away—and disappearing fast.

Later—much later—when car headlights pierced the gloom of her darkened living room, Jill eased away from a sleeping Kyle and headed toward the front door. A police car was inching up her narrow driveway, and for a moment Jill panicked. Had something happened to Keith, too? Fear clogged her throat and she stopped breathing. Not until she saw him emerge from the car did her lungs kick in again.

With a wave, he turned toward the porch, where a dim bulb illuminated the night. The car did a U-turn and headed back down the drive, the red taillights blinking as it wound through the forest, the crunch of gravel under the tires the only sound in the still air.

Not until he drew close did Keith realize that Jill was waiting for him on the porch. Pausing, he looked up at her and raked his fingers through his hair. "Rough night."

The weary lines scored on his face, the grease stains on his shirt, and the long, jagged tear in his jeans offered proof of that. Her first instinct was to throw herself in his arms, to comfort him as she'd earlier comforted Kyle. Instead, she jammed her hands in the pockets of her jeans and stayed where she was. "Can I get you some coffee?"

"No, thanks. I just want to sit a minute. How's Kyle?" He lowered himself to the porch steps carefully, every motion conveying his exhaustion.

She sat beside him. "He's sleeping on the couch in the living room. It took me a while to settle him down."

"I don't doubt it." He let out a long, slow breath and rubbed a hand down his face. "Things were hectic or I'd have called."

"It's okay. How is his grandfather doing?"

Clasping his hands between his knees, he stared down. "There's no easy way to say this, I guess. He didn't make it, Jill."

Jolted, she stared at him. "You mean he's…he's dead?"

"Yeah. I guess the jack slipped and the truck fell, pinning him underneath. When I got there he was unconscious but alive. I managed to reset the jack and get the truck off of him, but…he was pretty far gone already. The paramedics did what they could, but after a few minutes they gave up. There'll be an autopsy, of course, but I suspect the cause of death will be massive internal injuries."

Though her dealings with the man had been anything but cordial, and she'd resented his poor care of Kyle, Jill nevertheless took a moment to commend him to God, who was, after all, the ultimate judge. Yet even as she sent that silent prayer heavenward, she couldn't help but think that Kyle would be better off without the man. Except…who did he have now? His father didn't want him. His mother was dead. There'd been no mention of any other relatives.

"It's Kyle I'm worried about." Keith's comment echoed her thoughts.

"Me, too. I'll call Cindy in the morning. What will happen to him now?"

"He'll be placed in a foster home. That's the usual procedure in a case like this."

"But what about long-term?"

"He might stay in the foster system forever, unless someone adopts him."

Dismay washed over Jill. In his young life, Kyle had already known too much ill treatment, too much instability. In the foster system, he could very well be passed around like an unwanted Christmas fruitcake. What he needed was a secure, loving home, a place where he could learn to trust and relax and be a child again. An environment where he would be cherished and nurtured.

A place like Rainbow's End.

The solution was so obvious, so perfect—so right—that Jill didn't even have to think about it. "I could take him in."

In the dark, Keith turned to her. The porch fixture cast light on half of his face, leaving the other half in shadows. "I had a feeling you might say that."

There was a nuance in his voice that brought a furrow to her brow. "You don't sound too encouraging."

He gave a heavy sigh and raked his fingers through his hair again. "Don't get me wrong, Jill. I've seen you with Kyle. And with Dominic. And with the baby bird. I know what a caring, nurturing person you are. I think you'd be just what the doctor ordered for Kyle."

"But...?"

"But being approved as a foster parent isn't that easy. In general, the state looks for two-parent families."

"He didn't have that before."

"Biological families get away with a lot. Too much, in some cases. But foster and adoptive parents are put through the mill. Background checks...home visits...the whole nine yards. And it takes time."

"Kyle doesn't have time."

"I'm not the one you have to convince."

"I'll talk to Cindy tomorrow."

She started to rise, but Keith reached for her arm, holding her in place. "Don't get your hopes up, okay?"

"But I'd be a good foster parent."

"I know. Think about this, though. As much as Kyle needs love and nurturing, he also needs professional help after all he's been through. Medical tests and eye care and psychological counseling, for a start. That means a lot of trips into town. A lot of paperwork and dealing with bureaucracy. In other words, a lot of interacting with people."

Jill wanted to say that she could handle that. But hadn't she told Madeleine only a few days before that she wasn't sure she was ready to go to Seattle for even a one-night gallery opening? If she couldn't do that, how in the world could she cope with meeting all of Kyle's needs, which would require more than one quick visit to a city?

Her shoulders slumped. Tugging free of Keith's arm, she stood. "I'm heading to bed, and you should do the same. It's been a long day."

"I'm not trying to discourage you, Jill. I just think there are a lot of things to consider."

"Yeah."

She moved toward the door, turning when Keith's voice stopped her.

"If you want my opinion, I think you should go for it." He'd risen and was facing her now, the golden porch light illuminating his weary face as he looked up at her. "I think you can overcome the obstacles. I believe in you."

His words warmed her, and gratitude filled her eyes. "Thanks. I wish I had your confidence."

"Give it to the Lord in prayer."

The ghost of a smile played at her lips. "He's the first person I plan to talk to."

Chapter Twelve

"Cindy? Jill Whelan. I need to talk with you about Kyle Corbett."

Sinking into a chair where she could keep Kyle in sight as he watched a video Dominic had left behind, Jill combed her fingers through her hair, then reached around and massaged the stiff muscles in her neck. She'd spent the night on the floor next to the couch, wanting to be nearby in case the little boy awoke. Unlike her, however, he'd slept soundly. But at least she'd put the long, dark hours to good use. And after much prayer and soul-searching, she'd reached a decision.

"What's up, Jill?"

After explaining the situation to the social worker, Jill took a deep breath. "I assume you'll be putting him in foster care. And I'd like to volunteer for the job."

The surprised silence on the other end of the line lasted for several seconds. "That's a big responsibility, Jill."

"I realize that. I also realize that Kyle is in desperate need of love. And I have plenty of that to offer. Plus, I'm the only one he knows on the island, aside from Keith. Wouldn't it be better to place him in familiar surroundings where he's already comfortable?"

"Of course. But there's more to it than that." Cindy proceeded to give Jill a rundown on the requirements for foster parenting, echoing much of what Keith had said the previous night. "Are you up for all that?"

"Yes." The answer came without hesitation. Somewhere around four in the morning, Jill had decided that it was time to leave her sheltered, safe world and plunge back into the mainstream of life. She felt strong enough now to handle the pain of her past—and strong enough to deal with unkind strangers. If some people treated her differently because of her appearance, that was their problem. She had other, more important things to worry about. Namely, Kyle. With God by her side, she was confident she could find the courage to overcome her own challenges and make a difference in a little boy's life.

"Okay. Let me see what I can do to expedite things. I've already made one home visit. We've talked a couple of times. For now, I can leave Kyle with you, in the care of a neighbor, so to speak. We'll need to try and locate Kyle's father, too, but based on my conversation with Mr. Corbett I doubt he wants to be found. Let me get things rolling and I'll be in touch in a day or two."

As she replaced the receiver, Jill did have one final, fleeting moment of doubt. But this was where her prayers had led her. And Keith believed in her. With those two things to bolster her courage, she had to trust that all would turn out well.

"Would you mind doing the reading, Keith? The page is marked."

So lost in thought had he been as he stood beside the simple pine box containing the remains of Jeremiah Corbett that

Jill's request didn't register at once. When it did, Keith lifted his head and saw that she was holding out the Bible.

"I'd do it myself, but I have my hands full already." She dipped her head toward Kyle, who was pressed close to her side and clinging to her other hand.

Unable to think of a reasonable excuse to turn down the request, Keith reached for the book. He opened it to the marked page—the twenty-third psalm—and began to speak the lyrical prose so often used at commendations.

"'The Lord is my shepherd, there is nothing I shall want. In verdant pastures he gives me repose; beside restful waters he leads me; he refreshes my soul.'"

As the words drifted through the quiet air, Keith looked over at Jill without breaking rhythm, reciting the passage by heart. Her head was bowed, her eyes closed. Beside her, Kyle's attention was riveted on the pine coffin. No other mourners had come to mark the passing of the old man. If not for the three of them, the grave diggers in the background would have been the only ones to witness his burial. And if it hadn't been for Jill, their little trio wouldn't be here, either. But she'd insisted that whatever the man's faults, he should be sent to his rest with a prayer. When they'd been unable to establish any church affiliation, she'd taken it on herself to provide some words from the Good Book. Besides, she'd told him, Kyle needed the closure. Keith hadn't disagreed.

But he hadn't expected to find himself back in a role he thought he'd left behind forever. Nor had he expected it to feel so good. It was like putting on a pair of comfortable slippers after a long, painful walk in ill-fitting shoes.

Finishing the psalm, he closed the book and bowed his head. "Lord, we commend the soul of Jeremiah Corbett to Your care, confident in Your just and loving mercy. We also ask that You watch over those of us here today. Please give us strength and courage for the journey and challenges ahead. Amen."

When Keith looked up, Jill gave him a misty smile. "That was beautiful, Keith. Thank you."

In silence, they turned to go. And as he took her arm to guide her over the uneven ground, that, too, felt good.

The next weeks flew by in a flurry of activity. Jill was kept busy chauffeuring Kyle around for medical tests, eye exams, fittings for his new glasses and counseling sessions—the latter requiring a ferry ride twice a week to Friday Harbor, on the adjacent San Juan Island. She conferred with Cindy often, who informed her that she'd located Kyle's birth records, and that he should be starting school since he'd had his sixth birthday a couple of months before. However, both agreed he wasn't ready, given the trauma he'd endured and his lack of verbal communication skills. In light of Jill's teaching credentials, the best plan seemed to be for her to tutor him in the fall, then enroll him for the spring semester.

No family was located, which surprised neither of them. With Cindy expediting the paperwork, Jill became Kyle's official foster parent in record time.

Through it all, Keith provided her with much-needed moral support. Often he accompanied her on outings with Kyle, his steadfast presence at her side bolstering her courage as she ventured into public and forced herself to return shocked looks with a warm smile, making herself accessible instead of aloof. To her surprise, many people responded in kind, easing her reentry into society. But the smooth transition was due in large part, she knew, to the man who had changed her life by brightening her world with his simple acceptance and kindness.

And he was now working the same magic with Kyle, slowly breaking through the little boy's barriers. It was understandable that the youngster's trust level with men in particular would be low, given his bad experiences with his father and grandfather. But Keith seemed to have an instinctive ability to know how to go about it—and the patience to make the effort.

As Jill watched one day from the open kitchen window, Keith's interaction with Kyle reminded her yet again of what a special man had come into her life that turbulent, storm-tossed night in July. She'd sent Kyle out to the shed to retrieve a clay pot so that she could split a clump of herbs to share with Madeleine. As he trotted back toward the house, Keith called out to him from the corner of the studio. The boy's step faltered, and he turned toward Keith uncertainly, clutching the pot to his chest like a protective shield.

"Could you help me for a minute, Kyle? I need someone to hold the other end of this measuring tape while I check my numbers." Keith's tone was pleasant and gentle, his words a request, not a demand. When Kyle didn't respond, Keith tried again. "It sure would be a help to me, Kyle. Sometimes an extra pair of hands makes a big difference."

Still hesitant, Kyle glanced toward the house. Jill stepped back into the shadows, out of Kyle's sight line, but she maintained a clear view of the scene in the yard. After a few seconds, he slowly set the pot on the ground and stared at Keith.

"If you can hold this end, I'll be able to get my numbers." Keith offered the tape to Kyle.

With slow, cautious steps the young boy approached him, stopping a couple of feet away. Instead of moving closer, Keith pulled out the tape and stretched the end toward him.

"Can you put it there, next to the window?" Kyle edged toward the spot Keith indicated and pressed the tape against the wall, shooting Keith a tentative look. "That's perfect, buddy. Hold it right there."

Keith drew out the tape until it extended to the corner of the studio. Then he dropped to one knee to check the number, removing a pencil from behind his ear to jot down a few notes. "Just like I figured," he called out. "I need to put another nail in this piece of siding. You can let the tape go, Kyle. Would you mind handing me that hammer by your foot?"

The little boy looked down and reached for the tool. After weighing it in his hands, he headed toward Keith, holding it out from arm's-length distance when he drew close.

"Thanks, Kyle." Keith positioned a nail and gave it a gentle tap. Then he shook his head and examined his hand. "I'll tell you what, if I hold the nail, do you think you could get it started for me? I banged my thumb the other day, and it's kind of sore. I noticed that you had a good, strong swing when Dominic was here." He extended the handle of the hammer to Kyle, steadied the nail with one hand, and splayed the fingers of the other on the ground to balance himself.

Each request had drawn Kyle closer. Each had helped convince him that this man wasn't going to hurt him or criticize him or berate him, as the other men in his life had done. Just the opposite. Keith was not only building the boy's comfort level, he was helping the youngster feel good about himself. As if he had something to contribute.

Mesmerized by the scene unfolding before her, Jill positioned herself in the sunlight for a better view and held her breath as Kyle approached Keith in small, cautious increments. When he drew close enough to take the hammer, Keith dropped his voice and Jill could no longer hear the quiet conversation taking place. But Kyle's rapt expression told Jill that he was listening intently as Keith gave him some instructions. Then, his face a study in concentration, and wielding the hammer with both hands, he took a swing at the nail.

To Keith's credit, he didn't flinch—even though one small miscalculation could have resulted in smashed fingers. Instead, he smiled and encouraged Kyle to take another swing. And then another. Only when the nail—and their relationship—were secure did Keith remove his hand. Emotion tightened her throat, and she blinked several times to clear the sudden tears that blurred her vision.

At that instant, Keith looked up and caught sight of Jill framed in the window, sunlight sparking the fiery highlights in her hair. He hadn't realized he had an audience. His thoughts had been on Kyle alone. For days he'd been trying with limited success to ease the boy's fear of him. Today's inspiration had come to him in the spur of the moment, as he saw Kyle heading toward the toolshed. He hadn't been sure it would work, but he'd been determined to try. He wanted the little boy to realize that not all men were like his father and grandfather. That some were kind and caring and could be trusted. It seemed he'd taken a step in that direction today. And judging from her expression, Jill seemed to think so, too. In her eyes, he saw tenderness and gratitude and approval—and a longing so poignant, so intense that his mouth went dry.

Stunned, Keith stared at Jill. For weeks he'd tried to ignore his growing feelings for the woman who had given him refuge on that stormy summer night. When he could no longer suppress them, he'd tried attributing them to gratitude. But now he realized they ran deeper than that. Far deeper. Deep enough to stir to life an emotion that he'd thought never to experience again. An emotion that Kyle, too, had tapped into—in a different way.

Confused, Keith turned back to his young helper and murmured a few encouraging words. He wasn't ready to give a name to that emotion yet. But he did know one thing. Here, with Jill and Kyle, he felt at home. And at peace. As if this was where he belonged. It was almost as if they were a family. Or were meant to be one. And with each day that passed it was getting harder and harder to even think about walking away.

As Jill watched, Keith rose and laid a hand on Kyle's shoulder. Instead of recoiling, the youngster stood stock-still and gazed up at him, his eyes filled with hope. Keith smiled and said a few words. And when he turned to go, the little boy trotted after him, close on his heels, the clay pot forgotten.

Jill didn't mind. She could split herbs any time. But it wasn't every day that one witnessed a life-changing moment.

At Jill's suggestion, they began attending services at a nearby church. She'd gone on occasion in the past, supplementing her infrequent attendance with private Bible study and other spiritual reading. But now that Kyle was in her care she felt it was important for him to experience the routine of weekly church attendance, as she had. Her own faith had been built on that foundation, and she wanted to offer him the same opportunity. Though she hadn't necessarily expected Keith to accompany them, he'd surprised her by accepting the invitation. They were becoming a regular threesome at the small, white-steepled church.

Now, as they sat in the wooden pew with Kyle tucked between them, Jill felt a sense of deep contentment. Of rightness. It was the same feeling she'd had years before, when she and Sam and Emily shared a pew on Sundays. A feeling of belonging. Of family.

Family. A bittersweet yearning swept over Jill, and her throat tightened with emotion. It was an illusion, of course. She was only a foster parent to Kyle, and Keith would soon be moving on. They were merely three people brought together by circumstance for a brief moment in time. Nonetheless, it reminded her of all that she'd once had…and offered her a tantalizing taste of what she'd never thought to find again.

But…was it possible that she'd been too hasty in writing off the joy of a close and loving family? she suddenly wondered. Why couldn't she consider adopting Kyle? After all, Cindy had told her that few people wanted older children…especially children who came with baggage. The odds were that Kyle would spend his youth in the foster system—unless she stepped forward. Yet raising a child alone was a daunting task. And not encouraged by social services. Couples were much preferred as adoptive parents. Still, it might be Kyle's best chance for a stable home. The real question was whether she was up to a permanent commitment like that, assuming she'd have to do all the parenting alone.

And she had to make that assumption. Despite Keith's kindness, she held no illusions about her ability to attract a man. Whatever beauty she might once have possessed had been marred beyond recognition. And romantic love was based—at least in part—on physical attraction. That didn't mean you had to look like Miss America. But neither could you look like…well, like Jill Whelan. Maybe, someday, she might meet another man who could learn to overlook her scars and call her a friend, as Keith had. But that was the best she could hope for. If she chose to pursue an adoption, it would have to be with the understanding that she'd be on her own.

"Now let us stand and turn to number sixty-four in our hymnals as we raise our voices in song to the Lord."

The minister's words, and the sudden rustle of movement as the congregation rose, brought Jill back to the present. As the organ began the familiar introduction to "Amazing Grace," she turned to the correct page. At one time, she'd loved to sing. Now, her husky voice was suited to only the lowest notes. Still, she loved the words of this hymn. As must the minister, who seemed to include it in the service every week.

She opened her mouth to sing, but her voice faded when a new soprano joined in the refrain. Startled, her gaze dropped to Kyle, endearing in his new navy-blue blazer, his face clean, his cowlick dampened into submission. It was hard to believe he was the same little boy she'd first met, in worn, ragged clothes with a dirty face and uncombed hair. It was harder still to believe that the sweet soprano voice was coming from him. Though his spoken speech was still confined to a word or two here and there, in music he seemed to have found a release for the words bottled up inside. Jill looked over his head to Keith, whose pleasing, baritone voice had also been silenced by shock.

All at once, Kyle seemed to realize that the adults beside him had stopped singing. His voice faltered and he looked up at them, his expression uncertain. Jill forced a smile to her lips and squeezed his shoulder, then resumed singing. After a glance from her, Keith did likewise. A second later, Kyle joined in.

Not only did he have an uncanny ability to memorize lyrics and melodies, Jill realized, he also had perfect pitch. And if he could sing words, surely he couldn't be far away from saying them. She was anxious to share this latest breakthrough with his therapist. In the meantime, she expressed her gratitude in the quiet of her heart. *Thank you, Lord.*

As they left the service a short time later, Reverend

Campbell smiled and held out his hand in welcome. "Glad you could join us again today," he greeted them. His shock of white hair and lined face spoke of advanced age, but his grip was firm and strong.

"I enjoyed your sermon," Jill told him.

"Thank you, Jill." The man always surprised her with his remarkable facility for names. Even though she'd been an infrequent attendee in the past, and Keith and Kyle were new faces, the minister always remembered their names.

"It's good to know I'm not getting stale after all these years. But I must admit I'm looking forward to retiring next year. In some ways it will be nice not to have to write a sermon every week. Though I expect I'll fill in on occasion back on the mainland, to keep my skills fresh."

"You're moving?" Jill inquired.

"That's the plan. My son and his family live in Oregon, and the wife and I would like to be closer to the grandkids."

"I can understand that. Children are a great blessing." She rested her hand on Kyle's shoulders.

"Indeed they are. And I believe I heard you singing this morning, young man." The minister leaned down, putting himself on the boy's level. "You have a very fine voice, Kyle. We'll have to think about getting you into the youth choir one of these days."

When Kyle dropped his chin and didn't respond, the man stood again. "Keep that in mind, Jill," he suggested.

"I will."

"And it's good to see you, too, Keith. It's always nice to have new people in the congregation. I hope you'll be with us for a while."

"Well, the studio isn't finished yet," he replied noncommittally.

"Then I expect we'll be seeing you at a few more services."

"Yes."

"Good, good. And remember, if there's ever anything I can do to help, don't hesitate to call."

While the man directed the comment to all of them, he held Keith's gaze a second longer than necessary.

As they walked back to their car, Keith pondered the man's parting remark. It was almost as if he'd singled Keith out for special attention. As if he knew that the younger man was in need of assistance.

In truth, the minister's insight was sound. Time was ticking by. Soon Keith would have some decisions to make. Life-changing decisions. And he could use all the help and advice he could get.

In the end, it was music that finally unlocked the door to language for Kyle. When Jill shared her experience at church with Marni Stevens, Kyle's therapist, the woman began introducing more music to his counseling sessions. She also suggested that Jill play music around the house and encourage Kyle to sing along.

It took some experimentation, however, to find the kind of tunes that appealed most to the young boy. Jill tried gospel, country, pop, soft rock, jazz. A song here and there would catch his fancy, but none of the music sustained his interest. Until at last she hit pay dirt with the scores from the classic Broadway musicals. He could listen for hours to *Oklahoma, South Pacific, The Sound of Music, Brigadoon, Camelot…* they all captivated him. Soon he was singing along, finding release in the sometimes lyrical, sometimes lively melodies. And nothing warmed Jill's heart more than to hear him singing "Oh What A Beautiful Morning" at the top of his lungs in the living room while she prepared meals in the kitchen or worked on her latest painting in the studio upstairs.

Once he became comfortable with words in music, he began to use them in speech, as well. As his confidence grew, his halting single words gave way to phrases. She and Keith were still waiting for full sentences, but that would come, Marni assured them.

His schoolwork was also progressing. Jill discovered he had a sharp and agile mind, eager for information. He liked to learn and never fussed about spending time with books. She worked with him on his alphabet, while Keith took over simple math tutoring. He was such a keen student that Jill was confident he'd be ready for school after the holidays.

The bad dreams, however, were another story. His first few nights in her care had been quiet, giving her a false sense of security that at least the traumas he'd endured didn't plague his sleep. However, a few nights later he'd awakened her with wild sobbing and thrashing, and she'd had to face the reality. His exhaustion the first few nights had been deep enough to dispel his demons. But once he was rested, they'd returned.

Since it comforted him to have her nearby, she and Keith moved his twin bed from an alcove in Jill's bedroom closer to her bed. That helped. Still, some nights were rough.

Like last night. For whatever reason, he'd been more restless than usual, awakening in tears several times. In the end, Jill had lain beside him, gathering him in her arms until he quieted and at last slept in peace. She, however, had gotten no more than three or four hours rest. When she dragged herself out of bed the next morning, the dark circles under her eyes were testament to her weariness. She could only hope a cup of strong coffee would help.

Twenty minutes later, sipping from an oversize mug in the kitchen, Jill looked over the rim to find Keith at the back door.

"Morning. The coffee smells good."

"Help yourself." Even after all these weeks, he never entered the house without an invitation.

Stepping over the threshold, he headed toward the pot, then stopped in his tracks as he took in her wan appearance. "You look exhausted."

"Rough night." She shrugged and turned toward the stove to prepare breakfast.

Moving to the coffeepot, Keith studied her back, noting the weary slump of her shoulders. Considering how her life had been disrupted in the past few weeks, he supposed he shouldn't be surprised. She'd welcomed a stranger into her life. Taken in a troubled young boy. Reentered society after years as a recluse. All while she continued to pursue her painting. It would be a lot for anyone to take on, let alone someone who had endured the trauma Jill had. She had more spunk, more courage, more integrity than any woman he'd ever met. And her abundant kindness and compassion bestowed grace on all who touched her life.

Soon, the studio would be finished. But something else had begun while he worked to build a place where Jill could create beauty, he realized. Hope had taken root deep in his heart, along with another emotion, one that called for acknowledgment and yearned to be set free. Yet just as Kyle had been unable to give voice to words until he'd found the right avenue for release, neither could he give voice to what was in his heart until he put the past to rest once and for all. Only then could he, too, find release. Only then could he move on. He knew that now.

And he knew something else, as well.

It was time.

Chapter Thirteen

As the russet and golden hues of fall tinted the island and the studio neared completion, Keith began to spend more time alone. He accompanied Jill less on her outings with Kyle, and often disappeared in the late afternoon for hours at a stretch. Jill supposed he was preparing for a departure that couldn't be too far in the future, though she tried not to think about that. Or about the gap his parting would leave in her life. Instead, she reminded herself to be grateful for the gift of new life he'd brought to her. Without his acceptance, his encouragement, his kindness, Jill doubted whether she would ever have had the courage to emerge from the private, safe—but lonely— refuge she'd created, and to welcome Kyle into her life.

She'd always known Keith would move on, of course. He'd never made any promises about staying, never done anything to suggest he might become a permanent part of her life. After all, he had another life somewhere. A life she knew nothing about. And he continued to carry a sadness he'd never shared with her. That was what had led him to her island in the first place. He'd been running away—or toward—something when they'd met. And while the pain in his eyes had dissipated since his arrival, it wasn't gone. Keith Michaels still had issues to deal with. Secrets he held close to his heart. And it seemed he would take them with him when he left.

For Kyle's sake, Jill did her best to appear happy, confining her heartache to the wee hours of the morning when she often lay awake, thinking about Keith and yearning for something so impossible she refused to even consider it. It was important to stay focused on what was best for Kyle, she'd tell herself. He needed joy in his life, not sadness.

Keith continued to do his part to help the little boy heal, as well, which only endeared him more to Jill. With infinite patience he built Kyle's trust, until the boy became his shadow, trotting around behind him, imitating him, eager for his approval and his smiles. The downside to that, though, was that Kyle, too, would be devastated when Keith left.

Perhaps that was one of the reasons Keith had slowly begun to withdraw, Jill mused, as she stopped watering the plants on the front porch to watch his car cross the meadow late one afternoon, heading for the road. She lifted her hand to wave as he passed, and he returned the gesture. For a brief instant she thought the car hesitated, as if he had considered stopping to visit with her. But then he kept going. And that was a good thing, Jill told herself. She had dinner to prepare and a little boy to think about. Turning, she moved toward the door and disappeared inside.

Watching her go in the rearview mirror, Keith was tempted to stop and follow her. But he had things to do, calls to make, a past to reconcile. That had to be his first priority. Only when he'd put yesterday to rest could he allow himself to think about tomorrow.

Forty-five minutes later, as he waited at the booth in Eastsound for his father to pick up the phone, he flexed the tense muscles in his shoulders. A lot depended on this call.

"Bob Michaels here."

"Hi, Dad."

"Hello, Keith. I've been waiting for your call."

"Did you hear from anyone?"

"Sure did. It's all set up, just like you wanted. Two weeks from Sunday, nine o'clock sharp. Reverend Thomas was very cooperative. Sounds like a nice man. He said you wrote a fine letter, and he's willing to do anything he can to help make things right. He did say he'd like to talk with you before you come, though."

The tension in Keith's shoulders eased. "Okay. Thanks for coordinating this, Dad."

"Glad to do it, son. It's important for you to clear the air. Will you have time to pay me a visit while you're in the area?"

"Of course. I'll let you know the final timing when I have everything worked out. God be with you."

"And with you."

Feeling more at peace than he had in years, Keith headed back to his car and pointed it toward Rainbow's End. Jill had told him once that the worn, peeling sign had been there when she purchased the property and that she'd never bothered to remove it. He was glad she hadn't, because it described exactly the way he felt about the place. He hadn't found a literal pot of gold at Rainbow's End. But he had found the golden dawn of a new day. And that was even better.

As Keith passed the church where they attended services, he was surprised to see Reverend Campbell in front, planting some chrysanthemums around the sign. Keith slowed the car, then on impulse pulled into the small, empty lot beside the church and headed over to talk with the man.

"Afternoon, Keith," the minister greeted him, leaning on his shovel.

"Hello, Reverend. Nice day for gardening."

The man chuckled. "I doubt these'll last long once the deer discover them. But it doesn't seem like fall to me without a few chrysanthemums. Some things just go with certain seasons, you know? Crocuses in the spring, daisies in the summer, mums in the fall, holly in the winter. Course, I suppose if you grew up in Florida or California, that wouldn't make sense to you."

"I'm a Midwest boy, myself. So I understand."

"Midwest, hmm. Whereabouts?"

"I grew up in Missouri. And I spent several years in Ohio."

"That's a coincidence. I grew up in Ohio. Where did you live?"

"Maple Ridge."

"I passed through there once. Pretty little town, I recall."

"Yes, it is. So what brought you out here?" Keith didn't want to dwell on Ohio. Not today.

"The wife and I visited once and decided we liked this little island. Took quite a while to make the move, but in the end the good Lord must have wanted us here, because I got a call for this church. And I never looked back. It won't be easy to leave." He let his gaze wander over the small white structure nestled in the woods, his expression melancholy. Then he took a deep breath and smiled. "But it's time. Funny how God lets you know when the time is right for things."

"That's true."

"My only concern is finding a replacement. I'd like to get a younger minister in here. I think that would be good for the congregation. But young people would probably think this place is too far from the action."

"It is quiet."

"True enough. But sometimes it's easier to hear God's voice in the stillness. At least, that's how it worked for Elias."

A pensive look came over Keith's face. He'd thought of that passage often in recent weeks as he soaked up the tranquility of the island. "'And a great and strong wind before the Lord overthrowing the mountains, and breaking the rocks in pieces: the Lord is not in the wind,'" he murmured. "'And after the wind an earthquake: the Lord is not in the earthquake. And after the earthquake a fire: the Lord is not in the fire. And after the fire a whistling of a gentle air. And when Elias heard it, he covered his face with his mantle.'"

The minister gave him a shrewd look. "You know your Bible. Tell me, Keith, what did you do before you came to Orcas Island?"

A hot flush rose on his neck. "I was a carpenter. I worked with my dad."

"Hmm. Good, honest profession. Greatest man who ever lived was a carpenter. Well, you seem to have a real interest in the Good Book. If you ever want to talk more about that, look me up."

"I'll remember that. But first I...I have some things to work through. The past couple of years have been... difficult...and I'm still struggling to get back on track."

"Life can be a trial, no doubt about that. But let me share another favorite verse with you, one that's always given me comfort in hardship. 'God keeps his promises, and he will not allow you to be tested beyond your power to remain firm; at the same time you are put to the test, He will give you the strength to endure it, and so provide you with a way out.'"

"Corinthians."

The man nodded. "I thought you might know it."

"Sometimes, when things are really bad, even strong faith can falter."

"Very true. Consider that the disciples themselves had doubts. And they were in the Lord's presence every day. How much harder it is for us to believe without seeing. We're all Thomases to some degree, Keith. I think there are times in almost every life when we lose our way. I know that was true for me." A deep sadness stole some of the light from his eyes. "I mentioned my son to you not long ago, after services. But I also had two daughters. They were killed in a bus accident, on a mission trip to an impoverished area near the Mexican border. Sixteen and eighteen. Beautiful, intelligent, godly young women who had much to offer."

He folded his hands on top of the shovel handle. "For months after that I turned away from God. I didn't understand how He could do that to me, a man who had dedicated his life to spreading the good news. I felt lost and alienated. But when I let the anger go, when I sought God with a humble heart and laid my despair at His feet, He picked me up and led me home. I think He does that for anyone who comes to Him in sincerity and humility. But it can be a long, painful journey."

A lump rose in Keith's throat. This man, too, had suffered a terrible tragedy. And he, too, had felt abandoned and adrift. Yet in the end, he'd found his way back to God. And in doing so, was able to infuse others with hope. "Thank you for sharing that, Reverend."

The man laid a hand on Keith's shoulder. "I hope it helps you on your journey. I'll keep you in my prayers."

"I appreciate that. God be with you."

As Keith returned to his car, he pondered the chance meeting with the minister. Odd that he'd been out planting mums just as Keith drove by. Yet their impromptu meeting had given him new hope and opened up new possibilities for his future.

And as he drove away, back to a place he was rapidly coming to think of as home, he realized that maybe it hadn't been chance at all.

"Okay, Jill, I've put them off as long as I can. It's D-day. Yea or nay on the gallery show?"

Shifting the phone to her shoulder as she stirred a pot of soup, Jill knew she couldn't delay her decision any longer. Madeleine had been stalling the Seattle gallery for the past week as her client battled her doubts. While Jill wanted to take advantage of the great opportunity a show would offer, the thought of putting herself in the spotlight still scared her to death. It was one thing to venture out for Kyle's sake—with Keith by her side, ready to catch her when she faltered or stumbled after a particularly strong reaction to her appearance. And there had been a few. In Seattle, however, she'd be on her own. The center of attention. She wasn't sure she was quite ready to make that leap yet.

"Jill, are you there?"

Madeleine's voice pulled her back to the conversation. "Yes. Sorry. Thanks for being patient about this, Madeleine."

"I'd hate for you to pass up this opportunity. They don't come along very often. And you won't have to do this alone, you know. I plan to stick to you like glue. We want to generate some commissions out of this, and I intend to do some very aggressive selling. That's my job."

In fact, Jill knew it was more than that. Madeleine was also her friend—now that she'd opened the door and let her in. And even before that, the woman had been a strong advocate of her work. She'd also taken a chance on her at the beginning, when Jill had no credentials as an artist. Maybe she owed it to Madeleine to agree to the show. And to herself. *You can do this,* Jill asserted in the quiet of her heart. *With God's help—and the help of people like Madeleine—you'll find the strength.*

"Okay," Jill said, clutching the phone a bit tighter.

A couple of beats of silence passed. "Okay?"

"Yeah. Okay."

"Well, fabulous! The gallery will be thrilled. *I'm* thrilled! I'll call them right now and get things set up. Then we need to have lunch to celebrate. Check your calendar, and when I call back with the details on the show we'll pick a date. And I'm not taking no for an answer."

Memories of the horrible lunch with Deb crashed over Jill. So traumatic had the experience been that she hadn't stepped inside a restaurant since. But she didn't look quite as unsightly anymore. Even Dominic had noticed the improvement. And it had been a long time since she'd frightened a child. As for adult reaction—why should she let one mother's inconsiderate actions rob her of the chance to experience a nice meal with a friend in a restaurant?

"Okay."

Another beat of silence ticked by. "You know, this has all been a far easier sell than I expected," Madeleine admitted at last.

"Let's just say that it's time I made a few changes in my life. But I may need you to bolster my courage now and then." Jill tried for a teasing tone, but didn't quite pull it off.

"I don't think you have anything to worry about on that score, Jill. You're one of the most courageous people I've ever met." Madeleine's serious response surprised—and touched—Jill, but the woman moved on before Jill had a chance to reflect on the comment. "Okay, I'll be in touch. In the meantime, keep painting!"

That sounded more like Madeleine, Jill thought as she hung up the phone. Yet the woman's first remark replayed in her mind. While she was warmed by Madeleine's compliment, Jill knew that she wasn't courageous at all. She was more scared and uncertain and worried than she dared let on, overwhelmed and anxious about all the changes in her life and all the responsibilities she'd taken on.

But God seemed to be pushing her in this direction. Urging her to revise the plans she'd made for her life when she'd first come to this island more than two years ago. And it was important to remember one thing, she reminded herself. His plans were always better.

Chapter Fourteen

"How about a cup of coffee?" Keith looked over at Jill as Marni ushered Kyle into her office for a counseling session.

"This is getting to be a habit." Even as she spoke, she reached for her purse and jacket. In the beginning, Jill and Keith had stayed close by during the sessions. But Kyle had taken a great liking to Marni. Midfortyish, with large, owl-like glasses and a lively, engaging manner, the therapist had an innate ability to put people of all ages at ease. As a result, Jill and Keith felt comfortable stepping out during the sessions.

"I can think of worse habits," Keith countered with a grin.

"No argument there." Jill rose, and Keith held her jacket as she slipped her arms inside. Then he ushered her to the door, his hand in the small of her back. The protective gesture represented nothing more than simple good manners, Jill knew, but it felt good.

The late-October day was unseasonably warm, and they decided to walk the three blocks from the office to the café near the water. As they strolled down the sidewalk, Jill's attention was caught by a children's book on orca whales in a shop window. Dominic had been fascinated by the whales this year, spending hours searching for signs of them with his binoculars. A perfect Christmas gift!

"I'm going to run in and get that book for Dominic," she told Keith. "Why don't you go ahead and save us a table?"

"Okay. I'll see you in a few minutes."

Ten minutes later, the book tucked under her arm, Jill climbed the steps to the waterfront coffee shop. There was no sign of Keith—and only one unoccupied table on the terrace. Maybe he'd gotten hung up inside.

As she stepped over the threshold, it was clear from the line that snaked down the center of the café that the shop was doing a booming business. It was a popular spot with tourists whiling away the time as they waited for the next ferry. She spotted Keith near the front and turned to grab some napkins, planning to go out and secure the one remaining table for them while he placed their order.

"Reverend Michaels!"

A female voice boomed across the small shop, and Jill froze, then slowly turned.

The woman who was approaching Keith looked to be in her late fifties or early sixties. Jeans hugged her ample hips, and she wore a purple sweatshirt emblazoned with the words, Go, Falcons! in bright gold letters. A large tote bag was slung over her shoulder, and the camera hanging around her neck banged against her chest in rhythm with each ponderous step she took.

"Frank….Frank! Look who's here!" The woman threw the words over her shoulder and continued barreling toward Keith. A video-camera-toting man, with thinning gray hair and a slight build, scurried along in her wake.

The woman thrust out her hand, leaving Keith no option

but to take it. Some of the color had drained from his face, and his subdued response was barely audible over the buzz of conversation in the small shop. "Hello, Gladys. Frank."

"Well, imagine meeting you here, of all places! Isn't this the strangest coincidence, Frank?" The woman's voice carried easily over the din.

"Strange," the man agreed, confining his response to one word—as if he knew that was all he'd be able to squeeze in.

"My word, we do miss you, Reverend! Why, the way you just up and disappeared broke our hearts. Course, we understood the reasons. And we didn't blame you one bit. But I want you to know we never did believe that hussy. Not for a minute. Did we, Frank?"

"Never did," the man confirmed.

"And we were right, too. Do you know just a year after she caused you all that sorrow and trouble, she…"

The sudden, sonorous boom of the ferry horn set off a flurry of activity in the shop.

"Come on, Gladys. Can't miss the ferry, or we'll be stuck here all night." The older man rushed through the words in one breath, skipping the punctuation, as if afraid that any slight pause would invite an interruption. Taking his wife's arm, he urged her toward the door.

The woman hoisted her shoulder purse higher. "I guess we have to go, Reverend. But it was good to see you. I sure am sorry about all the bad things that happened. And I still pray for your dear wife, God rest her soul."

"I appreciate that."

"Take care, Reverend." The man held out his hand, and Keith shook it.

Within thirty seconds, the place had cleared out as the tourists dashed for the ferry, leaving Keith and Jill alone, surrounded by a sudden, unnatural stillness. Only then did he see her. At her stunned expression, his face went another shade paler.

"Sir? Sir, can I help you?"

Forcing himself to look back at the clerk, Keith gave their order by rote before turning back to Jill. "I'll meet you outside, okay?"

His voice was as shaky as she felt. With a silent nod, she headed for the deserted terrace.

When Keith joined her a couple of minutes later, Jill was still trying to come to grips with the conversation she'd overheard. If Keith was a minister, why had he kept it a secret? And why had he left the ministry? Who was the hussy the woman had referred to? What role had she played in Keith's problems? What had happened to his wife? Her mind swirled with questions as she looked over at him, but she asked none of them. For whatever reason, he'd kept his past a secret. She had no right to probe just because she'd been privy to a chance conversation. But she wished he'd felt comfortable enough to tell her about it. That he'd considered their friendship strong enough to withstand whatever he had to say. She thought they'd become closer than that.

As Keith set the coffee cups on the table and took his seat, he didn't need a degree in psychology to sense Jill's hurt or to know that she was overwhelmed with questions. He could read it in her eyes. And he intended to deal with both the questions and the hurt. Gladys's appearance had forced his hand, but it was one he had intended to play within the next few days, anyway. It was time he told Jill the reason for his year-long trek, time he shared with her the pain and sorrow, the humiliation and anger that had eaten away at him for two long years, until her gentle, healing kindness had touched his soul and begun to make it whole again, leading him back to God.

He'd come to that conclusion over the past three or four weeks, as the studio neared completion and he realized that he was fast approaching a decision point. He'd started spending more time alone, talking to God, seeking guidance, strength, direction—none of which had come overnight. After such a long estrangement, his communication skills with the Lord had been rusty. But when he'd taken his father's advice and simply spoken from his heart, the fog surrounding his life—and his future—had begun to lift.

Though patches of mist continued to obscure parts of the road ahead, one thing had become very clear. It was time to confront his past, deal with his unresolved issues, clear the air and forgive. And it was also time to stop asking "why" and let it go, as Jill had done. Only then could he determine his next steps.

With his dad acting as intermediary, and the cooperation of Reverend Thomas, the arrangements were now set for his journey to the past. He hadn't planned to tell Jill his plans in a public place, but the café was deserted. There was no reason to put it off. Especially in light of the conversation she'd witnessed.

"I'm sorry you heard all that, Jill." He gripped his mug with both hands as he looked at her.

She focused on the coffee she no longer wanted, tipping in a little cream to lighten the inky hue. "I didn't mean to eavesdrop, but she was talking really loud and…" When he reached over and took her cold fingers in his warm clasp, the words died in her throat.

"That's not what I meant. I'm just sorry you heard it in that way," he clarified. "I'd planned to tell you the story before I leave next week."

Jill felt as if she'd been slapped. She jerked her head up

and stared at him, her stomach twisting into a knot. "Y-you're leaving next week?"

At her bereft expression, Keith gave her fingers a gentle, reassuring squeeze. "I have some unfinished business to attend to. I won't be gone long."

Confused, she stared back at him. "You're…you're coming back?"

"I'd like to. If that's okay with you. I've got another job lined up, over in Deer Harbor."

He was staying! Maybe not forever, but at least for a while. *Thank you, God!* "Sure. T-the cabin will still be here."

The warmth of his smile sent a tingle all the way to her toes. But as he released her hand and took a sip of coffee, the curve of his lips flattened into a grim line. "There are a lot of things you don't know about me, Jill."

"Are you…are you really a minister?"

"I was. For twelve years. At a little church in Ohio. Ever since I was a young boy, I'd felt the calling to serve the Lord in ministry. And it was everything I'd expected. Life was good for a long time. I had a lovely wife, work that mattered and that fulfilled me, a close relationship with God, a congregation that supported me and valued what I did…everything was perfect. I felt very blessed."

Setting his coffee aside, he turned to stare out over the harbor, his troubled expression at odds with the sunny sky above and the boats gaily bobbing in the clear water. "Then things started to change. My wife, Ellen, and I both wanted children, but she suffered two miscarriages back-to-back. After the first one she became very depressed, which seemed normal to me. Who wouldn't be sad about losing a baby? I grieved over it, too. But I put it in the Lord's hands, and tried to console her. Nothing helped, though, until she got pregnant again. For a while things were good. Then complications set in, and she lost that baby, too.

"After that, the depression returned with a vengeance. I'd never witnessed despair that dark, and it scared me to death. Her behavior became erratic, and it got to the point that I was afraid to leave her alone. Her doctor said her melancholy was intensified by hormonal changes and prescribed some medication. But she'd often forget to take it, and she began to spiral deeper and deeper into darkness."

A chill rippled through Jill, triggered more by the ominous nature of Keith's story than the sudden change in air temperature caused by a passing cloud that briefly obscured the sun.

"I worried about Ellen all the time," Keith continued. "When I wasn't with her, I'd call every couple of hours, and I asked neighbors to stop in and check on her throughout the day. To say I was distracted would be an understatement. For the first time in my life, I felt unable to cope, and despite my prayers for guidance the Lord was silent. I couldn't imagine how things could get worse. Until they did."

A muscle clenched in his jaw, and his Adam's apple bobbed as he swallowed hard. "While all this was going on, I was counseling a young woman in our congregation. She was having marital problems, and she requested more and more sessions. I was so distracted by my personal concerns that I didn't realize she had begun to offer…more than sympathy for my situation. When her intent finally registered, I told her that I had no interest in the 'comfort' she was willing to provide and referred her elsewhere for counseling. I thought that was the end of it. But I was wrong. She didn't take kindly to being rejected. I just didn't realize how angry—or vindictive—she could be."

A cold, hard look gripped Keith's features, one Jill had

never seen before, and another chill chased its way down her spine. "A few days later, Susan—that was her name—called me. She sounded almost suicidal, and she asked me to meet with her once more. Since I was already dealing with Ellen's depression, I understood how unstable it could make a person, and I couldn't in good conscience refuse her request. Nor would I have been able to live with myself if I turned her down and she took some desperate measure. She suggested we meet in a public place, a park near the center of town. I figured that would be safe and agreed.

"I got there first. When she arrived, she seemed very agitated. I urged her to sit down, but she paced around in front of me, talking about how unhappy she was in her marriage and how she'd made a mistake…the same things I'd heard in our previous sessions. Then, all of a sudden, she started to sway, like she was going to faint. I grabbed her, and the next thing I knew she…she pulled me toward her and kissed me. Before I could react, she jerked away and slapped me. I remember her saying in a very loud voice, 'I told you I'm not interested, Reverend. I'm sorry you're having problems at home, but I'm a happily married woman.' And then she ran off."

Drawing an unsteady breath, Keith looked back at Jill. "It was a setup, of course. When I turned around, I saw one of the elders from our church with his family. Somehow Susan had gotten wind of the fact that they were planning a picnic in the park, and she arranged our meeting knowing that he'd witness the whole thing. To complicate matters, he'd never been one of my strongest supporters. He thought I was too traditional in my interpretation of scripture, and we'd often clashed. Anyway, the scandal swept through the town like wildfire. Of course I denied everything, but Susan stuck to her story, putting on an act worthy of an Academy Award."

When he continued, his voice went flat. "Bottom line, the board asked me to resign. After all the clergy scandals in recent years, they wanted to distance themselves from anything that even smelled of impropriety. Under normal circumstances, I would have fought such an unjust accusation with everything in me. But the scandal and the whispers and the pressure proved too much for Ellen in her already precarious mental state, and she...she took her own life." His voice broke. Resting his elbows on the table, he pressed his lips against his laced fingers and closed his eyes.

Horrified by his tale, Jill reached out and laid her hand on Keith's shoulder. She felt hate bubble up deep inside, hate for a woman she'd never met, whose vindictive actions had turned this kind, good man's world upside down and robbed him of both his wife and his work. Though she searched desperately for words of comfort, she knew there was nothing she could say to assuage his grief. All she could do was touch him, and hope that somehow he could feel her caring and sympathy through her fingertips, just as she could feel the tremors that rippled through his body.

When Keith at last opened his eyes, the moisture at their corners told her that he was using every ounce of his willpower to hold on to his composure. She yearned to gather him into her arms and comfort him, as she'd done with Kyle, to hold him until his shaking stopped and the world steadied. But it would take more than a simple hug to set Keith's world right.

"After Ellen died, I didn't have it in me to fight," he continued in an unsteady voice. "I was too filled with hate and anger—at Susan, at the congregation, at life...at God. So I walked away. Without even leaving a forwarding address. My father took care of tying up the loose ends for me. I wanted nothing more to do with that town or that church."

As Jill looked at Keith's ravaged face, feeling his pain as if it were hers, it occurred to her that there were many ways for people to be damaged. Some bore their scars in a manner seen by the eye; others in a manner seen only by the heart.

"I'm so sorry," she whispered.

"I was, too. For myself." He looked at her steadily, cutting himself no slack. "I didn't think that I deserved what had happened to me. That as a minister, I was somehow better than anyone else. It's taken me two long years to get past that. The first year I worked with my dad, hoping time would heal my wounds. When it didn't, I started traveling. Looking for answers. After almost a year of wandering, I reached the end of the road—literally—when I came to Orcas Island. I'd never been more down in my life than the night I arrived on your doorstep."

He leaned forward. "But I've learned a lot since then, Jill. About accepting God's will, about letting go, about moving on. That's why I need to go back to Ohio. To finish some business I should have taken care of two years ago. To set the record straight so that I can move ahead with my life."

But move where? Jill wanted to ask. However, her spoken words were different. "That makes sense."

For several long beats of silence, Keith's gaze held hers captive, as if he wanted to say more. But in the end, he checked his watch, took a final sip of his coffee and stood. "Kyle will be waiting for us." He reached for her hand and drew her to her feet, his face inches from hers, those blue eyes warm and inviting. "Thanks for listening, Jill."

His husky tone and tender expression played havoc with her metabolism. She had to clear her throat twice before she could respond, managing no more than a whisper. "Thank you for sharing."

He gave her hand a squeeze, then led the way to the steps, guiding her down with a clasp that was sure and strong.

And even after they reached level ground, he didn't let go.

Chapter Fifteen

It was a day of mixed emotions, starting off in a celebratory mood with an "official" ribbon-cutting ceremony for Jill's studio. A homemade cinnamon coffee cake was cooling on the kitchen counter, and she'd strung a yellow ribbon in the studio doorway. When the time came, they trooped across the yard to the new structure and she handed the scissors to Kyle, who stood between her and Keith.

"Will you do the honors, Kyle?"

Wide-eyed, the little boy stared up at her. "Me?"

"Yes. You've helped Keith so much that I think you should cut the ribbon. Don't you, Keith?"

"Absolutely."

A flush of pleasure colored the boy's cheeks as he took the scissors. "Okay."

"But first, I'd like to say a few words of thanks." Jill bowed her head and linked fingers with Kyle, then reached for Keith's hand to complete the circle. "Lord, we stand before You today in gratitude for the many blessings You have given us. We thank You for bringing us together, in this time and this place, to share and to learn and to grow. We ask that You guide us in the months and years ahead so that we may walk in Your path at all times, and we ask that You help us always to remember to share with others the many gifts You have given us. Grant us Your strength when we falter, Your compassion when we err, Your consolation when we are hurting. Fill us with Your love so we never forget, even on dark and lonely days, that we are never alone; that You are always by our side. And finally, Lord, help me to use this special room that Keith and Kyle have built to honor the glory of your creation."

When she finished, Jill looked over at Keith. "Would you like to add anything?"

"I think you said it all." He stroked his thumb over the back of her hand before he released it. "That was beautiful, Jill."

His smile was like the sun on a warm spring day, and the husky quality of his voice set off a flutter in her stomach. "Okay, Kyle."

Using both hands, the little boy lifted the scissors and snipped the ribbon while Keith recorded the moment with his camera. As the two ends fluttered to the ground, he and Jill applauded. Then she stepped over the threshold and surveyed her dream of a studio, brought to life by Keith. She'd been inside during the building process, of course, but the finished structure, now cleared of construction debris, almost took her breath away. Although Keith had worked from her drawings, he'd enhanced and embellished her ideas, creating a space that was as beautiful as it was practical. Skylights in the vaulted ceiling were positioned to best catch the light, and three sides of the building featured banks of windows. The overall effect was almost like being outdoors.

"It's too pretty to mess up with my paints." Jill's tone was awed as she moved around the room, her face alight with joy. "In fact, I'm tempted to move in here."

Keith grinned. "I'm glad you like it."

"Like it? I love it!" She twirled around, and on impulse reached out to hug the man who had made her vision a reality. His arms went around her, and he briefly pressed his cheek to her hair, inhaling her pleasing, fresh scent, before she pulled back and smiled up at him.

As he studied the woman whose goodness and sweetness had helped him find his way out of darkness, Keith marveled at the changes that had been wrought in her, as well. If he'd never believed in miracles before, he now had proof of one in his arms. Like a butterfly, she'd left her cocoon, transformed, with wings that were ready to soar. Where once she'd hidden her face under a hat and stayed in the shadows, she now embraced the sunshine. Despite the bright light that outlined every flaw, she was unselfconscious about her scars. At least with him. His throat tightened with tenderness, and he was tempted to express the depth of his feelings in a way that left no doubt in her mind that she was a beautiful and appealing woman in every way that mattered.

Jill saw a spark ignite in Keith's eyes, and for an instant she stopped breathing. Like that night on the porch, when he'd interrupted the tense scene with Kyle's grandfather, she had the distinct impression that he wanted to kiss her. Then, she'd thought the urge had been driven by consolation, by a need to reassure her that the danger was past. In this case she wasn't as sure about the motivation. Of course, she knew he liked her. But liking and attraction were two different things. He was probably just caught up in the excitement of the moment. Responding to her euphoria. It couldn't be anything more. Could it?

"This is…really nice, Keith. It's bright and sunny and… h-happy. I…I like it a…a whole lot."

So lost was Jill in Keith's eyes that it took several seconds for Kyle's words to register. When they did, she blinked once, twice, and tried to regroup. Had Kyle said a whole sentence? Not just one, but three?

Forcing herself to turn and step out of Keith's arms, Jill lowered herself to Kyle's level and gave him a glowing smile. "So do I. You guys did a great job."

Keith dropped down beside her, and from the look he gave her she knew he hadn't missed the significance of Kyle's milestone. "I couldn't have done it without you, buddy." He laid his hand on the youngster's shoulder.

A flush of pleasure warmed the boy's face. "What…what are you going to paint first?" he asked Jill.

"As a matter of fact, I have a very special project in mind. But since it's a surprise, you'll have to wait and see. And in the meantime, how about we go try that cake?"

The festive air continued as they trooped into the kitchen, which was filled with the enticing aroma of cinnamon. As they took their places at the table, Jill cut them each a generous wedge of the cake and passed out forks. Though they were celebrating the completion of her studio, the easy banter and laughter in the room was yet another blessing that filled her with gratitude.

Kyle was on his second piece when Keith shot her a look, and she nodded. This was one part of the day she wasn't looking forward to. Given Kyle's growing attachment to the man he'd once taken great pains to avoid, she and Keith had talked to Marni at length about Keith's upcoming trip, seeking her advice about how best to position it to ensure that Kyle didn't suffer any setbacks. Her counsel had seemed sound, and they planned to follow it to the letter. Jill prayed it would mitigate the effect of Keith's departure and reassure Kyle that the man he was fast coming to idolize was, indeed, returning.

"Kyle, I have a job for you to do," Keith began, keeping his tone conversational.

"Okay." The youngster looked at him expectantly as he put another bite of cake in his mouth.

"I have to go on a little trip. I'll be gone a few days, and I'd like you to take good care of my tools while I'm away. They're very important to me, because I can't do my work without them. If I leave my toolbox right by your bed, can you keep it safe until I get back?"

The little boy stopped chewing. "Y-you're going a-away?"

"Just for a few days. I'll be back real soon." Keith took the boy's small hand in his, never breaking eye contact.

"W-why do y-you…" Kyle stopped, leaving the rest of the question unasked.

"There are some things I have to do, back where I used to live. And I want to visit my father, too," Keith responded.

His hand trembling, Kyle set his fork down and stared at Keith with wide, fearful eyes. "H-he won't h-hurt you, w-will he?"

A muscle clenched in Keith's jaw, and he shot Jill a quick look. She could see the restrained fury in his eyes, prompted by an anger that any man—let alone a child's father—could treat a youngster as Kyle had been treated. But he shuttered them before he looked back at Kyle. "No, buddy, he won't. My father is a very nice man. I love him very much. When I was a little boy, he took me fishing and played catch with me in the backyard and brought ice cream home for us. I miss him, and he misses me. That's why I want to go and see him."

For several long seconds, Kyle digested that. "I-I don't

m-miss my dad." His voice was small, and he looked down at the table.

"That's okay. He wasn't very nice to you. Most of the time, we only miss people who are nice to us."

"I-I'll miss you. And I'd m-miss Jill if she w-went away."

Her throat tight, Jill laid a hand on Kyle's shoulder. "I'm not going anywhere, Kyle," she promised in a choked voice. And in that moment she knew that she could never send this fragile young boy to live with anyone else. That even if she had to be a single parent, she wanted to adopt him and do all she could to heal his wounds and give him the kind of home he had never known. "I love you, Kyle," she whispered. His head jerked up, as if he'd never before heard those words. "And I want us to stay together for always," she continued, blinking back tears.

She felt Keith's intent gaze, but she kept looking at Kyle. It was important that he see the sincerity in her eyes, to know without any doubt that he was wanted and loved and valued.

"You mean I…I can stay with you? F-for always?"

"I'm going to call Cindy, that nice social worker, and talk to her about it tomorrow. Would you like that, Kyle?"

"Yes." The tense line of his shoulders relaxed, and he gave Jill one of his rare smiles. Only when he picked up his fork once more and began to eat again did she risk a peek at Keith.

"I didn't know about that," he said quietly.

"I didn't either, for sure. Until just now. But I want to do this, Keith." Her gaze was steady and certain.

"Do what?" Kyle inquired.

For an instant, Keith's hard-to-read look had made her forget that Kyle was present. And very much aware of the conversation taking place over his head. "Just something I have to do tomorrow, that's all," she responded, forcing a smile to her lips. "I guess you like that cake, hmm?"

"Yeah."

"I think I'll have another piece, too. Keith?"

"No, thanks."

As she cut herself a second small slice and returned to the table, Jill had the nagging feeling that she'd somehow disappointed Keith. But she had no idea why. If she wanted to take on the job of raising Kyle, why should he care? It was her responsibility, not his. She was used to trusting her own judgment, making her own decisions. And this had been a good one, even if Keith didn't seem all that enthusiastic.

But her certainty couldn't overcome the sick feeling in the pit of her stomach that for some reason Keith disapproved of her decision. And when she picked up her fork, she realized that her appetite had vanished—along with the happy glow she'd felt at the ribbon-cutting ceremony.

Unless God was on their side, they were going to miss the ferry.

With a worried glance at her watch, Jill pressed harder on the accelerator. The boat was always on schedule…and it never lingered at the dock more than five or ten minutes, especially in the off season. There was very little margin for error. She thought they'd left the house in plenty of time, but she hadn't counted on the road construction that had required a detour over Dolphin Bay Road, which was partially unpaved—and slow going.

"We'll make it, Jill."

She took her attention off the road long enough to give Keith a quick, anxious look. "I'm not so sure. We should have eaten lunch sooner, but no one seemed hungry after the coffee cake this morning. If you miss the ferry, you'll miss the bus in Anacortes and you won't get back to Seattle in time for your plane." Why had his car picked yesterday to die?

Reaching over, he laid a reassuring hand on her arm. "Let's leave it in God's hands, okay? I know in my heart He wants me to do this. We'll have to trust that everything will work out."

Good advice. And Jill tried to follow it. But since she was in the driver's seat, she felt more than a little pressure to fulfill her role in God's plan to get Keith to the boat on time.

As it turned out, they made it…with mere minutes to spare. The hulking craft was still moored at the dock when they pulled into Orcas Village. But no cars were lined up waiting to drive on, meaning the loading was complete and the horn would sound any second to signal the boat's departure.

"See? I told you we'd make it," Keith noted with a smile.

"I won't feel sure about that until you're on board." She set the car brake and released the trunk latch. "Why don't you grab your bag while I run over and let one of the crewmen know they have another passenger. Kyle, stay with Keith, okay?"

Without waiting for a response, Jill dashed toward the boat.

Only when Keith and Kyle joined her a couple of minutes later did she feel the tension in her shoulders ease. "You'd better board," she told Keith, jamming her hands into the deep pockets of her jacket.

Ever since Jill had revealed her plans to adopt Kyle this morning, Keith had sensed a certain awkwardness between them. Due, he supposed, to his reaction to her announcement. In retrospect, he realized that she might have interpreted his surprise as disapproval. In fact, nothing could be further from the truth. He was all for the idea. It was just that he'd expected them to talk it over first. But why should she feel compelled to discuss choices about her future with him? He'd never given her any indication of his growing feelings.

Or his hopes that he might be part of her future. It hadn't seemed appropriate to do so until he was free of the past, until the way was cleared for him to make some promises about tomorrow.

But he couldn't leave on this uncomfortable note. Although departure preparations had kept him busy most of the morning, he'd hoped they'd have a few minutes to discuss the situation. That didn't seem to be in the cards now. For one thing, time was short. For another, it wasn't a subject he wanted to talk about in front of Kyle.

Then inspiration struck. He dug in his pocket and withdrew a handful of change, holding it out to Kyle. "Why don't you run into the store and get one of those ice-cream bars you like?" he suggested. Often in the past, as they waited to catch the ferry to Friday Harbor for a counseling session, they'd indulged in a treat from the neighborhood store at the dock. Kyle's face lit up as his small fist closed around the coins.

"Y-you won't leave till I get b-back, will you?"

"No. I still have a couple of minutes," Keith promised.

As Kyle took off at a run, Keith turned to Jill. She had her hat on today, and the brim hid her face as she stared out at the blue water, the surface sparkling like diamonds in the sun.

"Jill." At the sound of his voice, she turned to him. "I'm sorry if my reaction this morning to your announcement about adopting Kyle upset you."

"It's okay." But her stiff shrug as she once more turned away told him it wasn't. "I know I can't give him an ideal home. He won't have the kind of family I had. But it will be better than being passed around in foster care his whole life. And I do love him, Keith. As much as if he was my own child. I hope that helps compensate for the other things he'll lack."

Setting his case on the ground beside him, Keith reached

for her arms, urging her with gentle pressure to face him. "Jill, I don't disapprove. I can't think of anyone who would take better care of Kyle or give him a more loving home. He belongs with you. I was just surprised that you'd never mentioned it. But I guess I've never given you any reason to think you should discuss those kinds of decisions with me." He paused, trying to find the words to express all that he felt for this special woman. "The thing is, I…"

The ferry horn boomed, cutting him off, and the crew moved into position to release the tethers that anchored the boat to the dock.

"You need to go," Jill told him. "They won't wait."

Keith didn't loosen his grip. He couldn't leave like this, couldn't walk away from Jill without giving her some indication of how he felt. This wasn't the time or the place for emotional declarations, but he had to at least offer her a glimpse into his heart.

"You need to leave, Keith." Jill's voice grew more urgent. The ferry horn sounded again and she tried to draw away, but he held her fast. Prepared to object, she looked up at him. But the words died in her throat as he lowered his lips to claim hers in a tender, gentle kiss.

For several eternal seconds, time seemed to stop. She was too surprised to respond, to object…to do anything but cling to his arms for support. When at last he pulled back far enough to look into her eyes, she stared at him in confusion. "W-why did you d-do that?"

Reaching up, he brushed a soft strand of hair back from her face and responded in a voice that was as unsteady as the small boats bobbing in the harbor beside the hulking ferry. "Why do you think?"

At her stunned, perplexed look, Keith realized that she

really didn't understand the message he was trying to communicate. "Why does a man usually kiss a woman, Jill?" he prompted, his voice as soft, as tender, as a lover's caress.

She knew the answer to that, of course. But in her case it didn't fit. No man could be attracted to a woman so disfigured. Putting a hand to her cheek, she turned away in silence, blinking to clear the sudden film of moisture in her eyes.

His expression troubled, Keith studied the woman beside him. She'd made such strides in her reentry into society…it simply hadn't occurred to him that in their relationship she'd still harbor such insecurities. Be so conscious of her disfigurement. Yet her reaction affirmed the depth of her scars. Not just the visible ones, but the ones etched on her heart, as well.

Truth be told, she was far more conscious of her disfigurement than he was. Sometime during these past few months, as he and Jill had shared meals and conversation and trips with Kyle, her scars had faded into insignificance for him. Her inner beauty was what attracted him. Her warm heart, her loving ways, her deep faith, her generous and giving spirit. Those were the things that made her special. And long after the years robbed them both of physical appeal, those qualities would continue to shine in her, ageless and new, still able to tighten his throat with emotion and fill his heart with love.

But there was no time to say all those things now. They would have to wait until…

"Keith! Keith!"

Kyle was running toward them, as fast as his short legs could carry him. "I…I heard the horn." He screeched to a stop in front of Keith, puffing, and thrust a small package of licorice into his hand.

Confused, Keith stared at the cellophane bag. Instead of

getting his favorite ice-cream treat, Kyle had chosen the candy that Keith always bought for himself when they purchased snacks for their ferry trips. Keith was overwhelmed by the unselfish going-away present from a little boy who'd known little or no generosity or kindness until he met Jill. Blinking away the sudden moisture that clouded his vision, he dropped down and pulled the boy close, burying his face in his slight shoulder. "Thank you, Kyle."

He held him as long as he dared, and when he rose his intense gaze sought Jill's. "We'll talk more when I get back."

And then he was gone, sprinting for the boat, boarding with mere seconds to spare. He remained on the deck as it pulled away from the dock, his overnight case by his side, until the ferry shrank to a distant speck in the distance. Only when it disappeared from sight did Jill and Kyle turn toward the car.

As she took his hand, he looked up at her. "He's really c-coming back, isn't h-he, Jill?"

"Yes, Kyle, he is."

"Promise?"

"Yes, I promise."

It wasn't a pledge Jill took lightly. Nor was it one she had any qualms about making, she realized as her heart soared with fragile, newfound hope. Because the look in Keith's eyes just now, before he'd raced for the ferry, had been filled with that very thing.

Promise.

Chapter Sixteen

The early-November afternoon was blustery and cold, but Jill welcomed the feel of the brisk, invigorating air against her face. Ever since they'd seen Keith off at the dock yesterday, she'd been restless and jittery. The tremulous hope that had followed his kiss had quickly evaporated, leaving uncertainty, fear—and questions—in its place. Sleep last night had been elusive, and the long dark hours of wakeful pondering hadn't brought any resolution. What she needed was a long, secluded walk by the sea to sort things out. When she'd dropped Kyle off for his therapy session twenty minutes ago, she'd asked Marni if she knew of such a private spot. The therapist had directed her to the perfect place—a deserted, windswept stretch of driftwood-strewn beach fronting an expanse of open sea.

A sudden gust of wind whipped by, and Jill pulled up the collar of her jacket, tucking her hands into her pockets as she set off along the shore, determined to straighten out her tangled emotions. Except she wasn't sure where to begin. Until yesterday, she'd been able to convince herself that the look she'd seen in Keith's eyes on several occasions hadn't been attraction, but simple kindness. She could no longer delude herself with that notion. Though their conversation had been cut short at the ferry landing, and Keith hadn't had time to verbalize what was in his heart, she'd seen it in his eyes. And felt it in his kiss.

He was in love with her.

That insight had been astonishing and exhilarating and exciting. Not to mention scary.

But there was something else that was even scarier.

She was in love with him.

Trying to pinpoint the exact instant when their relationship had made the leap from friendship to love was impossible. It had been a gradual thing, happening in almost imperceptible increments, until one day she'd realized that Keith had stolen her heart. But until yesterday, she hadn't been sure about his feelings.

Now that she was, she knew that the solitary life she'd constructed with such care was on the verge of being reshaped. Assuming, of course, that he wanted to explore those feelings and follow a path that would deepen their relationship. But if he did, would she have the courage to upgrade her life, just as she'd upgraded her studio by adding a new structure that had changed her work space, yet in the process made it bigger and brighter and even better? Did she have the courage to trust this man with her heart, to believe that his love would be true and constant, that he would always be able to look past her scars and see her inner beauty? Did she have the courage to let go of the past? To say goodbye?

As she turned to the Lord in prayer, seeking answers, a gull swooped low in front of her, its raucous cry echoing above the breaking waves. And all at once she was transported back in time, to a trip she and Sam and Emily had taken to the seashore the summer before the fire. While her husband and daughter had built a sand castle nearby, Jill had taken refuge from the sun under the small patch of shade afforded by the beach umbrella, enjoying their easy repartee and Emily's giggles as Sam teased her.

After a while, a lone gull had circled above, raising its discordant voice and diverting Emily's attention. Jill could hear the conversation as if it were yesterday.

"Listen, Daddy. The seagull is singing."

Chuckling, Sam had reached over to tousle her hair. "Most people wouldn't call that singing, sweetie. Seagulls don't have a very pretty voice."

Enthralled, Emily had shaded her eyes to follow the bird's graceful flight. "Well, it may not be pretty, but it made me notice him. And when I watch him up in the sky, I forget about his voice because he has such beautiful wings. He makes me want to fly, Daddy."

"You can, sweetie. God gave you wings, too," Sam had responded as he added a turret to the castle.

Puzzled, Emily had transferred her attention to her father. "Where are they?"

"Right in there." Sam had given her chest a gentle tap. "By your heart. And God is always with you when you use them."

Emily had puzzled over that for a few minutes, her face thoughtful as she sifted the sand through her fingers. "When you love somebody…is that kind of like flying?" she'd asked at last.

"That's exactly right," Sam had replied with a smile. "Love is the very best way to fly, in fact." He'd turned toward Jill then, and she could still recall the tender look in his eyes as his gaze met hers. "Your mommy has a very special gift for loving. The kind that makes you want to fly. I'm glad she shared it with us, aren't you?"

The image of that warm, summer day faded as another cold gust of wind whipped past, chilling the tears that were streaming down Jill's cheeks. Startled, she reached up with a shaky hand and brushed them away. It had been a long time since she'd taken any of her precious memories out of their sealed storage box deep in the recesses of her heart. And longer still since she'd cried over one of them.

If Sam had been right, and Jill had a special gift for loving, it was a gift that had long gone unshared, locked away in a dusty box, just like her memories. But now a little boy who needed her love had entered her life—along with a man who wanted her love. And both had managed to find that dusty box in her heart and pry open a corner, like a child in search of hidden Christmas presents.

As she stared out at the sea, Jill's jumbled thoughts began to untangle. Like Emily's seagull, she was ready to spread her wings. Despite her fear, it was time to trust her heart—and to trust that the Lord would give her the courage she would surely need in the days and months and years ahead.

Suddenly, with perfect clarity, she realized that she hadn't come here today to seek direction.

She had come to say goodbye.

Startled by that insight, Jill sank onto a large piece of driftwood and stared out at the undulating waves. Then, clenching her hands in her lap, she closed her eyes. *Help me through this, Lord,* she prayed in silence. *Let my message find its way to the family I loved.*

When at last she began to speak, her choked, whispered words were caught and lifted by the wind.

"Sam, Emily, I came here today to tell you how much I love you. How much I'll always love you. Not one day has passed since you left me that I don't feel you close to my heart and wish we were together again, with thousands more memories to create and to share. But that wasn't God's plan for us. I take comfort in knowing that you're both in His care now, surrounded by His love for always. And I know someday we'll meet again.

"But in the meantime, I'm still here. And there are two people who need my love. One is a very special little boy who has been hurt emotionally and physically. With each day that passes, I feel more certain that God brought him to me so that I could give him the kind of love he's never known, the kind of love that will help him heal and thrive and blossom. You would have liked him, Emily. He's curious and kind and loving, just like you were. I think you would have been great friends.

"The other person who needs my love has also been hurt. I didn't go looking for his love, Sam; it came to me in a way that I first attributed to chance, but now believe was something more. I think God led him to me, just as He did Kyle."

Clasping her hands around her knees, Jill searched for just the right words. "I never thought I'd love again after the wonderful life we shared, Sam. I never wanted to. But Keith is very special. I've known that almost from the first day we met, when he commented on my scars. In fact, they could be the reason he took a closer look at me, like the day Emily noticed the seagull because of his raucous cry, but then looked past it to see his beautiful wings and admire the way he could fly. Keith did that with me. He looked past my scars and saw beauty underneath. The kind of beauty that really matters...of character and spirit and heart.

"I want to help Keith and Kyle fly, Sam. You said that day on the beach that I have a special gift for loving. I hope you can understand why I want to share it with these two special people. Why, after all these years of mourning, of hiding in the shadows, I'm ready to step into the light again and make some new memories. But they won't diminish the love we shared. You and Emily will always have a special place in my heart, reserved only for you. That will never change."

Drawing a shaky breath, Jill opened her eyes and looked up at the clear blue sky. "I have to go now. That little boy I mentioned is waiting for me. But wherever I go, part of you will go with me. For always. I love you both so much."

Tears once again blurred her vision, and as she groped for a tissue, a nearby piece of driftwood caught her eye. The size of an orange, its gnarled wood bleached white, it had been wrought over time by the ebb and flow of the sea into the shape of a heart.

With trembling hands, Jill reached for it, stroking her fingers over the smooth wood as she followed the curving shape. How odd that among the thousands of pieces of driftwood on the beach one bearing this shape would be lying at her feet.

Her expression thoughtful, she tucked the symbol into her large tote bag. From this day forward, it would hold a place of honor in her home, reminding her always of the transforming power of love. Of God's abiding presence when we spread our wings to soar. And of the simple truth that sometimes saying goodbye to the past is the only way to embrace the future.

"It's good to see you, son."

Wrapped in a bear hug, Keith was too choked up to respond at once to his father's greeting. It had been almost a year since they'd been together. But the link was as strong as ever. Maybe stronger. After seeing firsthand in Kyle what could happen to a child who didn't have the benefit of a loving, supportive father, he gave thanks that he'd been blessed with this special man in his life.

"I'm glad to be back, Dad."

His father released him at last, surveying him with a critical eye. "Come in, come in. You look good."

"I feel good." Keith crossed the threshold and shrugged out of his coat. "Better than I have in a long time."

"I have some homemade stew waiting. But from the look of you, I don't think you've missed too many meals lately."

"Are you saying I've gained weight?"

The older man's eyes twinkled as he took Keith's coat and slipped it on a hanger. "Yep. Another couple of pounds, you might be back to where you used to be. That landlady of yours must be a good cook."

As his father turned to put the coat in the hall closet, Keith stuck his hands in his pockets. He hadn't planned to discuss this subject with his father so soon, but the older man had given him the perfect opening.

"To be honest, Dad, she's more than a landlady to me."

Chuckling, his father turned back. "Can't say I'm surprised."

Startled, Keith stared at him. "Why not?"

"There was something in your voice when you talked about her on the phone." Bob Michaels shrugged. "Intuition, I guess. I'm happy for you, Keith."

A soft warmth flooded Keith's face. "Yeah. Me, too. There's a lot I want to tell you about."

"And I want to hear it all. We'll have a nice chat over dinner. But first, I had another call from Reverend Thomas. He wanted me to pass on a reminder that he'd like to talk with you before your visit."

"I figured I'd call him from here, if that's okay. I didn't want to have that conversation at a pay phone. Or at Jill's."

"Sure. You want to do that first, or after dinner?"

"Do you mind if I do it first? I'd rather get that out of the way so we can concentrate on other subjects."

"Like that nice landlady of yours?"

"Yeah." Keith's lips quirked up.

With a wave, the older man directed him to the den. "Help yourself. The stew will keep."

As Keith settled into his father's worn leather desk chair and tapped the minister's number into the phone, he drew a long, slow breath. Things were finally falling into place. Just one more piece of old business to clear up, a record to set straight, and then he could move ahead with his life, make a fresh, new start. His plans depended on Jill, of course. But he felt confident that she returned his feelings, even though they'd never given voice—or expression—to them until their parting at the ferry. Her eyes didn't lie, though. Yes, she was scared. And uncertain. And apparently unconvinced that any man could find her attractive. But he was sure he could put those fears to rest when he returned. And that couldn't be soon enough for him.

A man's greeting on the other end of the line snapped him back to the present and he refocused his attention. "Reverend Thomas? Keith Michaels here."

"Reverend Michaels! I'm glad you called."

The long-unused title jolted Keith, as it had when Gladys had hailed him with it. "My father said you wanted to speak with me before Sunday. Is there a problem?"

"No, no. Not at all. I just wanted to pass on some information. I wasn't sure how much you knew about events that transpired here after you left."

"I don't know about anything that's happened since then," he replied, his voice flat. "I wanted a clean break, Reverend. I had no interest in staying in touch with anyone."

"Call me Steve, please. And I understand your position, given the circumstances. But there are a few things you should be aware of that could affect your remarks."

Keith doubted that. He knew exactly what he wanted to say when he addressed his former congregation: what he *should* have said in his own defense two years ago, when the scandal broke. He wanted the people he'd once shepherded to know the truth, which they hadn't heard from Susan Reynolds or through the rumor mill. His course of action was clear in his mind. He would lay the facts on the table, set the record straight, clear his name and move on. But this man, this stranger, had agreed to let Keith speak from the pulpit that was now his. He owed him the courtesy of a hearing, at least.

"All right, Steve. I'm listening."

"I can sum it up pretty quickly for you. Since I didn't arrive until a few weeks after the…controversy…that led to your departure, I only had secondhand information and conjecture about what took place."

"That's all anyone had. Including Ted Mackland, the so-called eyewitness." Keith couldn't keep the bitterness out of his voice.

"They have more now. A year ago, Susan Reynolds accused the coach at the high school of the same thing when they were caught in a similar 'compromising' situation."

A shock wave rippled through Keith. "Mike Schwartz?"

"Yes."

"That's ridiculous!" Keith knew that Mike and his wife had been having some marital problems two years ago, but he also knew the man had strong morals and would never break his marriage vows.

"Yes, it was. And he was determined to expose Susan. So he turned the tables on her. He confronted her in private, and they had a very interesting—and revealing—conversation. Which Mike recorded. Plus, he'd brought along a witness who remained out of sight until the conversation was over. When Susan realized that her vindictive scheme had backfired, she left her husband and disappeared from town. No one's heard from her since. Needless to say, that escapade pretty much led any doubters in your case to conclude that you'd been a victim, as well. With far more tragic consequences."

In the silence that followed the man's revelation, Keith tried to process the unexpected turn of events. His status had changed from disgraced to vindicated. And it had changed a year ago—just about the time he'd started his travels, searching for answers and direction. Had he not cut all ties with the church, he might have discovered the truth sooner. Saved himself a wasted year of anguish and wandering.

Then again, if the truth had surfaced sooner, he would never have met Jill. Or Kyle. Or found the place, he knew in his heart, he was destined to call home. In the past twelve months, he'd learned to love again. And he'd found his way back to God. The year had hardly been wasted. In retrospect, it had been time well spent.

Still, that left him with a dilemma about his address to the congregation. But that wasn't the minister's problem. He was just grateful that the man had tipped him off in advance.

"I wasn't aware of any of that," he told the pastor. "And you're right—I'll need to rethink my remarks. Thank you for sharing the information. And thank you, also, for letting me borrow your pulpit for a few minutes on Sunday."

"It was your pulpit long before it was mine. And I'm happy to do my part to help make amends for the injustice you suffered."

When Keith rang off and joined his father in the kitchen, the older man was setting the pot of stew in the center of the table.

"Just in time. Hope you're hungry."

"Uh-huh."

Bob Michaels stuck a ladle in the pot and cast a shrewd look at his son. "Bad news?"

"No. But I'm going to have to rewrite my remarks for Sunday."

"Why is that?"

"I'll tell you all about it while we eat."

After a brief blessing, Keith relayed the conversation to his father. "So I'm not sure what I'm going to say," he concluded. "I'd planned to tell my side of the story, to do my best to set the record straight. But it seems that's already been done for me. I'm beginning to wonder if I should even go back."

"Interesting turn of events, I'll grant you that." His father helped himself to another serving of stew, his expression pensive. "You're here, though. And scheduled to speak. Maybe the Lord wants you to share a different message."

Twin furrows creased Keith's brow. "Like what?"

"Well now, I'm not the preacher. That's your department, son. And I'm sure you'll figure it out. Why not pray about it, ask the Lord for direction? If He has another message in mind for you to pass on, I expect He'll let you know. In the meantime, tell me about that nice landlady of yours."

The abrupt change in subject disconcerted Keith for a moment. But thoughts of Jill always managed to distract him, and it didn't take long for him to shelve his preaching problem for later resolution and switch gears. A smile curved his lips and he rested his elbows on the table, his meal forgotten.

"She's very special."

"I kind of figured that. Tell me all about her."

Keith was happy to comply. And when he finished, his father's smile mirrored his own.

"This sounds pretty serious."

"It is. And that brings me to a favor I'd like to ask."

His father listened as Keith explained what he had in mind. Then he laid his work-worn hand on top of his son's, his eyes misty, his heart filled with gratitude for his answered prayers. "Consider it done."

"Pretty remarkable, isn't it, when you lay them all out like this?"

Stunned, Jill stared at Kyle's drawings. They'd been done during therapy sessions over the past few weeks, and Marni had lined them up in sequential order on the conference table in her office. The heavy, dark tones of the early pieces had lightened and brightened with each subsequent drawing.

"It's amazing," Jill replied.

"He's making good progress, and I credit most of that to you." Marni began to gather up the drawings as she spoke. "Isn't it incredible how even a little love can bring sunlight into a dark world?"

"I got chocolate!" Kyle burst into the room, his eyes glowing behind his horn-rimmed glasses. He held up a fistful of foil-wrapped kisses, retrieved from the receptionist's "treat" drawer.

"That is something special!" Jill dropped down to his level and smiled. "You can eat those when we get on the ferry. But first I promised Keith we'd pick up some pictures for him at

the drugstore. And I have to stop at the market. So we need
to hurry or we'll miss the boat."

Standing, Jill turned back to Marni. "Thank you for sharing
that." She inclined her head toward the stack of drawings.

"Considering your profession, I thought you'd find it very
interesting."

"And encouraging. Is there anything more I can do to help
the process along?"

The woman smiled. "As the saying goes, if it ain't broke,
don't fix it. Just keep on doing what you're doing."

With an answering smile and a nod, Jill reached for Kyle's
hand. "Okay, sweetie, let's head out."

After picking up Keith's prints and visiting the grocery
store, they made it to the ferry just as the departure horn blew.
Once aboard, Jill followed Kyle up the steep steps to the passenger lounge. She juggled the bag of film and her purse in
one arm and hefted a large, frozen turkey in the other. When
she reached the top she took a moment to catch her breath,
keeping an eye on Kyle as he dashed toward the observation
window to watch the departure. Then she headed toward one
of the benches, anxious to lighten her load.

But as she leaned over to set the turkey on the seat, the four
packs of photos slipped from the bag in her other arm,
spewing images across the floor in a kaleidoscopic montage.

Muttering under her breath, she bent to scoop them
up…only to freeze, mesmerized by the pattern they revealed.
It was almost a replay of what she'd seen less than an hour
earlier in Marni's office, she realized. Like Kyle's drawings,
Keith's photos showed a marked change over time. The first
roll was easy to spot. It contained images that had been taken
elsewhere, before Keith arrived on the island. Brooding and
dark, many shot in low light or during stormy weather, they

resonated with a sinister, threatening power. A power that could smother and crush and break. Those images frightened her, driving home how bleak Keith's outlook had been when he arrived on her doorstep.

But subsequent photos showed a distinct change. Since she was keenly attuned to the foliage and colors of the island, the seasonal sequence was pretty easy to follow. As the summer had passed, the images changed. Dark gave way to light, dull gave way to bright, despair gave way to hope. The most recent prints, including the one of Kyle cutting the ribbon on the studio, were filled with joy and warmth.

Though Jill had observed Keith taking photos on several occasions, she'd never seen any of his work. And she was impressed by his talent. He had a great eye for composition, and many of his photos were evocative, resonating with imagery and meaning.

But most of all, she was awed by what they revealed about the man. Something wonderful had happened to Keith during his stay at Rainbow's End. The proof of that was spread out before her.

Jill wasn't a psychologist. But Marni was, and her earlier words echoed in Jill's mind.

"Isn't it incredible how even a little love can bring sunlight into a dark world?"

Deep inside, Jill believed that. She'd seen it happen in her own life these past few months. And it seemed to have happened for Keith, too. The transformation in both their lives was confirmation of the truth in those familiar words from Paul: "Love never fails."

Overwhelmed with gratitude, she gathered up the images and tucked them back into their envelopes. And in the silence of her heart she gave thanks.

Chapter Seventeen

"This morning we have a guest speaker, a man most of you know. He asked for a few minutes of our time today, and I was happy to oblige. Reverend Michaels, the pulpit is yours."

As Reverend Thomas finished his introduction, Keith entered the sanctuary. A murmur spread through the congregation, like ripples from a pebble dropped into still water, as he stepped up to the pulpit and surveyed those gathered before him, assessing their reaction. Some people stared, their eyes wide with shock and surprise. Some flushed in embarrassment and looked away—including Ted Mackland, seated in his usual place, front and center. Some fidgeted, their discomfort evident. Others smiled in welcome. Ever since he'd decided to speak to the flock he'd once shepherded, Keith had been determined not to let the congregation's response sway him from his message. He was no less resolute now.

That message, however, had changed over the past couple of days, following his conversation with Steve Thomas. He looked toward the minister, who had taken a seat off to the side, and bolstered by his encouraging smile, Keith turned his attention back to the congregation. Most of the faces were familiar. Gladys and Frank were in their usual spot, just to the right of center, and Gladys smiled at him, then nudged Frank when Keith looked their way. The new members seemed confused by the undertone of tension in the church.

"Good morning." A slight tremor ran through his voice, and he took a slow, steadying breath to dispel it. When he resumed speaking, his tone was composed and measured. "Most of you know me. For those of you who don't, my name is Keith Michaels. I was the pastor here for twelve years. Two years ago, I left both this church and the ministry under difficult circumstances." The confusion on the unfamiliar faces in the congregation began to dissipate, confirming that they'd heard the stories about him.

"Over the past two years, as I tried to put my life back together and make some sense of what had happened, I realized that I had unfinished business here. And that I wouldn't be able to move on until I shared with you my side of the story and set the record straight. I didn't know if you would believe me, but I knew I had to try. Reverend Thomas was kind enough to grant my request for a few minutes at the pulpit.

"But in the past couple of days, I found out that a year ago another incident occurred, similar to the one in which I was involved. Same perpetrator, different victim. Except this time the woman was exposed. I pray that all of you can now accept the truth of my innocence, as well.

"When I learned this news, I almost canceled my visit today. It seemed my message had already been delivered, in a far more convincing and conclusive way than mere words could ever convey. Then a very wise man suggested to me that perhaps the Lord wanted me to keep this date—but to share a different message."

Gripping the sides of the pulpit, Keith took a deep breath. "I puzzled over that for a while. What else could the Lord want me to talk about? I began aimlessly paging through my Bible, looking for inspiration, and all at once the words of St. Paul to the Ephesians seemed to jump off the page at me: 'Be kind to one another, and merciful, generously forgiving one another, as also God in Christ has generously forgiven you.'"

The silence in the church was as still as a morning on Orcas Island. It was almost as if the members of the congregation had stopped breathing, so rapt was their attention.

"I knew, then, that this was the message the Lord intended me to deliver. And that it was meant as much—if not more—for me than for you. The fact is, many times in life bad things happen to us. Unfair things. Things that disrupt our world and reduce us to tears, to anger, to bitterness. No one is immune to those kinds of tribulations. Including me. But anger and bitterness are destructive emotions. They isolate us from each other and from God. Where anger and bitterness have taken root, love cannot grow. Nor can the seeds of forgiveness or hope or peace find fertile ground.

"I know this firsthand. For two years I asked God why He had taken from me so many of the things that mattered, that gave my life value. Over and over I pleaded with Him for answers, and over and over the only response was silence. In the end, I turned away from the Lord.

"Then I met someone who had also endured great trauma. Who had struggled with the same unanswered question, but who had finally found peace. When I inquired how, the reply was simple: 'I stopped searching for answers. I stopped asking why.'

"That's when I began to realize that often there is no answer. At least, not one we can understand in our imperfect human state. I also realized something else: God doesn't call us to understand. Instead, he calls us to trust and to accept. And most of all, he calls us to forgive. To let the hate and anger and bitterness go and to open our hearts to His life-giving love.

"My friends, that's not an easy thing to do. I still struggle with it every day myself. But it's the path He calls us to. And that's the message I want to leave with you today. A message of hope and of love. And a belief that both of these things can be ours if we learn to accept without understanding, to forgive and to put our trust in the Lord."

Once more Keith's gaze swept the room. "When I left here, I felt I'd been wronged and betrayed both by the people I had tried to help and by the God to whom I'd devoted my life. I was filled with bitterness and hate. But after a long struggle, I'm learning to let those destructive emotions go. And to forgive, as the Lord taught us. I ask that you pray for me as I continue that journey. Just as I will continue to pray that all of us will take the Lord's message to heart so that we can live in the fullness of His grace every day of our lives."

When Keith finished, there was silence. But as he turned away from the pulpit, the crowd rose as one and applause rang through the small church. It followed him as he moved to the side and shook hands with Reverend Thomas. And it continued as the minister took his place behind the microphone. Only after a sustained ovation was the pastor able to resume the service.

Later, when the final hymn had been sung, Keith joined the minister in front to greet the worshippers. He was surrounded at once by members of the congregation who either wanted to assure him they'd always believed he was innocent— Gladys and Frank were in that group—or who wanted to apologize for doubting him. Many of the elders fell into the latter category, including Ted Mackland. However, he waited until most of the people had gone before he approached his former pastor.

As the man drew close, Keith realized that he'd aged a great deal. He was more stooped than he'd been two years before, and his slow, uneven gait was steadied by a cane. His once-ruddy complexion had faded to an unhealthy pallor, and deep creases crisscrossed his face. A significant weight loss had robbed him of the hearty, imposing presence that had once allowed him to dominate the board of elders. Bottom line, he looked like a spent, sick old man. Someone more to be pitied than hated.

"You gave a good…talk today, Reverend." Ted's stiff posture conveyed his discomfort with the situation, even as his slightly slurred, halting speech and the slack muscles on one side of his face explained his changed appearance. He'd had a stroke.

Keith gazed at the man who'd confirmed the story of his "indiscretion" to the church elders, whose staunch refusal to believe his pastor's version of the events had swayed the board to withdraw its support and urge him to resign. From all appearances, he'd been through a tough time. Keith knew that if Jill was here, she'd find it in her heart to show compassion, just as she had for Kyle's grandfather in the end, despite the man's faults. Surely he could do no less. *Help me, Lord, to follow her example,* he prayed.

"Thank you, Ted. I appreciate the kind words."

The older man gave a stilted nod and steadied himself, placing one hand atop the other on his cane. Or perhaps he was bracing himself, Keith speculated, as Ted stood a bit straighter and looked the man he'd accused in the eye.

"I'm glad you…came back, Reverend. When that…

woman left town last year, I wanted to…try and contact you. Then I…had this stroke." The apology in his eyes communicated his remorse even before he spoke the words. "I wanted to say…how sorry I was about…all that happened. You and I, we didn't…always see eye to eye. But you're…a good man, Reverend. I made a terrible…mistake. One I'll have to…live with until…the day I die. I've tried to…make my peace with the Lord. I only hope that someday…you can find that forgiveness you spoke about…this morning. Even though I surely don't…deserve it."

There was no question in Keith's mind that the man's contrition was deep and real. The price he'd paid in regret and sorrow was etched on his face. How could Keith add to the already heavy burden that weighed down his heart?

All at once he felt the cold, bitter anger he'd harbored against the man for two long years begin to dissolve, melting like snow touched by the spring sun, leaving the ground ready for new life.

"If only those who deserved forgiveness received it, all of us would be lost," Keith responded in a gentle voice. "It doesn't do any good to hold on to resentment. Or guilt. I'm learning to let mine go and move on with my life. It's time you did the same. With my blessing."

Keith extended his hand, and after a moment Ted reached for it.

"God be with you." Keith grasped the man's feeble hand in a firm grip.

"Thank you…Reverend." Ted's voice was a mere whisper. But his sincere gratitude warmed Keith's heart.

As he limped away, Reverend Thomas joined Keith. "Ted has suffered a lot this past year. Not just physically," he murmured, watching the man depart.

"I could tell. I hope he finds some peace now."

"I have a feeling he will. And how about you, Keith? Did coming back here give you the closure you were seeking?"

His expression thoughtful, Keith turned back to the minister. There was a kindness in the man's eyes, and an understanding in their depths, that touched his soul. Though the sprinkling of gray in the dark hair at Steve's temples suggested that he might be ten or twelve years older than his guest, Keith sensed in him a kindred spirit. And knew that this was a man he could have called friend under different circumstances.

"To a large degree, yes," Keith responded. "But I still have a little more work to do. Would you mind if I spend a few minutes in the chapel before I head back to Missouri?"

"Not at all. I left it unlocked. Just pull the door shut behind you."

"I appreciate your support and hospitality today. Thank you." He extended his hand.

"I was happy to help." Steve returned the handshake. "Have a safe trip back."

Left alone at last in front of the church he'd once thought of as his own, Keith slowly made his way back inside. Choosing a pew about halfway back, he sat on the polished wood and lifted his gaze to the simple cross that hung against the wall, facing the congregation. Finding his way home had been a long, arduous journey, fraught with loneliness and despair. But good had come out of it, too. His faith was deeper now. He had a richer, fuller understanding of the darkness that could plague even a believer's soul. That, in turn, had enhanced his compassion and empathy. He'd found the peace of mind that comes only from true communion with the Lord, from surrender to His will. God's love once again flowed through him, filling his life with light and hope.

And along the way he'd also found human love. From a special woman and an endearing little boy, who even now awaited his return. And he was anxious to go. To leave the past behind and focus on the future. But first, he needed to say thank-you. He needed to take one final step on his journey toward forgiveness. And he needed to say goodbye.

Bowing his head, Keith clasped his hands between his knees and closed his eyes. He started with the thank-you— the easiest of the three tasks before him.

Lord, I thank You for the blessings You've given me these past two years. Even when I was mired in doubt, even when I was lost in darkness, even when I turned my back on You, I realize now that You were by my side. Just waiting for me to turn to You, to ask for help without demanding answers. To take Your hand in trust, as a child takes the hand of a loving father, knowing that he will be protected and cherished and guided safely through danger. I'm sorry it took me such a long time to see the light. To understand and accept the very words I preached in Your name for so many years—Come to me, all you who labor and are overburdened, and I will give you rest.'

I've found that rest now, Lord. And so much more. My time of trial and fire was difficult, but like gold in the smelter, I've been refined and purified. I'm a better person now than I would ever have been without the suffering and pain I endured. I know I have a long way to go, but at least I feel I'm on the right path. And with Your help, I plan to stay the course.

After a few minutes of silent contemplation, Keith turned to his next task. Forgiveness. He'd spoken of it earlier. And he'd made great progress. But could he take this final, most difficult step of all? For two long years, Susan Reynolds had been the primary object of his hate and anger. While he now accepted the trials that had befallen him, and could acknowledge the good that had come from them, it was hard to forgive the woman who had wreaked such havoc and destruction in his life. Whose vindictive actions had led to his wife's death. Whose malice had driven a wedge between Keith and the God who had been the center of his life.

And yet…could he blame Susan for all those things? Yes, she'd been the catalyst for them. But Ellen had spiraled into deep depression due to events that had nothing to do with the scandal. Keith had already been anxious about her emotional and mental stability. Had worried that she might take some drastic action. That was why he'd been calling home so often, why he'd had the neighbors checking on her. If the scandal hadn't triggered her death, wasn't it possible that something else would have? The answer was obvious: yes.

As for his relationship with God…if it had been as strong as he once thought, would it have faltered in the face of tragedy? Of course he would have reeled from the blow. Stumbled, even. Anyone would have. But if he had truly believed everything he'd preached from the pulpit every Sunday, would he have let his anger at God destroy their relationship? Would he have turned his back and walked away? This answer, too, was clear: no.

Finally…what of Susan? What had led her to take such terrible actions? He'd known she was unhappy in her marriage. But mere unhappiness couldn't explain her compulsive need for attention, nor her attempts to implicate good, decent men in indiscretions sure to ruin their lives. Evil did exist in the world, of course. And perhaps that was what had motivated Susan. But a more plausible explanation seemed to be that she had simply been a very troubled and disturbed young woman who sought validation in the wrong places and took inappropriate action when her advances were rebuffed.

Keith wasn't a psychologist. The puzzle of Susan's mind was beyond his ability to assemble. But he was a Christian. And he knew what the Lord wanted him to do, difficult though it was. Calling forth every ounce of his compassion, Keith once more bowed his head.

Lord, I acknowledge now that I can't blame Susan for everything that went wrong in my life. Ellen's problems weren't her fault. Nor did she bear responsibility for my shaky faith. Her actions were wrong, and they triggered tragedy, but it was tragedy waiting to happen. Help me to always remember that. And I ask that You soften Susan's heart, wherever she is, so that she can feel the healing touch of Your spirit. Help her to find a healthy way to deal with the problems she has. Open her mind to Your words, and let Your love flow through her soul. Please forgive her, Lord…as I have done.

A burden seemed to lift from Keith's soul as he finished the simple prayer, and as the healing grace and love of God flowed through him he drew a cleansing breath.

Now it was time for his final task of the day. Saying goodbye.

Sitting back in the pew, Keith stared at the stained glass windows that flanked the cross, his thoughts drifting back to the day he'd met his wife in this very place. That was seven years ago now. When he was thirty-one. She'd just moved to town to take a teaching job, and was visiting area churches to select a congregation to join.

He'd noticed her right away, sitting alone in a back corner one Sunday, her chin-length hair swinging loose around her face. He'd sought her out after services, on the pretense of welcoming her. But in fact, he'd been intrigued—and interested. It wasn't often that a single, attractive woman dropped in for services.

Once she'd joined the church, Keith had spent several weeks mentally sorting through and reconciling potential conflicts that could arise between pastoral obligations and a personal relationship. Only when he'd worked through that to his satisfaction had he asked her out. But she'd turned him down. She was too busy with her new teaching job, she'd told him, and still trying to settle in. Besides, she wasn't sure she wanted the attention and scrutiny that went along with dating a minister. She didn't like being in the spotlight, she'd said.

He hadn't pushed. But neither had he given up. He'd continued to make his interest clear, seeking her out after services, offering a helping hand when she had car trouble, clipping education-related articles he thought she might find interesting. In the end, she'd taken the initiative by inviting him to accompany her to the faculty Christmas party. A year later they had married.

Even before they wed, however, Keith had realized that she had some issues. Estranged from her mother, she had no siblings, and her father had died years ago. He sensed that she'd had an unhappy childhood, but he could never get her to talk about it. In time, when his gentle questions began to meet with increasing hostility, he'd stopped probing about her past.

He'd also been aware of her desire to start a family, which he shared. However, he'd soon realized that her need for children bordered almost on compulsive. After they were married, long before she ever conceived, she'd begun to devour books on pregnancy and child-rearing. He'd learned to accept that, assuming that her desire to create a family sprang from the lack of one in her own life, from a need to compensate for something she'd never had. And he'd supported her decision to quit teaching so that she could concentrate on getting pregnant. They'd agreed that she'd be a stay-at-home mom, anyway, once they had children. It hadn't mattered to him if she wanted to get a head start on that life-style.

The real problems started when she lost the first baby, two years into their marriage. The depth of her subsequent depression had shocked—and frightened—him. He'd had no idea how to cope with her withdrawal or her constant tears, and he'd been relieved when a second pregnancy a few months later seemed to solve the problem. But after that, too, ended in a miscarriage, the situation had deteriorated. Not only had Ellen refused to leave the house, on some days she wouldn't get out of bed.

The toll on their marriage had been immense. Over time, as the woman he'd wed began to disappear bit by bit, Keith had become more of a caretaker than a husband. And he'd begun to realize that the unassuming, gentle manner that had first attracted him to Ellen had masked a very troubled, melancholy spirit. Desperate, he'd been on the verge of having her hospitalized when the scandal broke. And then she'd taken matters into her own hands.

Through the three and a half years of his brief marriage, Keith had tried his best to be a good husband. But in the end, he'd failed his wife. He should have recognized far sooner that she needed professional help. When he'd finally suggested that she see a counselor, her thought processes had no longer been rational and she'd refused. In retrospect, he realized he should have forced the issue. Except at that point he'd been too distracted by his own problems.

But it was too late now for recriminations. For second-guessing. Ellen was gone. And in all honesty, the woman he'd fallen in love with had vanished long before death gave her the peace she never seemed able to find on earth. All he could do now was express his sorrow, say farewell and try to remember her as she'd been those first few months—quiet, gentle and kind.

"I'm sorry I couldn't give you what you needed, Ellen," Keith whispered. "For all the ways I failed you, I ask your forgiveness. I pray that in God's loving presence, you've found the serenity that eluded you while you were with us here. Goodbye, dear one. May the Lord keep you in His eternal care."

For a long time, Keith sat in the silent church, letting the peaceful stillness refresh his unburdened soul. But finally he checked his watch. He'd promised to return his father's car early in the evening, and it was a long drive back to Missouri. It was time to go.

Rising, Keith took one more look at the sanctuary. Already, it seemed part of his past. A past that had shaped who he was, but which no longer had the power to deny him a future.

Moving to the back of the church, Keith stepped outside without a backward look, pulling the door shut behind him with a decisive click. Now he could face tomorrow with a clean heart and a soul attuned to the Lord's voice.

And if God granted his prayers, he would do so with two very special people by his side.

Chapter Eighteen

As the hulking ferry nosed its way into the dock on Orcas Island, the steady rain and gray, low-hanging clouds reminded Keith of the July day when he'd first set foot on this lush speck of fir- and juniper-covered land. Then, like now, the beauty of the island had been hidden, cloaked by mist and fog—just as his heart had been. And the dismal weather had matched his spirits.

Not anymore. Despite the dreary sky, despite the distinct chill in the November air, his heart was warm and sunny.

The ferry nudged the dock, and Keith hoisted his overnight bag to his shoulder. As he headed down from the observation deck to disembark, a surge of adrenaline shot through him, dispelling the weariness from his long day of travel by car, plane, bus and now ferry. In a matter of minutes, he'd be back with Jill and Kyle.

He'd be home.

When the ropes were lowered, Keith was the first one off the boat. As he stepped onto the ramp, he saw the two figures waiting at the end, wrapped in warm coats and huddled under an oversized umbrella. Even through the gloom, Keith could feel the warmth of Jill's welcoming smile, could see the excitement on Kyle's face. Oblivious to the cold, penetrating rain, he broke into a jog, each step bringing him closer to his little piece of heaven.

"Here he comes!" Kyle's eager voice carried through the still air, and before Jill could stop him he dashed from under the umbrella and made a beeline for Keith.

Dropping to one knee, Keith braced as Kyle launched himself into his arms. Still, the force of the little boy's welcome, and his fierce grip, was almost enough to topple Keith—physically and emotionally. "Hey, buddy. I missed you a whole lot." It was difficult to get the words past the tightness in his throat.

"We missed you, too. It was…lonesome while you…were gone."

"Well, I'm back now. And I plan to stay around a long, long time." The last comment was directed at Jill, who was waiting patiently in the background, her face alight with pleasure at the tender scene. A flush suffused her cheeks when she realized Keith was speaking to her, and a soft smile curved her lips.

Swinging Kyle up into his arms, Keith reached for his bag and closed the distance between them, never breaking eye contact.

"You're both going to be drenched." Flustered by his intent look, Jill lifted the umbrella higher and moved to one side. "I think we can all fit under here."

Keith didn't need any urging to get closer to the woman who had stolen his heart. He ducked under, and as the rain continued to fall around them, it felt almost as if the three of them existed in a separate world.

"Hi." Keith smiled at Jill, their faces inches apart, their frosty breath mingling in the crisp air.

"Welcome back." Her gaze held his, filled with welcome, with joy—and with a longing that wreaked havoc on his equilibrium and made him yearn to greet her in a way that left no doubt in her mind that the feeling was mutual.

However, with Kyle in one arm and his bag in the other—not to mention the presence of other ferry passengers nearby—that greeting would have to wait until later. But at least he could tell her in words how he felt. "It's good to be home," he murmured, his voice husky with emotion.

Of all the things he could have said, none could have given Jill more pleasure—or done more to ease her mind. During his absence, doubts had begun to assail her—most often in the wee hours of the morning, when sleep had been elusive. Could her lonely heart have misinterpreted his signals, read more into his eyes, than he intended? she'd wondered. Just because she'd fallen in love with him didn't mean her feelings were reciprocated with the same intensity. Or that he wanted to take their relationship to the next level. Yes, when he'd left a few days ago he'd said they would talk when he returned. And he'd kissed her goodbye. But with each day that had passed, she'd grown more uncertain about the significance of that gesture and comment. Perhaps he'd just wanted to talk about his plans for the future, and the job he had waiting. Perhaps the kiss had been a simple, perfunctory goodbye, the kind one friend gave to another.

But the look in his eyes now went way beyond friendly. And his words resonated with meaning.

The relief that eased Jill's face, the slight relaxing of tension in her shoulders, didn't escape Keith's notice. She'd been doubting his intentions, he realized. He'd hoped his parting kiss had reassured her; now he realized it hadn't been enough. Well, before this day ended he planned to make his intentions crystal clear. And he prayed that when he did, the Lord would give her the courage to place her trust in him and believe in his love. For always.

"Are we going home now?" Kyle asked. "We're having turkey...for dinner. And dressing. And mashed...potatoes. And Jill baked a...chocolate cake."

"Sounds like Thanksgiving." Keith shot Jill a quizzical look.

"We have a lot to be thankful for. I thought it would be nice to anticipate the holiday a little."

"I agree." His eyes softened as he gazed at her. Once more he was tempted to kiss her. Once more he held off for a more appropriate time, when he could do the kiss justice. "Would you like me to drive?" he offered.

"No." She led the way back to the car as they huddled under the umbrella. "You've had a long day. Why don't you just sit back and relax?"

"We have a...surprise for you," Kyle told him as they reached the car.

"Oh? Are you going to tell me about it?" Keith leaned down to help the boy buckle his seat belt.

"No. It wouldn't be...a surprise then." Kyle gave him a gap-toothed grin.

"Say...what happened to the tooth?" For the first time Keith noticed that one of his front teeth was missing.

"It fell out. It was just a...baby tooth. Jill says a...new tooth will grow there now. That means I'm...growing up."

"Not too soon, I hope. There are lots of little-boy things I want to do with you first."

Once on the road, Jill covered the distance to the far end of the island in what seemed like record time. Kyle kept up a steady stream of banter, his excitement causing him to stumble more than usual over his words. Still, the sound of his voice was music to their ears. When they reached the entrance to Jill's place, he leaned forward in his seat, almost bursting with anticipation.

"Do you…see it, Keith?" he asked.

"See what, buddy?"

"The surprise!"

Confused, Keith scanned the woods in the deepening dusk. Nothing looked different.

"Up ahead," Jill cued in a muted voice, angling the car to let the headlights shine on the surprise.

Once more Keith was transported back to that stormy July night when he'd arrived on her doorstep, lost and despondent. He'd almost missed the turnoff, he recalled, until the sudden appearance of a black-tailed deer sent his car skidding—and pointed his headlights directly toward the weathered, peeling sign for Rainbow's End.

Now, as then, the sign was illuminated. But like his life, it had been transformed. The words were bold against a sky-blue background, written in a flowing, graceful script, and a vibrant rainbow arched over them.

"I helped with…the rainbow," Kyle announced from the backseat.

"And you did a fine job," Keith praised him. "It's beautiful." He cast a curious glance at Jill. "What prompted this?"

"When I first came here, I thought the name was ironic," she said softly, turning to him. In the dim light he couldn't read her expression, but the joy in her voice was unmistakable. "I don't think that anymore."

"Can we eat now?"

There was nothing like a child to dispel a sentimental moment, Keith reflected with a wry grin. He reached over and gave Jill's hand a squeeze, then turned toward the backseat. "I'm with you, buddy. They don't give you a whole lot of food on airplanes these days. I'm starving."

As Keith expected, the meal was wonderful. And Jill had gone all out to create the perfect, festive ambiance. Her best dishes were set on a pristine linen cloth, and she'd fashioned a fall centerpiece from the bounty of the meadow and forest. Keith couldn't remember when he'd had a more wonderful evening.

And the best was yet to come.

It wasn't until they'd finally settled a keyed-up Kyle in bed for the night, however, that they had a moment alone.

"You must be exhausted," Jill said as they descended the stairs toward the living room.

He heard the tremor in her voice—of excitement, anticipation, uncertainty…he couldn't be sure. But he intended to erase any doubts in her mind without further delay. Grabbing her hand when they reached the first floor, he turned her toward him. "Oh, I have a little life in me yet. And the evening's young. Besides, I've been waiting way too long to do this."

Before she could say a word, Keith pulled her close and lowered his lips to hers in a gentle kiss meant to set the stage for what he had to say, a kiss that would be a preamble for those that would follow later, after he'd clarified his intentions. After he'd assured Jill that his love was sure and strong and true—and that it always would be. After he'd put to rest any doubts she might still harbor about her appeal as a woman.

But somehow he forgot all of those plans. Because Jill surprised him. She needed no coaxing to return his kiss. Quite the opposite. From the first instant his lips touched hers, she responded, holding nothing back. When he deepened the kiss, she didn't protest. Instead, her lips asked for more. And he complied, giving full expression to the love that was in his heart.

Keith wasn't the only one surprised by her response. Jill, too, was taken aback by her boldness. But she was unable to contain the love she felt for this special man, who had given her back her life—and made it better. She wanted him to know, in a way that spoke more eloquently than words, how much she needed him. How much she trusted him. How much she loved him.

In the end, it was Keith who broke contact, though he kept her in the circle of his arms when he drew back. They were both trembling, and as she searched his face, Jill worried that she'd come on too strong. It wasn't like her to be so assertive. Nor was it a side of her Keith had ever seen. In fact, it was one *she'd* rarely seen. A flash of uncertainty flickered in her eyes, and she lowered her head. "I'm sorry. I didn't mean to be so…"

"Hey." Keith lifted her chin with a gentle finger, forcing her to look at him. "Don't ever be sorry about loving me," he told her in a fierce, soft voice. "Or demonstrating that love. Okay?"

Her throat constricted with emotion. "Okay," she whispered.

"And just for the record, you can kiss me anytime." Taking her hand, he tugged her toward the couch, pulling her down beside him. "However, I need to say a few things before you take me up on that. But at least that preview gave me a little more confidence about making my speech."

Angling his body toward her, he cocooned her hands in his. "You know my story, Jill. I told you why I came here back in July. But I haven't told you why I want to stay. I guess I'm hoping you've already figured that out. But a woman deserves to hear it put into words. So I'll do my best to say what's in my heart."

He stroked his thumbs over the backs of her hands, and his compelling gaze captured and held hers. "When I arrived on your doorstep, I was as low as anyone could be. I felt as if everything I'd cared about and believed in had been taken from me. I was angry and bitter and resentful. And fast losing any hope that I would find my way out of the darkness that had closed around me.

"Then I met you. A woman who'd endured more than her own share of tragedy. A woman who'd lost as much, if not more, than I had. And yet you'd found a way to go on. Instead of turning your back on your faith, you found a way to strengthen it. Instead of responding to tragedy with bitterness, you countered with compassion and kindness. Even though you'd withdrawn from the world, when the world came to you, hurting and in need, you found the courage to step back into the mainstream and do what you could to help. Your strength and generosity and humanity inspired me, Jill. You softened a heart that had grown hard, and diffused anger with gentleness."

He stroked her disfigured face, his touch as soft as a butterfly's wing. "I know you've always thought that these scars are an impediment to romance. That no one could ever see past them, to the loveliness that lies underneath. But I can, Jill. When I look at you, I see a woman filled with compassion and spirit and character. I see beauty. I see the woman I love."

Withdrawing his hand, Keith reached into the pocket of his slacks and withdrew a small black velvet box. When he flipped it open, a large, square-cut diamond flanked by two smaller stones winked back at them from an old-fashioned platinum setting.

"This was my mother's engagement ring. It belonged to her mother before her. I always hoped to give it to the woman I married. Since Ellen preferred modern things, I never asked my father if I could have this ring. Until last week."

The intensity of his eyes took Jill's breath away. "I don't have much to offer you in the way of material things, Jill. I'll be starting over. But I can offer you all my love…for always. And a promise that whatever I have in the future will belong to you. I can also promise you that I'll do my best to be the kind of father Kyle deserves. The kind of dad my father was to me. I never expected to be blessed with a second chance at love. Nor a ready-made family. But I'll be grateful every day of my life that God brought me to your door on that stormy night."

Easing off the couch, Keith dropped to one knee and took her hand. "Jill, would you do me the honor of becoming my wife?"

Tears blurred Jill's vision as she looked at the wonderful man kneeling before her. The man who had given her just as much as he claimed she'd given him. A new life, for one. A life she wanted to share with him.

"I love you, Keith," she whispered, her voice choked.

A smile whispered at the corners of his mouth. "Is that a yes?"

"Yes. Yes, yes, yes, yes!"

As his smile blossomed into a grin, he slipped the ring over her finger. "What would you think about a Christmas wedding?"

"That's the best present I could ever hope for."

"Then let's seal this engagement the proper way."

When he reached for her, Jill went willingly into his arms. And as his lips claimed hers, she gave thanks for the gift of love that had graced her life. For a faith that sustained her through the dark times. And for the clear, bright dawn of a new day.

Keith, too, said a silent prayer of thanks as he pulled her close. Two years ago, he thought his life had ended. But here, in this place apart, he'd found a new life. A new love. A new family. And he'd found his way back to the Lord. The journey had been long and difficult, the destination often obscured by the fog of doubt and anger and bitterness. But in the end, that fog had been diffused by the warmth of God's love, like mist kissed by the sun. And His wondrous light had shone once again in Keith's heart.

In his old life, Keith had often preached about the presence of everyday miracles. Of how the ordinary could become extraordinary if viewed through the lens of faith.

That was how he viewed the love that had transformed his life. Given in a simple, heartfelt way, the gift of a lovely, lonely woman and an abandoned little boy, it had rescued him from the darkness, illuminating his life with goodness and hope. If he lived to be a hundred, he knew it would always remain the greatest blessing he had ever received.

And as Jill's sweet lips surrendered to his, as he lost himself in the warmth of her embrace, he thought once more of the sign she'd painted with such vibrant colors. Rainbow's End.

How apt. For here, in this place, he'd found the golden light of faith, hope and love.

And that was a far greater treasure than any leprechaun's pot of gold.

Epilogue

Eighteen months later

Keith adjusted his clerical collar, slipped his arms into the sleeves of his black suit jacket and turned toward Jill, who sat on the bed. "Ready?"

Distracted, she replied without looking up. "Mmm-hmm."

A tender smile curved his lips, and Keith sat beside her to fold back the edge of the soft pink blanket in her arms. Sarah Elizabeth looked up at him with wide blue eyes, gurgling with pleasure when he extended a finger. She wrapped her tiny hand around it and squeezed, her strong grip always surprising and delighting him.

"She's perfect, isn't she?" Jill stared at her daughter in awe.

"Yes. Just like her mother."

At last Jill transferred her attention from her daughter to her husband. He was looking at her now, the soft light of love warm and tender in his eyes, his gaze caressing her face, making her feel beautiful despite her scars. As he always did.

She reached out a hand to him, too overcome with emotion to speak, and he took it, pressing a kiss to her palm.

"Hey up there! I think we have a christening to attend, don't we?"

Deb's voice floated up the stairs, and Jill tugged on her hand. When Keith held fast, she gave him a quizzical look.

"We'll pick up here later," he promised, brushing his lips across her forehead before relinquishing her hand with obvious reluctance.

"Hey! Anybody home up there?" Deb tried again.

"We'll be right down," Jill called. Lowering her voice, she leaned close to Keith. "I'll remember that."

With a chuckle he rose and lifted his daughter. "Come on, Miss Sarah. It's your day to shine."

As they descended the steps, Jill looked around at the group assembled for the christening. Deb had come, with her burly, raven-haired husband Tony, in tow, a big teddy bear of a man who Jill had loved as a brother since the day Deb brought him home. Bob Michaels was there, too. And a number of friends would join them for a celebration afterward, including Madeleine and Cindy.

"Where are Dominic and Kyle?" Jill asked.

"Who knows? They were here a minute ago. It's impossible to keep track of their comings and goings," Deb replied, rolling her eyes.

"I'll round them up," Tony offered.

"Now isn't that a pretty sight," Bob Michaels said, reaching out to stroke a finger down Sarah's cheek as Keith handed her back to Jill.

"I have to agree. But then, I'm partial," Jill admitted with a smile.

"To be honest, I was talking about the baby *and* the mother," Keith's father responded.

Grinning, Jill turned to her husband. "Flattery must run in the family."

"Not at all. The Michaels men are just an honest bunch," Keith replied with a wink.

"Hey, Mom, can I hold Sarah?" Kyle skidded to a stop directly in front of Jill, Dominic close on his heels.

"We need to leave now. But you can hold her when we get to church," Keith promised.

"Okay. Can I ride with Dominic, Dad?"

"If Aunt Deb says it's okay."

"Sure. The more the merrier," Jill's sister replied with a grin.

"Good. I wasn't finished telling Dominic about the garden Dad and I are planting."

"Don't you two ever run out of things to talk about?" Deb teased.

The two boys looked at her as if she'd sprouted two heads.

"How could we run out of stuff to talk about?" Kyle asked. "I haven't even told Dominic about the whale I saw last week, or about the baby hawk Mom and I found that had a broken wing, or about the field trip I took at school to see the English Camp on San Juan Island, or about the solo I sang with the school choir at the final assembly or…"

"Okay, okay, I get the picture!" Deb held up her hands, laughing. "Sorry I asked." She grinned at Jill. "And you were worried about the language thing."

That was true. But it was also history. Once Kyle had started to talk, there had been no stopping him. It was as if he was trying to say all the words he'd stored up for so long. Which was perfectly normal, according to Marni. And perfectly fine with Keith and her.

"I think we'd better hit the road," Keith reminded everyone.

A few minutes later, while Keith's father climbed into the back of Jill's car—keeping one protective hand on his new granddaughter's car seat—the other foursome headed toward Tony's rental car. By the time Keith and his father double-checked all the latches securing their precious cargo, the other car had begun to ease down the gravel driveway, disappearing from sight with a merry toot.

When Keith stood at last and closed the door, he turned to find Jill watching him, the May breeze caressing her soft, lustrous hair.

"You look very handsome, Reverend," she said, a serene smile lifting the corners of her lips. "The collar suits you.

"It still feels a bit odd to wear it again. But good. And right."

That was another way he'd been blessed, Keith reflected. Reverend Campbell's retirement had paved the way for him to ease back into the ministry. The congregation hadn't really needed a full-time minister, and the members had been amenable to their former pastor's suggestion that following his retirement, Keith take over his duties on a part-time basis. Splitting his time between carpentry and ministry had given Keith's life a perfect balance.

"It shows. You seem very content."

"So do you, Mrs. Michaels."

In truth, she was. Surrounded, sheltered and uplifted by Keith's love; adored by her son; entrusted with the gift of a new life to nuture…how could she not be? And as icing on the cake, her work was receiving critical acclaim. Plus, her commissions were mushrooming as a result of her show in Seattle and another, a few months later, in Portland.

"Hey, you two, I think this little lady has a date at church."

Bob Michaels's voice pulled them both back to the

moment, and they looked down to find the older man watching them through the open window with a twinkle in his eye.

"If we don't get a move on, it will take a miracle to get us there on time," he added.

Keith and Jill exchanged a look, and the luminous smile on his wife's face confirmed that they were thinking exactly the same thing.

They'd make it to the church on time. Because they believed in miracles.

After all, they were living one every day.

* * * * *

*If you enjoyed RAINBOW'S END by Irene Hannon,
look for 2 new stories in the brand-new*
HEARTLAND HOMECOMING
miniseries available soon.

A DREAM TO SHARE
February 2008

WHERE LOVE ABIDES
May 2008

*Available wherever books are sold, including most book-
stores, supermarkets, drugstores and discount stores.*

QUESTIONS FOR DISCUSSION

1. In *Rainbow's End,* all three of the main characters—Jill, Keith and Kyle—are scarred. Some of their scars are visible, some are not. Discuss how each character deals with his or her particular scars. What behavior do they have in common at the beginning of the story?

2. Discuss the importance of the setting in this book. How does the location enhance the story?

3. Jill's disfigurement makes it difficult for many to see past her damaged face to the whole person beneath. Why are people who are disabled, disfigured or merely different sometimes avoided or shunned? How did Jesus treat outcasts? Why is it important to respect and appreciate the uniqueness of every individual?

4. When Keith's life is turned upside down, he feels betrayed and his heart is consumed with anger and bitterness. In the end he realizes that in order to reconnect with God—and with love—he must learn to forgive. What does the Lord teach us about forgiveness? Why is it often so hard to pardon those who have wronged us?

5. Keith's father and Jill's sister provide moral support for their respective relatives in the story. How do their caring and encouragement help Jill and Keith survive their traumas? Discuss the value of a strong, loving support system. Can you think of some examples in your own life when a friend or loved one helped you through a difficult time? How did their support make a difference?

And now, here's a sneak preview of
A COWBOY'S HONOR by Lois Richer,
coming from Love Inspired *in April 2008.*

Hope was a wasted effort, thought Gracie Henderson as she walked through the park at the Dallas arboretum. There, on a hillock, she found the spot she remembered clearly. The spot where she'd first met her cowboy six years ago.

Now, staring at the exact spot where he'd first entered her life, she noticed a man crouched in the grass. Birds gathered around him, swooping down from the sky.

The man's face was turned away from her, but something about the way he sat, something in his frozen stillness would not let her look away.

He pulled off a morsel of whatever was in his hand. Without so much as a muscle twitch, he held it out, wordlessly coaxing the birds nearer until they lit upon his hand and pecked the food from his fingers. Entranced children flocked near him, trying to emulate his success as their bemused families watched.

Gracie blinked, checked her watch. Not a lot of time to spare. Since the wrought-iron bench she sought out was unoccupied, she sat down. In this particular place, in the warm rays of the May sun, her aching soul felt soothing relief.

Gracie had been back in Texas only a week, but that was long enough to dull her memories of the cooler North Dakota spring she'd left behind. It was almost long enough for Dallas's southern heat to evaporate the chill encasing her heart.

She pressed her back against the warm metal and soaked in the lake-view vista in front, breathed in the heady scent of blooming alyssum and freshly mowed grass, listened to the breeze rustle the lush leaves of a nearby cottonwood. All of it combined sent her thoughts headlong into the past, into emotions she'd struggled to bury.

She'd been so happy that day, so trusting.

Reality dumped a cold-shower reminder that her blissful joy had lasted eight short days. At least she'd learned from that. Now she took precautions, made sure before she leaped.

With effort, Gracie pressed back the hurt and opened her lunch. From the corner of her eye she noticed the man rise. He ambled across the grass, pausing to sniff at a bed of flowers.

Gracie bit into her sandwich and closed her eyes, allowing herself a moment to savor the taste. Simple joys. She'd learned not to take them for granted.

"It's a beautiful place, isn't it?"

Gracie blinked, stared at the owner of that butter-smooth voice.

Her heart stopped.

He looked so real standing in front of her, watching her with a quizzical stare. The man in her dreams. Her cowboy.

"Dallas?"

Gracie's heart beat in a painful rhythm that sent her hand down to grasp the edge of the bench for support.

"It's a pretty city, but I didn't know it would be so hot." He swiped a hand across his forehead, smiled. A familiar dimple peeked out from the corner of his mouth. "And this is only spring."

How she'd missed those bittersweet eyes.

"You've chosen the prettiest spot. Do you mind if I share it?"

Gracie shook her head. Her limbs trembled with excitement until terror, cold as Arctic ice, grabbed hold, plunging her from delight to dread in two seconds flat. Something was wrong.

She didn't know what to ask first.

Dallas didn't try to break the silence between them. In fact, he seemed to relish it. A faint smile curved his lips as a bird flitted closer to beg for food.

It was a mirage, a dream. It had to be. Only, Gracie couldn't wake up.

So many times, through long sleepless nights and terror-filled days, she'd longed to share her burden, to talk to him, to lean against his shoulder and know she wasn't alone, that she didn't have to be afraid ever again.

Gracie had never grieved for Dallas. And after the first year alone, filled with questions that were never answered, she'd shoved him out of her mind and never permitted herself to imagine him coming back.

Now here he was.

"Where have you been, Dallas?" Rage replaced curiosity. "Did you even consider how worried I was? Surely you could have called, written—something?"

He jumped up from the grass, terror on his face. He was afraid? Of her?

"I didn't mean to bother you, ma'am. I'm sorry."

Brown eyes brimmed with shadows she didn't understand, but his fear was obvious. A riot of emotions flashed in his eyes, a wariness she'd never expected. As if she was a stranger.

Gracie stood and reached out, touched his arm. "Don't you think you owe me some kind of explanation, Dallas?"

He fidgeted as if he found her touch painful. Then he stilled and his eyes met hers for the first time.

Empty eyes.

"You know me?"

She might have missed his question if she hadn't been standing inches away.

"Of course I know you. What are you playing at, Dallas?"

He struggled to speak. "So my name is Dallas."

Gracie pulled back. This was not the man she knew. This was a stranger in his body. He showed no signs of recognizing her. She longed to shake him, to finally pry loose the answers she'd been denied. But his uncertainty, the watchful way he looked at her—Gracie gulped down her bitterness.

"My last name. What is it?"

"Henderson."

Gracie waited for an apology, an explanation. Something. But he continued to regard her with a blank stare.

"Who am I?"

His whisper sounded deadly serious, but Gracie couldn't quite believe it. And until she figured out if he was playing some kind of game, she had to be cautious.

"Let's sit down on the bench. You can share my lunch. Please?" she added when it looked as if he'd refuse. "Are you hungry?"

"Not really."

"I am. Maybe you could wait while I eat my lunch." Gracie drew him toward the bench, motioned for him to sit. She needed to buy some time, figure out what to do next. "I have some coffee. Would you like some?"

"I love coffee."

He always had.

She handed it over. Dallas removed the lid, sniffed and closed his eyes as he savored the aroma. The familiar gesture brought tears, but Gracie dashed them away.

She would not weep. Not then. Not now. Not ever.

"This is good coffee. Thank you, ma'am."

If he'd had a hat she knew he would have doffed it. Like a gallant cowboy. Her cowboy. The sting pierced deep and hard, but Gracie was used to pain. She ignored it, focused on getting the answers she craved.

"Can you tell me where you've been?"

"California."

"What did you do there?"

"I worked with animals."

That made sense to Gracie. It didn't matter why he'd been there. She knew it would have to do with the rapport Dallas had always shared with animals. But that was the only part of Dallas she recognized. At least for now.

"Did you come here straight from California?"

He nodded, accepted half of the sandwich she held out, munched on it before speaking.

"Yes, I had a memory. Of this park, I think. It was different, but it was the same day as today. May first." He glanced around, frowned. "I know that sounds weird."

The significance of the date might have escaped him, but Gracie couldn't forget. She held her breath as she asked the next question.

"Dallas, do you know my name?"

He turned sideways to study her. "No."

"My name is Gracie."

"Hello, Gracie." He held out a hand, shook hers with solemn formality. "Pleased to meet you."

"Thank you." She detected no sign of recognition. Her heart jerked.

"Do you know me well?" Dallas asked.

"I thought I did."

His gaze searched her face. "How did we know each other?"

"We met in this park." Gracie wasn't sure how much to reveal. "Over there. Where you were feeding the birds. I was here on a vacation during college."

"So I came back to a familiar place." He nodded, his brown eyes pensive. "The doctors said I might."

Doctors. So he'd been in a hospital?

"Do you remember anything about being here before? About me?"

"Nothing is clear." He rubbed his temple.

"It doesn't matter. We don't have to talk about it now."

"You're the first person I've met who knows me. I want to talk." He paused, then spoke haltingly. "When you knew me, what did I do? For a job, I mean."

"You're an animal behavior specialist. You worked with horses."

"I was a cowboy."

You were. My cowboy.

You were supposed to come home to me.

"Please tell me what you know. Please tell me where I belong."

The ache underlying those words was Gracie's undoing.

"You belong to me," she whispered. "We were married in this park five years ago today. I'm your wife."

* * * * *

Though Gracie has found her long-lost husband,
a tragic accident has claimed his memory.
How will they rekindle the love they once shared?
Can they ever be a family again?

Don't miss A COWBOY'S HONOR by Lois Richer.
Available April 2008.

Love Inspired®

DELIVERS HEARTWARMING, INSPIRATIONAL ROMANCES.

A Cowboy's Honor
by Lois Richer

On sale April 2008

Available wherever books are sold, including most bookstores, supermarkets, drugstores and discount stores.

Love Inspired ®
SUSPENSE
RIVETING INSPIRATIONAL ROMANCE

These contemporary tales
of intrigue and romance
feature Christian characters
facing challenges to their faith...
and their lives!

**Four new Love Inspired Suspense titles are
available every month wherever books are
sold, including most bookstores, supermarkets,
drug stores and discount stores.**

Steeple
Hill ®

Visit:
www.steeplehillbooks.com